"STARBUCK. REPORT IN."

Starbuck's voice came on the line. On the small screen, his face looked worried.

"It came from the asteroid, all right," he said. "A high energy beam of coherent light. Very intense. It's some sort of laser weaponry, the kind with the pulsar effect—but this time, believe me, it must be a *giant* pulsar weapon. Big enough to destroy *anything*!"

"Starbuck," Boomer's voice cut in, "we've lost contact with Cree. We're missing another ship!"

"Breaking transmission, *Galactica*," Starbuck cried. "I'm going in!"

THE CYLON DEATH MACHINE
The newest adventure from the
spectacular TV space epic

SEND FOR YOUR BEAUTIFUL FRAZETTA
COVER ART POSTER NOW!
15 by 20 inches in full color!
$4.00 each, plus 75ᶜ postage.
Frazetta Prints
Box "R"
Marshall's Creek, Pa. 18335

Please specify poster #103 when ordering.

Berkley Battlestar Galactica Books

BATTLESTAR GALACTICA
by Glen A. Larson and Robert Thurston

BATTLESTAR GALACTICA 2: THE CYLON DEATH MACHINE
by Glen A. Larson and Robert Thurston

BattlestaR GALACTICA 2
THE CYLON DEATH MACHINE
NOVEL BY
GLEN A. LARSON AND ROBERT THURSTON

Based on the Universal Television Series
BATTLESTAR GALACTICA
Created by
GLEN A. LARSON
Adapted from the episode
"The Gun on Ice Planet Zero"
Teleplay by MICHAEL SLOAN &
DON BELLISARIO & GLEN A. LARSON
Story by JOHN IRELAND, JR

A BERKLEY BOOK
published by
BERKLEY PUBLISHING CORPORATION

Copyright © 1979, by MCA PUBLISHING, a Division of MCA Inc.

All rights reserved

Published by arrangement with MCA PUBLISHING, a Division of MCA Inc.

All rights reserved which includes the right to reproduce this book or portions thereof in any form whatsoever. For information address

MCA PUBLISHING, a Division of MCA Inc.
100 Universal City Plaza
Universal City, California 91608

SBN 425-04080-1

BERKLEY MEDALLION BOOKS *are published by*
Berkley Publishing Corporation
200 Madison Avenue
New York, N. Y. 10016

BERKLEY MEDALLION BOOK ® TM 757,375

Printed in the United States of America

Berkley Edition, JANUARY, 1979

BattlestaR
GALACTICA 2
THE CYLON DEATH MACHINE

FROM THE ADAMA JOURNALS:

Croft.

Who is he? Where did he come from? Am I really a part of his memories, or just a substitute for authority figures in general? Even when he described the incident where we crossed paths, and I pretended to remember it because he needed for me to remember it and I needed him for the mission, I could not recall a single aspect of the brief adventure.

Later, when I had some time, I went to my quarters and requested from *Galactica*'s computer a printout of my journals covering that time period, the time when he claimed I'd supervised the capture of his gang and the ship containing their booty while they were fleeing from their raid on the Cylon platinum mines. Studying the pages, the only reference I could find to the incident, or an episode which could have been the incident, was this:

Routine was interrupted today by an apparent pirate ship that stumbled into our sector, seemingly the result of a miscalculation in course. Ship tried to escape, but when they had our pursuers in their sights, their commander refused to fire on us, and ship and crew were easily netted. Tigh says their

holds were quite rich in plundered cargo. I told him
to take care of the matter fairly and to send the
prisoners to the proper judges.

Could that commander have been Croft, could that cargo
have been the platinum? Why didn't I record the name of
a man who allowed himself and his gang to be captured
rather than firing on his own kind? Wouldn't the fact that
the cargo had been Cylon platinum be worth noting?

   The note seems to indicate I didn't even see these
particular brigands, yet Croft insists we had a face-to-face
confrontation. I should recall such a meeting vividly.
After all, wouldn't I have been impressed that the leader
of a pirate group had once been a full-fledged commander
of a garrison, and wouldn't I have recorded my
bewilderment that such a vital and intelligent man had
corrupted his worth in a petty crime? The escapades of
such a daring renegade commander deserve more than
just a passing mention in my journal, I think.

   There is nothing in the surrounding entries to indicate
that I was busy with some more important matters that
might have prevented my entering a full report of the
incident. Further, the journal note that remains is so
routinely worded, so militarily matter-of-fact, that I can't
believe that I wouldn't have let at least a hint of Croft's
personality or the uniqueness of his exploit enter my
journal. What could have been going in my head at the
time that caused me to miss the essential point of the
episode? I can only believe that internal evidence suggests
that the entry is about a different group of crooks and that
Croft has mistaken me for somebody else, some other
commander performing his normal duty.

   Still, if it was Croft and his gang, I am sorry I do not
remember him or the details of his capture that have been
so large an obsession for him during his confinement
aboard the prison grid barge. To Croft that episode seems
to have been the major event of his life. It's too bad that,
while he dwelt on his hopes for revenge so fiercely, our
confrontation was only a forgettable moment for me, an
entry in my journal that calls forth no pictures of the event
it describes.

CHAPTER ONE

This time the trap must work.

It must, the Imperious Leader of the Cylons had commanded, snare the human fleet completely. The humans should not be able to execute one of their sneaky last-minute escapes. There could be no overlooked malfunction in the trap's mechanisms. For too long now the Cylon forces had chased after Adama's assemblage of mismatched ships (a captured prisoner had referred to them as a ragtag fleet, a meaningless term since it could not be translated into the Cylon language).

His executive officers, tired of battling the human pest, had acceded readily to the Leader's plan to force the human ships, especially the *Galactica*, into the range of the awesomely efficient laser cannon on the ice planet Tairac.

Imperious Leader was particularly pleased that the final destructive assault should originate on Tairac because the garrison there was commanded by the exiled first centurion, Vulpa. It was fitting that the outspoken Vulpa should deliver the final blow. He would learn obedience and regain status at the same time.

The Leader recalled vividly the day he had been obligated to send Vulpa, one of his most valued officers, into exile.

"Perhaps we should abandon pursuit of the humans," Vulpa had suggested in the middle of a briefing. The executive officers closest to Vulpa had immediately moved away from him, knowing that the oddly ambitious first centurion had finally overstepped the proper bounds.

"Abandon pursuit?" the Leader had said. Vulpa took the question as an invitation to pursue the subject. The Leader knew he was drawing Vulpa into inevitable errors of Cylon decorum, and he was sorry to have to do so, but there was no other choice when a Cylon acted in an un-Cylon-like manner.

"I suggest," Vulpa had said, the arrogance in his voice quite above his station, "that we allow the humans to continue their foolish quest toward the far reaches of known space. As long as they do not contaminate any part of our own dominions, they do not pose a threat significant enough for the continued waste of Cylon time and personnel. We have, after all, achieved our goal. Except for that small band of fleeing survivors and the remaining enslaved humans on some outworlds we control, the human race *has* been exterminated. The war *has* been won."

"You wish to criticize my decision?" Imperious Leader had said politely, giving Vulpa a final chance to back down from his unsuitable position.

"Leader," Vulpa had replied, "your wisdom and judgment are vitally needed back on our home worlds. You would even be cheered for abandoning the—"

"Silence, First Centurion Vulpa! You assume my right of omniscient judgment. As long as a free human is left alive, the chance they could return in large numbers at a later time is a threat that cannot be abided. Humans breed faster than Cylons, even though their lifespan is shorter. Do you not remember how their resourcefulness made the war against them last too long, longer than it should have? Even now the human insects are winning battles and skirmishes against us. Remember how a small squadron of human viperships wrecked our attacking wall of fighters at the Battle of Carillon. I cannot rest until we have achieved the goal of human extermination. A period of exile, First Centurion Vulpa, should aid you to realize the importance of my objectives—and, perhaps, lessen your unfortunate impulses toward ambition."

As Vulpa had slunk off the command deck, Imperious Leader had almost felt sorry for the punished centurion. However, he had known for some time that Vulpa would draw such punishment eventually. Vulpa's excessive displays of ambition had to be countered. He clearly hoped to be the next Imperious Leader, and he did not lack qualifications for the position, if only he would stop exhibiting his ambition for it so openly.

Ambition was rarely observed among Cylons. Imperious Leader had not had an inkling of what the word meant until he had been awarded third-brain and absolute power over the Cylon Alliance.

Vulpa, however, had always been something of a renegade Cylon. As a fighter pilot, while still at first-brain status, he had been more aggressive than his peers, so suicidally aggressive that it seemed surprising that he had survived to second-brain and then executive-officer status. Normally Cylons at Vulpa's level knew how to maintain a showing of absolute obedience whether they felt it or not. Imperious Leader hoped that the exile would force some sense into him, since he so obviously did have the potential to become the next Imperious Leader, plus abilities that would make him exceptional at the job.

Now it seemed that Vulpa's exile would work out to the Cylons' advantage. He was the best possible officer to have on the ice planet Tairac. An officer with Vulpa's abilities was, after all, required at the mainspring of the trap.

As always, Imperious Leader enjoyed working out the details of his plan. Details were comforting. If his head, now covered by a massive communications helmet, could have been seen by the intricate network of officers arrayed around his pedestal, they would have observed a glowing aura shining from each eye. The few humans who had ever seen the impressive alien leader had felt both awe and revulsion toward him, partially because of the creature's many eyes, partially because of his uneven and out-of-balance body (which, in its bulk, resembled a pile of

jagged and lumpy stones), and partially because of the
large-pored aspect of its swamp-gray skin. As his abilities
to mimic human thinking processes increased, he
discovered just how repulsive he looked through their
eyes. Their perception of him as an ugly beast made him
hate the human pest even more. Especially since, to him, a
human was the ugliest sight imaginable in a universe that
contained a diversity of ugliness.

As he awaited the first reports of the beginning of his
present strategy, a sneak attack on the fringe of the ragtag
fleet, the Leader reviewed his overall plan. He could find
no flaws, but there were gaps. He needed to acquire the
kind of information that would prevent such gaps from
becoming another of the humans' lucky escape routes.
Another session with the simulator might provide him
with data about human behavior that could lead to key
insights about their seemingly erratic patterns of
motivation and action. He had already learned several
odd lessons about them from conferring with various
simulacra. He ordered an executive officer to have the
simulator transmitted to the command chamber. It was
there before him, on his pedestal, exactly at the end of his
request.

Nodding toward the telepathy-template at the center
of the simulator console, he requested mentally the
simulation of Commander Adama, head of the human
fleet. As usual, Adama proved too difficult a task for the
simulator. The edges of his simulacrum were fuzzy. Too
little was known about the commander—there was not
enough information about him stored in the simulator
data banks, and so it could not provide a successful
duplicate. Whatever the Leader asked of it, the indistinct
form of Adama supplied insufficient data. Frequently it
was not able to answer at all and just stared at the Leader
indifferently. No insights or revealing associations of
thought could be gleaned from the Adama simulacrum.
Brusquely the Leader ordered it away, called instead for
Adama's son, Captain Apollo. The resolution of the
Apollo simulacrum was sharper. Humans regarded the
young man as handsome. Knowing that made the Apollo
simulacrum more repellent to Imperious Leader. Fortunately, he could disengage synapses within his third-brain

to cut off physiological reactions to the simulation. He asked the Apollo a few questions, but could discover little more than he had learned from the simulacrum of Commander Adama. Apparently the simulator's information concerning the son was nearly as scant as that concerning the father.

Imperious Leader called for a scan of information that might suggest names about which the simulator had accumulated more data. Since most of the Cylons' information about humans was extracted from prisoners, the simulator often contained better information about key officers in lower positions of command, those who had more direct dealings with combat warriors. On the scanner's list, he recognized the name of Starbuck, an heroic sort of human (or at least they thought so), mention of whom seemed to occur often in Cylon interrogations. He ordered the template to provide a simulation of this Lieutenant Starbuck.

Suddenly seated in front of Imperious Leader was a human with eyes so bright and searching they reminded him of the rays of light that emanated from Cylon warrior helmets. The Starbuck figure immediately broke into a broad smile. Humans seemed to derive some odd sort of pleasure out of smiling. The Leader was glad he had cut off physiological reaction to the sight of humans, or else he might not have been able to endure the sight of this smiling bright-eyed human.

"Hi, chum," the Starbuck simulacrum said. The greeting surprised Imperious Leader, since simulacra—programmed, after all, from simulator data banks—rarely initiated conversation.

"I am addressing Lieutenant Starbuck of the Battlestar *Galactica*, am I not?"

"Knock it off and tear it up, Cylon. You know I'm no more Starbuck than you're a blooming lily of the valley. I'm a reproduction and I'd strangle you if my hands had any substance."

The Leader glanced briefly toward the simulator template, wondering if something was wrong with the device. It was highly unorthodox for it to program such independence into a simulacrum—unless, of course, that independence was so much a part of the man's character that it could not be removed from the mental, emotional, and physiological profile that had been extracted by the simulator. It was possible, Imperious Leader thought, that this Starbuck might be extremely useful, if only as a study of independence of thought in humans. Much could be learned from the brashness and insulting demeanor of this young officer replication. Connections might be established that could fill just those gaps in Imperious Leader's strategy.

"How many ships remain in your fleet, Lieutenant?"

The Starbuck laughed.

"As many as the specks of dirt between your toes, Cylon."

"Cylons do not have toes."

The Starbuck seemed genuinely surprised.

"Then maybe we don't have any ships," it said.

"Come now, Lieutenant, we know that there are still many ships in your—"

"Then you'd better inspect the dirt between your toes more closely, Cylon."

"But I told you Cylons don't—"

Imperious Leader stopped talking. Not only did the Starbuck simulacrum initiate conversation, it also *interrupted.* This interrogation was going to be difficult, and perhaps extremely unpleasant.

When the Cylons' sneak attack came, Commander Adama was in a classroom aboard the research-ship *Infinity,* lecturing to the greenest-looking bunch of flight cadets he'd ever seen. They looked to him like grade-school children who should be learning the history of the twelve worlds rather than the intricacies of viper aerodynamics and warfare maneuvers. One of the youngsters in the first row appeared to be not much older than Adama's adopted grandson, Boxey. From the glazed look in the cadet's eyes, the commander wondered if he might even trust six-year-old Boxey at the controls of a viper more than this dazed young man. He had been assured that the new crop of cadets were all of proper legal age, but the dangers they'd have to face after graduation from their abbreviated course of training were so considerable, so awesome, that he wished they did not have to be quite this young. Still, they were all volunteers. When the call went out to the hundreds of ships in the fleet, the command staff had received enough applications to man the ships and flight crews of at least a hundred squadrons. If only they had enough ships to form a hundred squadrons.

The desperate plight of the fleet was not made any brighter by the inadequate and makeshift conditions in which the new warriors were trained. A research ship didn't substitute for a fully equipped and staffed space academy, even though the faculty had been able to convert enormous labs into gymnasiums, mock-flight areas, and simulated battle-condition testing chambers. Adama recalled the space academy he'd attended on his native planet, the destroyed Caprica. The Caprican Academy had been manned by the most brilliant military strategists in all the twelve worlds; the classes aboard the *Infinity* were conducted mostly by officers too disabled to maintain their posts and pilots who'd been severely wounded in combat. The Caprican Academy had boasted the finest technology available. Any flight, combat, or support situation could be reproduced within its walls or at its many stadiums for war maneuvers. The facilities on the *Infinity* were acceptable so long as you didn't inspect them twice.

However, such improvisation was the key to the fleet's continued success in evading the main force of their Cylon pursuers. Every person on every ship was putting in double time to improve the efficiency and speed of the overall fleet. Half a dozen freighters had been converted to flying foundries, which in turn converted scrap metal and other materials into vipers for the *Galactica*'s crew of fighter pilots. Everyone in the fleet had become a scavenger, searching for metal and electronic supplies within their ships and on the few planets they encountered with obtainable material. Considering the sources for their construction, the viperships now leaving the foundry were remarkably well-manufactured vehicles. It was true, of course, that they were more often subject to technical and mechanical failures than those vipers from the

original squadrons. That was only natural, considering
the haste of construction, the substitutions, the strain on
already overused metals, all of the compromises that
made the newer vipers a bit less maneuverable, a bit more
subject to the kind of malfunctions that often accompanied improvisation.

Still, Adama was continually amazed at what
experienced pilots could do, even with substandard
equipment. A pilot like Starbuck, Boomer, or Apollo
could do wonders with any flying crate put under his
control. But space-academy cadets didn't have the
instinctive abilities to correct course, or whirl out of a
spin, or work a smooth landing when all the equipment
around you was sending out sparks. At that, their record
under fire was not bad so far—a tribute to the command
abilities and protective instincts of the experienced pilots
and flight officers. Starbuck, for example, inspired so
much confidence in his squadron that a cadet on his first
launch out of the *Galactica* tubes frequently accomplished miraculous aerodynamic feats. Even Apollo,
more militaristic than other young officers, more distant
from the crews under his command, had performed
wonders in helping the new cadets. It was just too bad that
they were unable to train them better, unable to give them
more flights just for practice. Fuel conservation and the
constant danger of Cylon attack made flights that weren't
concerned with battle, scouting, or planetary exploration
impossible. Too many cadets were being lost in
skirmishes that experienced warriors would have survived.

The main theme of Adama's speech was the need for
caution, a message that he had to reiterate often even with
his experienced officers. It was not cowardly, he insisted,
to draw back from a planetary or intraspace phenomenon
when your instruments recorded even the slightest threat
of danger. It was not cowardly to retreat from a battle
with Cylons when the alien forces outnumbered you by
fantastic odds. It was not cowardly to carry back an
important message to the fleet even when it meant leaving
some of your fellow pilots behind to fight an apparently
hopeless battle.

Looking down at the cadets' faces, Adama could see that although they strived to look respectful to an officer whose name was legendary among them, they still were not ready to accept his message. Adama wasn't even sure he offered it with complete sincerity. He recalled Apollo's misery when the young man had been forced to leave his brother Zac under intense Cylon fire in order to return to the *Galactica* and warn the fleet of the impending Cylon ambush. Zac had been killed, and a long time passed before Apollo stopped feeling guilty over his brother's death. Even now, Adama wasn't entirely sure his son had surmounted his guilt feelings. But Apollo *had* acted correctly and his alerting of the fleet had led directly to the few human survivors' eventual escape from the massive Cylon war-thrust.

It seemed tragic, to Adama, that Apollo, perhaps the most heroic of all *Galactica*'s combat officers, never had a moment when his emotions allowed him to actually feel like a hero. It was just an epithet awarded him, like a medal he never took out of its storage box to wear proudly.

"I'm glad Apollo is so reticent about his heroism," Adama's daughter, Athena, had said when her father had broached the subject to her. "Never trust a hero who boasts about his heroism."

"Your *friend* Lieutenant Starbuck isn't reluctant to boast a bit about his exploits."

"Well, he's an exception to a lot of rules. And don't think I didn't take note of your sarcasm."

Adama knew his daughter felt something like love for Starbuck, so he didn't pursue the subject. She always pretended her feelings for the bold and immodest young officer were not as deep as Adama knew they were.

The alarm warning of the Cylon attack blared out in the middle of Adama's lecture. To their credit, the cadets were on their feet and on the move immediately. Adama dropped his notes to the floor and rushed to the launching bay where his shuttle, piloted by Athena, awaited him. As soon as he was secure in his seat, he felt the welcome lurch as the shuttle hurtled forward through the launching tubes and out of *Infinity*.

"What is it this time?" he asked his daughter, who was listening to the garbled series of messages coming over the shuttle's commlines.

"Nothing too frightening," she responded. "A bunch of Cylon fighters broke through a flaw in the camouflage force field. We might as well drop the force field for all the good it's doing us. Save the energy. The Cylons seem to detect us often enough."

"I'm beginning to wonder if they know where we are at *all* times."

"Think you might be right there."

Athena's agreement added to Adama's suspicions. She had command-level abilities and, in fact, had turned down important posts in order to remain aboard *Galactica*. He had always found her opinions valuable, even when they disagreed with his own instincts.

"What's the report on the ambush?" he asked her.

"Only one of our ships hit. The foundry ship *Hephaestus*. Some highside damage, nothing serious, nothing they can't handle."

"Cylon casualties?"

"Not specified. Boomer's message was, quote, we annihilated a majority of the creepy red-lights before they turned tail, unquote."

"We lucked out again then."

"Starbuck says he's donating a large bequest of luck to be spread over the entire fighting crew."

Adama's laugh was too short an outburst, and Athena looked over him, worried.

"Something's troubling you," she said.

"Luck's troubling me. We've had too much of it. We've stayed ahead of the Cylons for a long time. Some of that's skill, some of it's luck."

"Well, it's natural I suppose to worry about luck turning, but—"

"No, that's not even bothering me. Anyway, I think luck's just an instinctive control of our natural human resources. What's bothering me is that our luck seems a bit too pat, a bit too calculated."

"I'm afraid I don't—"

"Sometimes I get the definite feeling that the Cylons

have some strings attached to us and are just pulling at them like puppetmasters. As if their sneak attacks are not meant to succeed, as if they're just proddings to force us into certain course patterns, as if—"

"Mmmm, that's pretty fanciful. If I didn't know you better, I might say paranoid. *And* if I didn't know..."

She lapsed into a concerned silence, pretended to check gauges she had just checked a moment ago.

"Well, out with it," Adama said. "What were you going to say?"

She took a deep breath before answering.

"I reviewed a report on the last Cylon ambush, the one where our guys wiped out nearly the whole contingent of their fighters. Tigh underlined a part of it for me, put a question mark in the margin. Our scanners seemed to indicate—I emphasize *seemed*—that there had been no life form of any kind within a couple of the destroyed ships. Of course the scans were random, and they might be incorrect, especially since collected under battle conditions in which not all Cylon ships were scanned efficiently. Still..."

"Still, it's an interesting bit of data, and that's why Tigh wanted us to take note of it."

"Exactly."

"What do you think it means, Athena?"

"Not sure. What's the possibility that the fighters were remote-controlled, operated at a distance by Cylons inside the ships that escaped?"

"It's worth considering."

"Fits your puppetmaster theory rather neatly, don't you think?"

"As I say, it's worth considering."

Athena laughed.

"I detect a touch of mockery in your laughing, young lady."

"It's just that, even if your boots had wings on them, you'd resist jumping to conclusions, Dad."

"You're not supposed to call me Dad during duty hours."

"What do I get, company punishment for insubordinate affection?"

"A couple weeks pulling prison barge duty might do you a world of good."

"You've convinced me. Sir."

The *Galactica* now hovered before them, reminding Adama of some kind of brilliant gem (a steely, brightly glowing jewel set against black velvet in the Universal Museum on Caprica). Next to the *Galactica*, the rest of the fleet looked pretty much like paste items on a costume-jewelry necklace. These vehicles carried the only survivors of the vicious Cylon ambush that had destroyed twelve worlds and most of their people.

Adama felt a twinge of pain in his chest as he recalled the day when, helpless on the *Galactica* bridge, he had watched the twelve worlds go up in flames, had listened to the transmissions of human suffering, had observed the planets fall to the enslaving Cylon forces one by one, had sent out the clarion call to assemble those humans who could escape Cylon capture and bring ships to the fleet. The ships' continued survival in the face of Cylon assaults testified to the courage of the remainder of the human race, the inherent courage within all humans. Vessels designed for commercial, transportation, or supply purposes had managed to perform like fighting ships. One marked *Colonial Movers, We Move Anywhere* had, with makeshift armament, turned back a squadron of Cylon fighters single-handedly. Its achievement was already being transformed into song and legend among the people in the ships of the fleet.

Adama felt proud of the way his ragtag fleet had performed so far. However, the fear that one day there would be an attack in which human ingenuity and fortitude could not overcome the overwhelming Cylon odds haunted the dreams of the *Galactica*'s commander.

Every time Starbuck settled his neck back into the neckbrace and watched Jenny, his flight-crew leader, close the canopy around him, he wished the same wish. If only he could have a cigar right now...

Hundreds of times he'd asked Boomer, who was an expert on the botanical aspects of smoking devices, to develop a cigar that wouldn't be crushed against the front of the canopy or fill the small enclosed area with dense smoke, and could additionally be fitted through breathing and communication gear. Boomer had laughed heartily and said that while he thought it was possible to contain the smoke within a proper-sized burning cylinder, and even possible to find a way to adapt it to the breathing gear, he doubted whether Core Command would approve such a revolutionary device. Core Commands were always aeons behind in accepting the really innovative combat notions, Boomer had commented dryly.

"Lieutenant Starbuck, sir?"

The high voice, distorted perhaps by the static in the transmission, sounded adolescent, a bit whiny.

"What is it, Cadet Cree?"

Starbuck saw the boyish cadet's face in his mind. Childlike eyes, eager mouth, tousled hair—did he imagine it, or did Cree have a number of freckles across the bridge of his nose? No, there were definitely no freckles. Cree was just the sort of wide-eyed kid who looked like he should have freckles, that was all.

"Lieutenant, sir, what you said at the briefing—about exercising all caution and not firing until—"

"Yeah, yeah, kid. What is it, did I use too many two-syllable words or what?"

"No, not that. I understood. It's just that we were taught that there were times when aggressive initiative was—"

"Stow it, Cadet. That's academy lecture and it's all just so much felgercarb when you're in the cockpit of a colonial viper, get it?"

"Well, yes sir, but—"

Starbuck sighed. It seemed that every third or fourth cadet was like Cree—still not ready to join a squadron, too eager to spout ill-digested textbook lessons, and yet so unwilling to even consider death and pain.

"Look, Cadet Cree. When you've been on a few combat missions, you'll know all there is to know about *aggressive initiative*, okay? Until then, you obey Starbuck's Golden Rule."

"Golden Rule?"

"Keep your trap shut when somebody wants something from you, plan on how you're gonna get them later, and never volunteer even when the mission looks like the boondoggle of all time."

"That doesn't sound very—"

"Kid, now's one of those times when you keep your trap shut."

"Yes, sir, Lieutenant."

A soft chuckle on the line. Starbuck's wingmate, Boomer.

"I think the young warrior's learned a lesson," Boomer said.

"What's that?" Starbuck asked.

"Now he knows what it's like to be starbucked."

Starbuck smiled. In flight-squadron slang, to be starbucked meant to be maneuvered into a losing situation, whether in a gambling game, a battle, or an argument.

A blue light began beeping on the viper's control panel—the command bridge's warning that all ships were ready for launch. The deep mellow voice of Colonel Tigh, the commander's aide, came over the line:

"Deepspace advance probe. Blue Squadron up."

Starbuck tensed his body, knowing he was to launch first.

"Launch one!"

Starbuck was slammed back against the cockpit seat and neckbrace as his viper began its long accelerating thrust out of the launch tubes of Battlestar *Galactica*. On the line, Tigh's voice bellowed:

"Launch two!"

That would be Boomer's ship being catapulted out the second bay. Starbuck steadied his viper as it cleared launch tube and zoomed in a wide arc above the massive command ship. Out of the corner of his eye he saw Boomer executing the same maneuver with his fighter, then hovering beside Starbuck's viper.

"Flight Academy unit, stand by," ordered Tigh. "Cadet Cree, Cadet Bow, and Cadet Shields. Prepare to launch."

Each of the cadets' ships was launched in its turn and the five fighters of the advance probe formed a star formation in front of the *Galactica*. Starbuck tapped a signal button on his control panel to alert the other fliers to engage their turbos for forward thrust. All five fighters, even the three makeshift vipers fresh from the foundries, were accelerated evenly by their pilots. Behind them the command battlestar appeared to fade abruptly and become a distant point.

Starbuck felt cold shudders as he surveyed the apparently far-off empty space around him. Even the flickering far-off stars gave him no confidence that there was really anything out there. *Oh, there's something out there, all right*, he thought. *If there's nothing else, there're Cylons out there. Out there somewhere. Behind us, ahead of us. Even above and below us.* He laughed softly, thinking how Boomer was always saying, in off-duty bull sessions, that there were no such concepts as above and below, in front and behind, when you were alone in space. Each tilt of your ship, the smallest alteration of your flight angle, each failure of your instruments to record correctly—all of these changes shifted your reality as well. Boomer was fond of phrases like "altering reality." In a way, Starbuck's long-standing friendship with the courageous, intelligent, and skillful Boomer kept shifting his own reality in positive ways. Boomer steadied him whenever the angles of his own life tilted, rescued him when he got himself into really deep trouble.

Starbuck checked the scanner panel which now displayed, in electronic silhouettes, the flight formation. One of the ships had edged out of formation and appeared ready to veer off on its own.

"Loosen it up, Boomer," he said. "The man next to you is about to fly up your tailpipe."

There was a short pause before Boomer, evidently checking which pilot was out of line, spoke:

"Cadet Cree, is that you?"

"Yes sir," came the agonizingly adolescent voice of Cree.

"Come any closer you'll melt your front end off."

Cree's viper edged back slightly. But just slightly. Imagining the freckle-faced—no, not freckle-faced—kid screwing up his unlined brow in childish puzzlement, Starbuck was surprised to find himself simultaneously amused and annoyed by the foolish daring of the young cadet.

"Our instructor ordered us to keep tight," Cree announced with authority. *He probably has a blackboard in his cockpit with him*, Starbuck thought.

"Your instructor is back at the base, probably playing seven-eleven with a glass of grog at his elbow," Boomer said. "You, my fine young skypilot, are on a deepspace probe. There are risks that you don't get past by stopping your mock-flight vehicle and raising your hand to ask your instructor a question!"

"Our instructor never let us raise—"

"Cadet! Even this kind of routine flight is different from anything you experienced on the training ship *Infinity*. It's not like failing a simulation. Overheat and you evaporate. Pfft. Get off my tail, okay?"

Cree paused before answering:

"Yes. Yes, sir."

Starbuck studied the scanner, watching Cree draw his ship back and take his proper place in the star formation. The kid would have to be watched or he'd be converted to space debris the first time anything went wrong. No matter what the mission, there was always a complication—a ship so hastily built it couldn't stand the stress of battle, or a pilot who should be flying model ships in his hand across a playroom. Starbuck sighed. To some people the present difficulties of the *Galactica*'s fighting squadrons might be shrugged off as fortunes of war. He had too many problems seeing war in such terribly materialistic terminology. If there was any financially oriented figure of speech that applied, it was that war—at least the kind of battles Starbuck and his kind had to fight—was the gaming pot with each side anteing and raising until one displayed the winning hand. Or, as so often happened with Lieutenant Starbuck, the victorious player managed to avoid having his bluff discovered.

Adama watched Colonel Tigh trace a flight-path line on the starfield map. Tigh's long thin aristocratic fingers seemed to be about to create their own individual paths across the map. Long ago, during the thousand-year war that had ended so abruptly with the fake Cylon peace offer and their subsequent annihilative ambush, Adama and Tigh had been combat pilots together, sharing a reputation for bravado and accomplishment much like that enjoyed presently by the brash and daring young lieutenants Starbuck and Boomer.

The two combat teams, one from the past and the other in the present, were alike in hundreds of ways. Both teams had distinguished combat records. Both were the obvious choices for the most dangerous missions. Both were even composed similarly, each containing one white man, one black. And (Adama would have been embarrassed to admit) there were distinct similarities in the personality makeup of the past and present duos. Although he would never have acknowledged it to Starbuck, Adama had been a similarly brash young man, plunging recklessly into risky exploits, especially if they seemed designed to test him. And, in many ways, Tigh had been Adama's Boomer, courageous and equally daring. Boomer and Tigh, however, both knew when it was time to apply the brakes to adventurers like Starbuck and Adama, knew when caution should replace bravado as the watchword. It was a pity that Tigh had not won the battlestar command post he so richly deserved. He had been, unfortunately, as incautious in speaking his mind in the wrong places as he had been wary in battle, and the result was that the command posts had been denied him. Adama had reminded him time and again to measure his words, but Tigh always blurted out what was on his mind, usually with some eloquence, without regard to the situation. On the *Galactica* command bridge, Adama valued Tigh's frankness, depended on it in fact. Still, he deserved that command post—and Adama would have obtained it for him, if there had been any more battlestars left to command.

"We have our new flight path," Tigh was saying. "The corrected course is locked in."

Adama studied the course and the change of vector that Tigh's hand traced.

"I don't like it," he said softly.

Tigh seemed surprised.

"But it's the only course that makes sense, Commander," he said. "And look how it's keeping us even farther from—"

"Still don't like it. Anything that dovetails this simply, this conveniently, must be examined more closely. For our own safety."

One side of Tigh's mouth tilted upward in an ironic smile.

"I thought you'd be jubilant," Tigh said. "We destroyed sixteen Cylon ships in that last assault."

"How many of them were manned?"

Tigh hesitated before answering:

"We scanned five. No indication of Cylon pilots in any of those cockpits. But, Commander, in the middle of combat you know that scanners can't be accurate, can't be—"

"Yet it is not unreasonable to assume that the Cylons are sending unmanned craft against us."

"Well, as speculation, it's—"

"They may want to have us destroy those attackers. To lull us."

Tigh nodded.

"That *has* occurred to me, I admit. You read my report. On the other hand, their task force has fallen back to"—he pointed to the starfield map—"that point. It's a considerable distance, and seems to indicate they've lost track of us again."

Adama stared at the cluster of lights in the sector of the map which Tigh indicated.

"No, I doubt that. I think they're still there, right behind us. Just keeping their distance. And so are their base ships." He turned away from the star map. "One thing is sure, we can't go back."

"When have we ever done that?"

Adama understood the undertone of frustration in his aide's voice. Tigh often expressed his wish they could stop fleeing the Cylon task force, could just turn around, dig in, and blast the Cylon war machine out of the skies.

"Look here," Adama said.

Taking a small cylindrical tube out of his pocket and

setting its laser-directed light for a thin line, he directed
the ray toward the map, first raising it toward the top of
the starfield.

"Above us is the planet Cassarion, listed in the
warbook as a Cylon outpost. We cannot move in that
direction." He lowered the light, sent its beam toward the
lower portion of the map. "Below us, the Sellian asteroid
belt. Millions of fragments from the world the Cylons
destroyed. We couldn't get through it. Apollo, Starbuck,
and Boomer'd have no chance of blasting a path through
that mess, as they did back at that Carillon minefield."

"Our only course is clear then," Tigh said. "Straight
ahead. The point scouts report a safe passage."

"It was too easy," Adama said softly.

"Commander?"

Adama raised his voice.

"That last defeat of the Cylon attackers, their sudden
retreat..."

"But the *Galactica* was bearing down on them."

"Yes...so it appeared."

A glimmer of understanding came into Tigh's dark
eloquent eyes.

"And what is the truth?" he asked.

Tigh was challenging, demanding an absolute.

"Not truth perhaps," Adama said. "More than truth.
Instinct. I think we're being carefully maneuvered, *herded*
toward that...that *safe* passage ahead."

Athena, now standing by her father, suddenly spoke:

"But why?" She glanced toward the starfield map,
seeming to see in its lines, arcs, and flickering lights the
black void with its few stars that was the reality
represented by the symbols on the map. "What's out
there?" she whispered.

"I don't know, Athena. Ghosts maybe. Hostile planets,
friendly ones. Maybe this time we'll stumble on Earth, if
it's not after all the imaginary product of legend." He
turned back to Tigh. "I think we should send out more
scouting patrols. What is it, Tigh? You're reluctant.
Why?"

"Commander, we've pushed our star fighters around
the clock. They're bushed."

"We all are. You're worried about more than that, aren't you? Well, what is it?"

"Sir, it's just that, well, we're having to throw in more cadets from the academy now. Too many. It's dangerous."

Adama thought of the cadets he'd seen earlier, and the emotional exhaustion he'd felt from addressing them. He wanted to tell his aide to bring everybody in, recall all vipers. But that was impossible.

"Of course it's dangerous. But we're somewhat lacking in alternatives for the moment, with a Cylon task force probably tailing us, and who knows what out there."

Tigh nodded, the reluctance still showing in his saddened eyes.

"Colonel, we *must* increase the scouting contingent, even if it means sending up cadets."

"Dad?"

Adama glared at his daughter, showing disapproval at her familiarity on the command bridge. She caught his meaning, drew her slim body to attention.

"*Commander*. I'm checked out for scouting in a viper. Reassign me."

Both Adama and Tigh smiled.

"Athena," Adama said, "you're much too valuable here."

"Yes, sir," she said, clearly disappointed.

Tigh turned to a bridge officer and ordered that the duty roster be flashed onto the main screen, in order to see who was still available for scouting patrols. Starbuck's voice over the main commline interrupted Tigh's command:

"Blue Leader to Base. We're coming up on a small planet. Dead ahead. Can you give us a quick scan?"

Tigh nodded toward the scanner section leader, who immediately fed the lieutenant's request into the ship's computer system.

"Base to Blue Leader. Scanner readout coming up." He turned to Adama, concern in his eyes. "Commander?"

"What is it?"

"An object in Sector Sigma."

The officer switched the readout onto Adama's screen.

Grids flashed and words appeared in the screen's corner. The shape of the planet reported by Starbuck came into resolution. Adama ordered a deeper probe-scan. The planet was so dark, so shrouded in a nearly black cloud cover, that only a slightly more detailed resolution could be managed. As each category covered by the probe flashed by in a corner of the screen, the same conclusion was flashed: insufficient data.

"Starbuck," Adama said into his commline mike.

"Yo, sir."

"Do you observe a sun or any other astronomical or geologic phenomenon around the planet?"

"No, sir, not a blessed thing."

Adama turned away from the console.

"What is it, sir?" Athena asked. "Why doesn't Starbuck observe anything? It doesn't—"

"Perhaps it does, Athena, perhaps it does. We need more data."

"I don't understand."

"We have a small planet here, not much more than an asteroid. It seems to be floating through space on its own, no sun anywhere detectable. It might be the remnant of some exploded planet from a star system long since disintegrated. Or it might be ... something else."

"Sir," Tigh said, "are you thinking what I think you are? One of the Cylon asteroids?"

"Exactly, Tigh."

"Cylon asteroid," Athena exclaimed. "I don't get it. An asteroid's a geological—"

"That's correct. I forget, Cylon asteroids would be before your time. There was a time, early in the thousand-year war, when the Cylons discovered a way to power asteroids across space, sometimes at phenomenal speeds, for combat purposes. They became sort of geologically formed fighter craft. We were never able to discover how they did it, as we've been unable to discern a great deal about Cylon technology."

"And this could be one of their—what would you call it, war weapons?" Athena asked. "This minor planet?"

"Well, it's a bit large, but perhaps. This might be one of their abandoned units. Or maybe not abandoned."

Adama's voice had become ominous.

"We need more data. Probably it's just what it looks like, a drifting asteroid." Adama turned to a bridge officer. "What's the report on it show now?"

"Structure: Crystalline elements table M-one."

"Surface?" said Tigh.

"Frozen seas. Fields of ice. Blizzard conditions marked by di-ethene storms."

Both Adama and Tigh looked pained by the new information.

"Di-ethene?" Athena said. "I never heard of—"

"The word's a corrupted form of a much longer word," Tigh said. "One too long to memorize. It's a gas. A *Cylon*-manufactured gas."

"If I remember correctly," Adama said, "di-ethene is often formed as a waste product from the style of laser weapon the Cylons've evolved. Their weaponry pumps out di-ethene, usually into the ground, sometimes into the air. It's very dangerous, especially if it escapes to a planet's surface in the form of clouds or mist. In the proper density, it can be fatal to us—one of the few instances I know where the discharged elements from a weapon can be just as dangerous as the firepower of the weapon itself."

Athena hunched her shoulders.

"That gives me the cold creeps."

Adama smiled.

"Cold is the word for it, all right, at least on this particular planet. What's your view, Tigh?"

Tigh glanced briefly at father and daughter, then at the watching bridge crew, before speaking tersely:

"Environment: Hostile!"

When Starbuck finally got a good look at the dark cloudy planet, he felt his hands go cold. He wondered if he was reacting to the planet's spectral appearance or whether the intense cold that no doubt existed on its surface sent out actual penetrating waves of frigidity, perhaps to warn off intruders. He flicked on his commline to *Galactica*, and said:

"Nice place. Didn't I see it listed in the R & R guide?

You want us to orbit the equator or is there a torrid zone for—"

"Keep out of its gravitational pull," ordered Tigh in a solemn voice. Tigh didn't like flippancy in transmissions to base, but had long ago given up ordering Lieutenant Starbuck to maintain the proper gravity while communicating.

"Will do," Starbuck said. He cut off the *Galactica* line and switched over to direct-comm among the vipers in the formation. "Okay, guys," he said, "all youngsters move up ahead and lock in a holding pattern while Boomer and I get a closer scan of the surface. If you—"

"Lieutenant Starbuck. Sir."

The annoying squeak of Cadet Cree again.

"Yes, what is it, Cadet?"

"I made a first in Scanning Procedure finals at the academy. I could go along with you, get a little actual experience at—"

"This is no time for *practice*, Cree. I'll give you a spot quiz later. Meantime, obey your orders. Your instructor did tell you guys about obeying orders, didn't he?"

"Yes sir! Lieutenant, sir!"

"All right then. You guys, peel off. Cadet Bow, you're in command."

Starbuck could picture Cree choking at that last order. The overconfident young cadet obviously saw himself as command material. Well, he'd learn. Learn or catch a laser beam in the throat; there weren't many other alternatives for eager new cadets nowadays.

The vipers broke formation. The three cadet ships moved ahead as ordered, although Starbuck thought he could detect a shade of recalcitrance in the way Cadet Cree executed the maneuver.

"Let's go, Boomer!"

The ships of the two experienced lieutenants arched away from the cadet ships and edged cautiously toward the asteroid. On the commline Starbuck heard Cadet Bow:

"Shields . . . Cree . . . Keep visual contact. Hold formation, Cree."

Bow's voice was deeper, more mature than Cree's, but

there was still a cadetlike tentativeness in the sound of it.

On Starbuck's control panel, the *Galactica* commline light flashed on. He flipped the communication switch.

"*Galactica*, reading," he said.

Adama came on the line.

"Starbuck," he said, "the planet below you has an atmosphere. Some di-ethene content, breathable otherwise, although the cold can descend to unbreathable levels. I don't want you or any of your squad to get too close. The di-ethene indicates the possible presence of Cylons or other alien habitation. Be careful. Take a look and return."

"About the di-ethene. It's in cloud form?"

"Sometimes."

"Dense."

"Sometimes."

"You don't have to worry. We won't go anywhere near that planet. Right, Boomer."

"Do you have time to put that in writing?"

"Boomer, sometimes—"

Starbuck was interrupted by a sudden blinding flash of light that seemed to come from the other side of the asteroid. Where the cadet ships were.

"Bow!" he cried into the direct-comm. "What was that?"

"I wish I could tell you," Bow replied. "Biggest darn light show I've ever seen. I'm going to check it out."

"No, wait for us," Starbuck said, but he could see on control-panel scanner that Bow had already peeled away from the other two cadet vehicles and was heading toward the point where the light had flashed.

"C'mon, Boomer," he said, "let's hop to it. That kid'll—"

"Got you, bucko."

Both flight-command vipers curved into gradual loops and flew toward the cadet ships. As the cadet fighters came into view, Bow speeding far ahead of Cree and Shields, a brilliant bead of light suddenly emerged from the planet's cloud cover. Throbbing and fiery, it soared skyward, almost with a gliding ease. It headed toward Bow's fighter. Too late Bow started to brake the ship and change his flight angle. The beam of light intersected

Bow's foundry-manufactured viper, which now looked like a speck of dust dimly illuminated in the brightness of the gigantic light-spear. Bow's fightercraft was seared jaggedly down the middle before it erupted into a shapeless melting mass, then exploded. The explosion's flames seemed dim by comparison with the brilliance of the force that had destroyed it.

The light-beam sailed off into space, as if launched on a steady even course, leaving no trace behind of the disintegrated craft.

The words now coming over direct-comm from the remaining two cadet ships were jumbled, inchoate, hysterical. Both pilots had changed their courses to fly toward the area where, moments ago, Cadet Bow's ship had been.

"Cree! Shields!" Starbuck shouted. "Back off! We're on the way!"

"What happened?" Boomer said as he brought his viper up beside Starbuck's.

"He was picked off!" cried Cree. "It's some kind of energy beam. Got Bow, wiped him out, came at him like a pulsar—only bigger, much bigger!"

Remembering Adama's cautionary words, Starbuck said:

"What do you think, Boomer? Some kind of laser cannon? With, say, a pulsar-styled beam?"

"It can't be! We're way out of range. Never saw one that could pick off a target that accurately, from ground through a cloud cover. I never saw that good a tracking device, especially not for that distance and situation."

"Okay."

Starbuck flipped the communication switch to the *Galactica* and shouted:

"Blue Leader to Base! We're under attack! Ready the landing deck. We've lost a ship and we're coming in!"

As he began to set his viper for the return course, Starbuck checked the whereabouts of Shields and Cree. They were both heading toward the dark asteroid.

"Cree! Shields! Set for return course. *Now!*"

But both pilots, unheeding, headed their craft straight for the planet's cloud cover.

CHAPTER TWO

Silently, Apollo watched Boxey put Muffit through its intricate maneuvers. The furry daggit-droid was a manufactured replica of the animal the boy had lost during the invasion of Caprica. Actually, as Boxey had pointed out often enough, the droid did not replicate the original very accurately. The original Muffit, Boxey said, had been shaggy-haired and mostly gray. The reproduction's fur was thick and brown, and its body was larger. Larger, in fact, than any daggit Apollo had ever seen or owned. Nor did its visible metal patches add to the illusion. However, the lab that had manufactured this prototype had included the essential traits for any daggit model, affection and loyalty. In the time since Boxey had tentatively accepted the droid from the laboratory, he had come to love it as much as, if not more than, the daggit he'd lost.

Now, as the boy commanded the droid to sprawl on the cabin floor and do a sort of clumsy push-up, Apollo kept his eye on the youngster, amazed at how much the boy seemed to have grown in just the past few days. The difficulty of raising a growing and energetic child made Apollo wonder again whether he should have adopted Boxey. Homeless, without parents, the child needed somebody. But perhaps a flight commander was not the most suitable father. With the *Galactica* constantly under Cylon pursuit and unknown threats ahead, there was always the risk that Boxey could be orphaned again, and Apollo didn't know whether the boy could recover from still another loss among the many losses he'd already sustained. Thinking of the boy's tragedies led Apollo to remember the losses in his own family. His brother Zac dying, left behind by Apollo in a damaged ship to die under Cylon fire while Adama watched on *Galactica*'s monitors. Later, both father and son had traveled to the surface of Caprica to find that Ila, wife and mother, had disappeared without a trace.

"Dad?"

Apollo almost didn't react to Boxey's question. He was still not used to being called Dad by the boy.

"Yes, what is it, Boxey?"

"You, well, you sort of went away from me there for a minute."

"Sorry, Boxey, just thinking. A bad habit. What do you need?"

"Don't need anything. Just wanted to make sure you're still here."

Apollo smiled at the boy, but could not keep from feeling sad. Even Boxey was aware of the risks. He didn't want Apollo to go away even when he was physically present. But there were more battles to come, more missions. *I have to go away, Boxey*, he thought, *and there's no way I know how to explain that to you.*

The boy returned his attention to Muffit.

"Hey, you daggit. I said twenty figure-eights. Stop shirking!"

Apollo was amused by the authoritative tone in the boy's voice as he barked commands at the droid. The boy was always saying how he planned to be a colonial warrior, a fighter pilot like his dad, and it had become part of his play. Well, he certainly looked to be starfleet material, even at the age of six. He'd already shown an unusual bravery so many times in the—

Apollo's thoughts were interrupted by the blaring of the alert claxons. As he leaped toward the door, saying a quick good-bye to Boxey, he heard Adama's voice echoing from many speakers:

"Battle stations!"

Hurrying onto the bridge, Apollo was quickly briefed by one of the officers. He rushed to his father's side.

"Fighter control reporting," he said. "All squadrons standing by."

Adama nodded, clapped a hand on his son's shoulder.

"Starbuck's probe ran into something," he told Apollo. "He's lost a ship." He turned to Tigh, asked: "Situation?"

Tigh leaned in toward the telecom screen, flipped a switch.

"Starbuck," he said. "Report in."

Sounding out of breath, Starbuck's voice came on the line. On the small screen, his face looked worried even in the telecom's unsure resolution.

"It came from the asteroid, somewhere in the upper quadrant. A high-energy beam of coherent light. Massive, very intense, blinding...we think it's some sort of laser weaponry, the kind with the pulsar effect—but this time, believe me, it must be a *giant* pulsar weapon. Tigh, it's—"

"Starbuck," Boomer's voice cut in, "we've lost contact with Cree. Visual *and* scanner."

"Stand by, Colonel. We're missing another ship."

"And Shields now!" Boomer yelled. "I've got no contact with Shields either!"

"Breaking transmission, *Galactica*," Starbuck cried. "Back with you in a flash."

As Starbuck's voice faded, Apollo turned to Adama.

"Father," he said, "let me take my squadron out after them, to protect them from—"

"No, not yet," Adama said softly. "Not till we know more. But put your squadron on alert, Captain Apollo!"

Apollo rushed off the bridge, grabbing a flight jacket held out by an aide just before he leaped through the hatchway to the corridor.

• • •

Starbuck frantically racked through all communication channels, trying to find a sound-trace of the missing cadets. "Cree! Come in! Shields! Where are you?"

"Got them!" Boomer shouted. "They're just inside critical gravitational pull."

Boomer flashed Starbuck the coordinates identifying the location of the two ships. The static on the commline faded, and the cadets' hysterical voices replaced the firelike crackle.

"Cree! Shields!" Starbuck cried. "Come back! You can't go down there!"

Cree's response was strident:

"I saw where it came from! I'm going after it!"

"Turn back!" Starbuck said. "Do not enter the atmosphere. I repeat, for both of you, do not—"

"Bow was my roommate!" Shields gasped, tears in his voice.

"That's an order! Both of you turn back!"

Starbuck's control panel scanner showed the two cadet ships not veering a millimeter from course.

"I'm locked on target," Shields said, his voice cooler now.

"Right behind you," Cree said.

Starbuck set his viper downward, toward the asteroid cloud cover.

"Boomer," he said, "we can't let them go down alone!"

"Maybe we can't, but we have to! Starbuck, pull out!"

"No, you know me better, Boomer. Join me or return to command ship."

A pause before Boomer answered:

"I never know whether you really mean that option. I'm just behind you, bucko."

The two vipers zoomed toward the cloud cover. Boomer's level voice came over the commline:

"They're in the clouds. We'll never get a visual on them."

"Record their short-range telemetry. Maybe we can get a fix."

Involuntarily, Starbuck sucked in his breath as his ship penetrated the gray, almost black cloud cover, and he felt himself enveloped in a nightmarish darkness.

●　　●　　●

First Centurion Vulpa, Warrior of the Elite Class, sat regally in his command chair and gruffly barked orders at his first-brained subalterns. Some kind of intruder had been discovered above the clouds of Tairac. A beam from the laser cannon atop Mount Hekla had struck and destroyed a ship. Subsequent activity of other ships had been detected.

Vulpa felt uncharacteristically nervous. Cylons rarely felt agitation of any sort. But then, Vulpa was not a characteristic Cylon. When he had been a first-brain fighter pilot, he had had occasional glimmerings that there was something special about him. And he faintly perceived that his specialness had little to do with his spectacular abilities to maneuver a Cylon fighter and destroy hundreds of enemy spacecraft. No, the qualities he felt had more to do with the way he could perceive the universe, the way he could make simple mental connections that seemed impossible for other first-brain Cylons. In some combat instances he had been able to execute strategy that he *knew* was the equal of anything a second-brain officer might have done. When he had tried to express these strange feelings to other warriors, they had not been able to comprehend. A number of times his conversations were reported to superiors, and he had been called in for discipline. Thus he had learned to conceal his awareness of his own select rank among his fellows. His inner isolation had also brought him feelings of loneliness, another emotion not usually felt by Cylons.

After the ceremony in which he had been awarded his second brain, his perception of himself increased more than twofold. He had been right, there was for him the potential for a special destiny. He knew immediately that he was one of the few second-brain Cylons whose intricate body mechanisms would not reject the implantation of a third brain at a later evolved stage of his life. Most Cylons could not survive one more brain implantation, and therefore only few were ever scanned as eligible to be raised to Imperious Leader status. Of those few, many were simply not suited for overall command level because they were not qualified in other physical, mental, or emotional aspects. Vulpa discovered later that his own

eligibility was endangered because of his tendency toward
forthright commentary, a pronounced arrogance in his
manner, and a need to bully other officers into agreement
with him. The present Imperious Leader had cautioned
him several times about these traits, saying that if he did
achieve third-brain status, he would comprehend at once
the reasons why such traits could, from an overall
objective view, be regarded as deficiencies.

Nevertheless, Imperious Leader had admitted, Vulpa's
assertive tendencies might just be overlooked, since in
certain situations they resolved themselves into ingenious
positive actions. Vulpa tried to obey Imperious Leader's
admonitions, as any good Cylon must. His ambition
increased, soared higher than any hopes ever displayed by
his fellow executive officers, who could just barely
express ideas of ambition, who perhaps were not in fact
ambitious. That knowledge made him feel lonelier than
he had ever felt in the days when he had had only a single
brain.

In spite of his own cautiousness, Vulpa encountered
situations in which his negative traits came to the fore,
and he cursed himself for his loss of control. He did not
want to fall off the thin line he was treading, since it led
directly to the monstrously high pedestal on which the
Imperious Leader throne rested, and Vulpa needed
desperately to continue along that line. His last outburst
had nearly finished him, and had resulted in the
disciplinary assignment to this frigid, distant, appropri-
ately lonely outpost. Although there was considerable
honor in being assigned command of the most massive
weapon ever devised for Cylon use, Vulpa nevertheless
felt the shame of the discipline deeply. He vowed to
perform actions here so heroic that Imperious Leader
would have to call him back to the command base star.
There he would prove himself worthy of the throne until
the time came when he would actually ascend to it.

The time when a new Imperious Leader would be
chosen seemed frustratingly a long time away, but Vulpa
would have to endure it. Anyway, it might not be so long.
If the present Imperious Leader continued his obsessive
quest to destroy all fleeing humans, to exterminate the

grubby little race in fact, there were all sorts of openings, all sorts of possibilities that the Leader would tumble from his throne ahead of his time or even be destroyed by one of those crafty little human pests. It was doubtful, but an ambitious being tended to contemplate lines toward the future with an un-Cylon-like eagerness.

Now, perhaps, his chance had come. As soon as the message that the escaping human fleet was being maneuvered toward his sector arrived, informing him that it might be necessary to engage the immense firepower of the laser cannon, Vulpa had put his garrison on alert. Destroying the remnants of the human race might just put Vulpa into the strategic position he had hoped for. It would draw Imperious Leader's approval and definitely put Vulpa in the forefront of all Cylon executive officers. It would—

A technician interrupted the first centurion's reverie:

"Two fightercraft. Colonial. Entering defense perimeter."

Rising, Vulpa examined the hexagonal screens for himself. Good. This confirmed the previous reports of anomalies, and verified that the destroyed ship had also been colonial in origin. The two ships now onscreen had cleared the dense cloud cover and were skimming along the vast gray underlayers, seemingly flying with purpose toward an objective. The foolish filthy little creatures! They were planning an assault on Mount Hekla and the laser cannon. Vulpa might have laughed aloud, if such laughter were not regarded with such suspicion among Cylons.

"I want one of them alive," he said to his subalterns.

Starbuck's ship cleared the clouds, with Boomer following a moment later. The asteroid's surface was nearly as dark as the interior of the cloud cover. The only discernible lights were a fairly bright spherical glow in the foothills of a dimly outlined mountain that ascended to the clouds, and the contrails from the ships of the two cadets far ahead of them.

"I got 'em, Boomer."

As they closed in on the slower vipers of the two cadets,

Starbuck punched up a general terrain scan. He was immediately impressed with the mountain. Although the great ranges of Caprica had contained mountains more awesome than this one, here on this small asteroid, rising up from a relative flatland, it was an awe-inspiring sight. Its ragged outlines and glacial surface suggested quite a challenge even to an experienced mountaineer.

And the vipers of the two cadets were heading right for it!

That's the last thing I need right now, Starbuck thought, *to crash-land on a mountain like that chasing two brainless kiddie-pilots. I never planned on getting any mountaineering time into my files and records.*

He punched up a closer scan of the mountain. As the screen displayed the summit, some ungeological formations were indicated. The information at the bottom of the scanner screen made Starbuck inhale sharply.

"What is it?" Boomer said.

"On the top of that mountain, it's a gun emplacement. Huge. It's like it's carved out of the ice and rock. The weapon itself's in a, in what appears to be a steelcrete bastion. And, Boomer, if my figures are correct, it's every bit as massive as we suspected. And, look, it's moving now. As big as it is, it ain't stationary—it's as maneuverable as . . . as a telescope in an observatory. I mean, the scale shows it as *enormous*, maybe the largest laser-style cannon anywhere, Boomer. It's bigger than—oh my God!"

The vipers of Cree and Shields were now slipping upward, zeroing in on the weapon itself. At the same time the barrel of the cannon swung slowly around, pointed in their direction but just above them. Starbuck bellowed a curse as Shields's ship eased into the weapon's lower range. Suddenly an uncanny, luminescently bright beam of light pulsed out of the cannon's barrel, lighting up the skies and causing thousands of glittering rays to form a mazelike network across the immediate icy surfaces of the planet. It enveloped Shields's viper, which seemed to remain in shadow outline for a brief moment, then disintegrated into a blazing fireball. The beam passed to the left of Starbuck's and Boomer's ships, continuing to illuminate the surface of the planet in a daylike brightness, then entered the clouds, briefly lighting them in a red-streaked but quite peaceful-looking aspect that reminded Starbuck of the kind of fluffy clouds that had sailed over Caprica on a warm summer day.

"Shields!" Starbuck screamed, even though he knew the cadet was dead.

"Too late," Boomer said, "he's gone. I've lost Cree's signal too."

"It's there. I saw him. But it's being jammed. They know we're here, too, Boomer. Stay low, that canron can't reach us down here."

"Right, bucko!"

Starbuck's scanner showed a trio of what were clearly Cylon fighters rising from an area beyond the weapon. From the first shots they fired, at a target near the left side of the mountain, Starbuck knew immediately where Cree was.

Vulpa ordered the launch of three fighters to make the remaining enemy pilot crash-land. The command pilot of the lead Cylon fighter carefully sent a shot across the viper's bow. In the gelid atmosphere, the streaks of laser fire had the look of fiery icicles.

"Invader," the Cylon flight commander said, "release control of your ship to us."

The human's answer was to open fire. Vulpa ordered his flight commander:

"Force him down!"

The three Cylon ships converged on their common enemy.

Starbuck and Boomer had to watch the Cylon ships force Cree down. Cree's pitiful voice came through an interruption in the jamming crackle of static:

"Starbuck! I'm surrounded!"

"Hang on," Starbuck replied, even though he suspected the poor cadet couldn't hear him. "We're coming, kid."

"Starbuck," Boomer pleaded, "forget it. It's too late now to do anything for Cree. By the time we get there, he's either dead or taken by those Cylon creeps."

"But—"

"No buts about it. We have to get back and warn the *Galactica*. This weapon's like nothing in any of our warbooks. They've gotta know!"

"I've lost two men. I'm not going to lose Cree."

"Forget it, Starbuck. We don't stand a chance against that weapon. We have to get to the *Galactica*. One life against thousands! Starbuck..."

For a moment Starbuck, furious, was tempted to disregard Boomer's cautions. But, knowing that his wingmate was right, he muttered another dark curse and, following Boomer, swung his viper around.

Seeing that the human enemy had been effectively trapped and captured, Vulpa returned to his command chair. One of the monitoring centurions announced:

"Two more fightercraft approaching, flying low."

"Destroy them as they come into range," Vulpa said.

The monitoring personnel kept close watch on the two new ships, then saw them swing around and slip over the near horizon.

"Fightercraft retreating," the technician said.

"That may be to our advantage. If we can use them to locate their command ship."

"Sir, that will be impossible. They have already managed to elude our instrumentation."

Vulpa nodded. The red streak of light moving back and forth across his helmet slowed, almost stopped.

"Bring me the captive," he ordered.

Imperious Leader turned to the simulation of Starbuck, which now seemed to lounge insultingly in its chair, an ugly stick humans called a cigar clenched between its teeth.

"Well, Lieutenant," Imperious Leader said, "your compatriots suspect nothing. They seem to have fallen blithely into my trap."

The Starbuck took the cigar out of its mouth, flicked ashes from it as if the cigar had real substance, and said:

"You got 'em in your slimy little claws?"

"No, but we will have them at any—"

"Then you ain't trapped 'em, bug-eyes."

"You are not programmed to insult me, Lieutenant."

"Sorry. Oversight. Sometimes even illusions can't help expressing the obvious."

Imperious Leader's hands gripped the sides of his throne more tightly, trying not to show anger at this unusually autonomous simulation.

"I would like to speak to you about your commander," he said.

The Starbuck's eyes lit up and he broke into that annoying smile.

"Ah. You mean, old Ironhull Adama."

"I do not understand. Hull made out of iron. I had never understood that he wore metallic battlesuits, as we Cylons do. There is nothing on record to suggest that."

The Starbuck's irritating smile broadened.

"Ironhull is a figure of speech. Do you Cylons have figures of speech?"

"We employ such in our poetry, but not ordinarily in our normal speech."

"You guys write *poetry*?"

The Starbuck seemed amazed. Imperious Leader was impressed by how sharply outlined this simulation was, as if one could reach out and actually touch it. He almost wished to make the test, but knew his hand would go right through Starbuck's incorporeal form.

"We have a faction of our society who use figures of speech in the poetry they chant. It is never written down. Cylon law does not allow that. But much of it is, I understand, preserved orally."

"But Cylons do *have* a written language?"

"Naturally."

"Why don't you let the poets write their work down?"

"It is custom, and has been custom since times more ancient than your puny race has apparently existed. Poets do not write down their poetry. It would be unseemly."

"Unseemly? Why unseemly?"

"Poets are not...not among the most desirable elements of our society. They are misfits, often criminals. We have found that assigning them to the poetry enclaves defuses their dangerous criminal traits that threaten the order of our society."

"You said *defuses*."

"I believe I did, yes."

"That was a metaphor. Figure of speech, Imperious Leader. Dangerous. Watch yourself."

"I should order your beheading."

The Starbuck laughed heartily.

"Try it. I'd like to watch the blade slip through my neck. It would be like a viper sliding through the clouds. Pardon the figure of speech."

Imperious Leader reviewed the annoying conversation, found his way back to the point of the discussion.

"We were talking about Ironhull. Your commander."

"Yep. Ironhull just means he's tough and not always penetrable to ordinary human eyes like mine. Around the crew, sometimes we call him Ironhull. Especially when we don't understand what's going on in his head. Is that any clearer?"

"It is clear enough. Commander Adama—is he likely to detect the outline of our plan? Will he know that our pursuit is a way of directing him toward a destination that we have chosen?"

"I think he might."

"Why?"

"You guys are hardly the subtlest creatures in the universe. You manage to be insidious, I'll give you that, and there are areas of, well, alien psychology in your makeup that keep throwing us for loops. But you are not especially subtle when it comes to warfare. You like the big moves, you like to display the heavy weapons, you prefer to destroy by outnumbering your enemy, depending on numbers instead of intricate strategy, you prefer direct attack to sleek aerial maneuvers—all of these things have often given us the edge in battles."

"In some battles, yes. But you should remember that, overall, we are the victors. Our methods have brought us the near-destruction of your military might, have brought us the annihilation of your twelve worlds, have given us the domination of the universe."

The Starbuck stopped smiling and nodded gravely.

"Yes, you're right there. By sneak attacks, torture, and a total lack of mercy you've nearly won it. But not quite all of it, bug-eyes. We're still there, and we're on the run now. But someday we may turn and face you, and then you'll..."

"You hesitate. Why?"

"Your data banks here cannot provide me the words that would effectively allow me to speak the disgust I feel for you."

The Starbuck sounded almost mechanical. The edges of the simulacrum seemed to blur.

"I believe, Lieutenant, that your day to turn and face us will never come. Your commander is headed on a course that will result in the final annihilation of your race. When it comes into range of our weaponry upon Tairac—"

"We've beaten you before. We'll do it again."

"This trap, Lieutenant, is what your people call foolproof."

The Starbuck's eyes seemed to narrow as he said:

"Well, with any luck, Imperious Leader, perhaps you can catch yourself a couple of fools."

Pressing a button on the side of his throne, Imperious Leader made the Starbuck simulacrum disappear. Its vague outline seemed to remain for a moment even after the image had abruptly vanished.

I never knew Lieutenant Starbuck during his cadet days. However, stories—myths and legends of the academy— have come back to me. I can't verify their truth.

I heard that, on off-duty hours, he would often unlock the war-game room (with "borrowed" keys, of course) and turn the area into a vast amusement arcade, conducting lotteries on how many hits could be scored within specified amounts of time by a mock-flight vehicle shooting at images of Cylon ships, hiring the best hand-to-hand fighters to hold matches under simulated battle conditions (again, a certain amount of gentlemanly wagering was supervised by Starbuck), and using the numbers of randomly selected spot quiz questions of a testing computer for some sort of roulette-styled game. Even though he conducted the arcade with a clientele of about one-third of the students attending, nobody on the teaching staff could ever nab him. They tried. But each time they tried to catch him in the act, they entered a war-game room that was dark and silent.

Another time, it's said, a cheating ring developed among many of the cadets who were under so much pressure to succeed that stealing tests or sending in better students as substitutes to take the exams began to seem like the most reasonable way out of their plight. They figured that Starbuck, with his reputation for engaging anyone around him in a con, would go along with their plan and help them.

"Sure," he said, I imagine with that sometimes irritating sly smile on his face. "What do you need, chums? What's coming up? Let's see—Intermediate Military Strategy I, am I right? Tomorrow? Okay, you guys meet me in the Cylon throne room just before the test, I'll have copies of the answers ready for you there. No sweat. See ya around, kiddies."

("Cylon throne room" was an academy euphemism for the communal bathrooms at the academy.)

The next day the cadets in the cheating ring showed up in the throne room and, sure enough, Starbuck was there, a twinkle in his eye and a set of answer papers in his hands. He told the cadets that this first instance of the answer service would be free of charge, they could discuss terms when the students had evaluated the worth of the service.

I don't know how the cadets got the answers into the testing rooms. Perhaps they merely memorized them, or sneaked them into the place in some ingenious cadet fashion. Anyway, the tests were fed to each individual testing cubicle by the exam-transmission system. The tests had been kept under lock and key, and guarded, since the previous morning when instructors made them up. The examiner who told me this anecdote said there was no way any intruder could have gotten near the exams or discovered the answers. At least the staff thought so.

The cadets from the cheating ring eagerly set to work, marking answers with their electronic pencils at a rate that no monitor had ever before seen from a cadet class. It looked like many of the students would finish the test way ahead of time, something of a phenomenon with the monstrously difficult academy tests. A feeling of great confidence swept among the cadets who'd received the answers from Starbuck.

Then they turned to the last page of the test booklet. At the bottom of the page was scribbled a note which was unmistakably in Starbuck's handwriting. This note appeared *only* in the test booklets of the cadets who were part of the cheating ring, another maneuver which led the examiner to tell me he believed the story might be apocryphal. Anyway, the note read:

All of the answers which I supplied you in the throne room are incorrect. If you filled in each and every one of them, you just achieved a zero on this exam. However, since this is a test of intermediate military strategy—a fancy term for grace under pressure or the successful use of reason and instinct to stay out of trouble—those of you who deserve to pass, who deserve to succeed beyond cadethood, have this option: there is sufficient time for you to rush back through this exam, change your answers, read the questions properly and choose the correct answer, and—if you got my kind of luck— successfully achieve a passing score on this exam. But, before you do that, first erase this note. Bless you all. S."

The examiner who told me this story swore up and down that it couldn't possibly be true.

I have observed Starbuck closely, ever since he came aboard the *Galactica* as a green but crafty young ensign. I have watched him starbuck everybody in sight, including myself.

I believe the story.

CHAPTER THREE

If the tension on the command bridge had been flammable, one spark could have destroyed the entire *Galactica*. Athena, in an instinctive affectionate move, edged closer to her father, just out of range of his peripheral vision, simply to be there in case he needed her for anything.

Starbuck's hands had nervously fumbled with his flight helmet as he and Boomer reported in to the commander. Their words, although properly formal and military in phrasing, came out in angry bursts. At one point, Tigh put a calming hand on Starbuck's arm to steady him. Apollo could not stand still and he paced a small area of the bridge, sliding one hand along a railing as he walked. At the end of Starbuck and Boomer's report, Adama broke the shocked silence by saying to Athena:

"Show the tape of what Starbuck picked up from Cree's scanner."

Everyone on the bridge cringed visibly when the

pictures of Shields's viper being blown up were shown. Then, as Cree faced his ship toward the summit of the mountain and the awesome laser cannon was revealed, everyone inhaled sharply or swallowed hard or simply gaped in wonder.

"Good Lord!" Adama cried. "Athena, freeze on that weapon."

Quickly Athena stopped the tape and reversed it a few frames, then adjusted the resolution of the picture. Knowing her father would want figures about the weapon, she worked out the calculations immediately.

"Sir, I have a fix on the scale. The ramparts are fourteen metrons high. Destructive power nearly infinite within two hectares."

"We're just out of its range right now," Tigh whispered, examining Athena's figures. "It can't zero in on us accurately, although a random shot could still hit us."

"It could destroy the *Galactica* in a single pulse!" Adama said softly.

Apollo hit the railing beside him with a hard ham-fisted slap that rattled it on its moorings.

"It's fantastic!" he said. "The Cylons are a highly advanced, mechanized culture, yes, but their technology can't have reached those proportions. Their weaponry tends to be less—"

Starbuck interrupted angrily:

"Can't say it matters much to *me* who built it. It's *there*, and it took two of my pilots!"

Apollo and Starbuck glared at each other, each spoiling for a fight in their frustration over the deaths of Shields, Bow, and probably Cree. Breaking the line of sight between them, Adama stepped in front of Starbuck and said calmly:

"Combat losses are my responsibility. You took the only course of action you could by returning to the *Galactica* with these scans."

"Tell that to Cadet Cree!" he shouted furiously. Then, catching the disapproval in his commander's eyes, he added: "Sir."

Adama, his eyes saddened, nodded. Athena knew her

father could always sympathize with insubordination that originated from anger over combat deaths. He turned to Colonel Tigh and said:

"That's it then—this is why the Cylons squeezed us into this course."

Apollo, leaning on the railing, said:

"How long until their pursuit force catches up to us?"

"Depends on where their base ships are," Adama said. "We have too much fire power for their attack squadrons. They'll hang back, make their occasional sneak attacks. But you can wager it won't be long until they bring up base ships."

The officers of the bridge fell silent, until Starbuck finally spoke up:

"Commander, Blue Squadron can take out that gun."

That's Starbuck, Athena thought. *Although he advises all cadets never to volunteer, he's always the first to step forward when the* Galactica *is threatened.*

"To send in a squadron of fighters would be mass suicide," Adama said. "You've seen what that weapon can do."

"Still," Tigh said, pointing at the star map to the last known location of the Cylon pursuit force, "we cannot turn back."

"No," Adama said.

"What's left?" said Boomer.

Adama turned to Athena and ordered:

"Put up the geologic scan of the asteroid's surface."

"Yes, sir."

Adama examined the subsequent picture for a long moment, then pointed toward it, saying:

"We could land a small, highly specialized task force down on the surface. Find some weakness in their defense. Destroy the weapon."

Tigh, studying the geologic scan, said:

"We can't be sure there is a weakness..."

Adama nodded, raised his eyebrows querulously.

"Risk is high," he said. "As always, it seems."

"But... but that's suicide," Starbuck muttered.

Adama glanced at Starbuck, no anger for the young man's outspokenness visible in his eyes.

"I cannot see any alternative," Adama said. "I am open to other suggestions."

All anyone on the bridge could offer were a few coughs and a couple of murmurs.

"Program a search for qualified personnel," Adama said to a communications officer. "Anyone experienced in ice-planet survival. Experts in mountaineering. Specialists in heavy demolitions. Once the readout is assimilated, we will convene in the Briefing Room. Until then, everyone not on duty right now return to your cabins and get in as much sack-time as you can. Once the mission is initiated, there might not be a time for any of us to rest."

Athena exchanged a worried glance with Apollo, each of them sending to the other the message that the one person who should rest, their father, would be the only one to disobey that particular general order.

Light... red light... moving slowly from side to side against an icy metallic background . . . blurs . . . cold . . . intense cold freezing blood, stopping the flow of blood... the red light coming closer... Shields's scream as the beam hit his ship... all the pieces of his ship... how many pieces... uncountable... could they be put back together like in a puzzle... Shields dead, Bow dead, no that can't be... the red light up against my eyes, trying to draw me into it... red light, Cylons, the stupid red light on their helmets . . . cold . . . red light . . . cold everywhere... cold...

Cree came awake suddenly. The red light interfering with his dream was on the helmet of a Cylon staring down at his prone body. Everything came back to him in a rush of memory. The beam of light, the destruction of his buddies' ships, his own viper being forced down. The swirl of large-flaked snow as he climbed out of his ship and faced the four Cylons who surrounded him, their quartet of moving red lights alarmingly eerie in the cold gloom. One centurion had ordered him disarmed, and two others had performed the deed before Cree's seemingly frozen arms had been able to resist. What was it the centurion in command had said before the others dragged him away and he had lost consciousness? "Take him to Vulpa," the alien had said. He had definitely wanted Cree to understand, for he had spoken it in the language of humans and not of Cylons.

The Cylon now examining him was different from the ones that had captured him. There were more wide black strips across the metallic portions of his uniform. The black lines indicated rank in a Cylon officer, Cree had been instructed back at the academy. Then this one was a leader of the Cylons on this icy world. A much-decorated Warrior of the Elite Class, if his instructors had been correct in their interpretations of alien heraldry. What was a Warrior of the Elite Class doing on a distant barren icy outpost like this one? And where was the fleet? And did they know Cree came from the fleet? Maybe not. A cadet's uniform differed from a warrior's, and there was no *Galactica* insignia on it.

Quickly Cree reviewed in his mind the lessons he'd been taught about proper behavior in the event of capture by the enemy. Never give more than your name, rank, and classification numbers. Never succumb to the transparent attempt of an enemy to engage you in casual conversation. Always remember that you are a colonial fighting man and every kind of dealing you have with the enemy must be regarded as combat. Never speak at all unless there is no other choice.

Cree remembered his instructor pausing at this point in the lecture. "However," he had said, "in the event of torture, the fleet does not require your compliance with any of these injunctions. We would prefer you to withhold information, but you will not be condemned if torture extracts it from you." Another cadet had raised his hand and asked if perhaps suicide might be better than succumbing to torture. The instructor had replied, "It might, but choices like that cannot be dictated. The fleet recommends survival over suicide." Cree vowed now to let the Cylons kill him before revealing anything to them—nevertheless, a voice deep within his brain seemed to whisper, don't be so hasty.

The Cylon commander identified himself as First Centurion Vulpa, then in a guttural brusque voice said:

"You're a colonial warrior?"

Cree almost answered yes, and proud to be one—but that would be a response, a break in the armor of silence. Even though he greatly desired to stand up to this arrogant Cylon officer, he kept his teeth clenched and gave a hate-filled glare as his only answer.

Vulpa didn't seem at all disturbed by the cadet's obstinacy. He rose calmly from his command chair and approached Cree, speaking briskly:

"Only one vestige of your race remains, the battlestar *Galactica* and her fleet. Your insignificant, weak-willed, stupid, lice-ridden group of—"

"Go rust yourself," Cree interrupted, then cursed himself for breaking his vow of silence so soon. Such a childishly impulsive reaction did no honor to the cause of the captured colonial warrior.

Keeping in his emotions had always been difficult for him. Back at the academy Shields was always dropping by his cubicle and giving him gentle lectures about caution, about not questioning the lecturers so much. But what did Shields know, he had always thought. Shields didn't long to be a command officer. Like he said, he just wanted to fly the nuts and bolts off his viper.

The smiling, chubby-cheeked face of Shields seemed to materialize in front of Cree now, as if replacing his own reflection in the shiny metal of the Cylon's silvery uniform. Then he saw Shields in his cockpit, then he saw Shields's ship exploding into a million disintegrating fragments, and his eyes filled with tears. He blinked quickly twice, hoping that the Cylon hadn't noticed. Who could tell what Cylons noticed? What did they see with even? Was that red light drifting so lazily from side to side in his helmet an aid to Cylon eyes, perhaps a focusing mechanism that, in its scanning, brought a single vivid picture to the monster's organs of sight?

If Vulpa perceived Cree's tears, there was no way of telling. The Cylon merely continued to circle him and ask his infernal questions.

"How many viper fighters left in the fleet?"

Wouldn't you like to know, Cree thought. *And wouldn't the information that we have discovered methods to manufacture new vipers in our foundry ships be of use to you?* Cree tried to push such thoughts out of his mind. Formulating the answers the monster was trying to get out of him was a short step from actually articulating them.

Vulpa stared directly at Cree, his red light now gliding faster from side to side along the dark line at the top of his helmet.

"You are made of flesh and blood, human. You have a nervous system which carries impulses, the sensation of pain. Intense pain. Agony." He leaned his head closer to Cree, nearly formed the Cylon version of a whisper: "How many combat ships in the fleet?"

Cree, struggling to suppress his curses, kept silent. Vulpa leaned back, motioned to the two guards and another pair of the aliens who stood by a nearby entranceway.

"Do not let him lose consciousness," Vulpa said, then turned around, returned to his command chair, and sat down in the awkward cumbersome way of the Cylon. The other Cylons, arms raised, with many distorted reflections of Cree flashing off their outer armor, closed in on the young cadet.

Starbuck stood to the side as the others, huddled together, nervously awaited the results of the computer search. He could not stop thinking of the three lost cadets, especially Cree. He remembered each of Cree's naive and, at the time, annoying questions, and now wished he'd been less blunt, more avuncular with the curious trainee. Cree was probably dead, and whatever Adama said about command responsibility, the fault was Starbuck's. He didn't like drawing to a losing hand time and again, didn't want to chance losing another cadet.

Rapidly the computer sorted out the names of people whose qualifications fit the assignment as entered in the program. Athena ripped out the readout copy and said:

"Five specialists. Three support."

Adama nodded.

"Lock it in," he said.

"Here's the roster," Athena said, handing her father

the paper. He examined it briefly, then thrust it at Starbuck.

"This is the team, Starbuck. You and Boomer go get them. They might be a trifle recalcitrant. Give them a good pep talk, okay?"

As Starbuck started to leave the bridge, he glanced at the list. He stopped abruptly and whirled on Adama.

"Commander, there must be some mistake."

Adama raised his eyebrows, looking as if he had no suspicion of what the lieutenant meant. Starbuck moved closer to him and whispered:

"These are—they're criminals. They're aboard the grid barge."

A hint of a smile from the commander before he whispered back:

"You have the authority to collect them, Lieutenant."

"Yes sir, I know, but—"

"You have your orders, Lieutenant."

"Aye-aye, sir."

A worried look on his face, Starbuck gestured to Boomer to follow him. *Prisoners?* he thought. *Why in the twelve worlds of blessed memory would the computer come up with a list of prisoners? Grid-rats. Barge-lice. Is this the tribute we're giving to those three doomed cadets, sending a bunch of criminal misfits on a mission of grave importance?* Starbuck shook his head from side to side, wondering if the computer was suddenly under enemy control, and if this was a part of the trap that the commander had earlier spoken of.

"What's the matter?" Boomer muttered as they strode down the corridor. "Something serious?"

"No, we're just handing the safety of the fleet over to a bunch of murderers and cutthroats."

Boomer scowled.

"Well," he said, "as long as it isn't serious."

CHAPTER FOUR

Croft:

In my dream I seem to separate from my body and drift upward, through the walls of this lousy cell, through the superstructure of the prison barge itself. For a while I float above the ship, looking down on its dim gray exterior, its battered sections of unpolished uncaring metal—seeing simultaneously, it seems, the hundreds of poor wretches who are squirming within the squares of her grids, each prisoner trying to find one comfortable spot in which to rest. A con's greatest goal is the search for a comfortable area to rest in. You never find it, but you keep looking. You're like a rat searching for an enclosed safe niche and settling for a scratchy rope being blown from side to side in a stiff wind.

I can't stand staring at the barge any longer and I seem to catch a magical air current that has mysteriously snaked its way through the vacuum of space, just to find me and help me to escape. Escape, of course, escape. The only real dream a prisoner can have, no matter in what form his dreaming mind disguises it, is escape. He may escape from his body, as I do, or find himself in a dreamland of sweet pulpy food, beautiful people, and complete luxury.

I slide off into empty space, leaving the fleet behind me. Looking back over my shoulder I watch the ships turn into slowly flying insects, gradually diminishing to specks and disappearing. The *Galactica* is last to disappear; it is the largest insect of all. As I look forward again, I know that ahead is either the good dream or the nightmare. In the good dream I land at the summit of a mountain, alone and enjoying my aloneness. In full gear, my hand delighting in the feel of the sturdy ice-ax through the thickness of my gloves, my feet shifting about and digging hard-metal crampons more firmly into the summit's icy surface, the hood of my parka enveloping my head so that only a narrow view of the great craggy vistas is allowed, a monstrously fierce wind blowing into my face in spite of the narrow parka opening. And, unless the dream includes the climb or the descent (rappeling in an unlikely slow-motion slide), that's all there is to the good dream. It's good simply because I feel so good. I have been pardoned, redeemed, allowed to resume the only kind of life I've ever loved.

The nightmare is nearly identical to the good dream. Except the wind is hurtling at me in hurricane force, my parka is ripped to shreds, my ice-ax is tumbling away from me down the mountainside, my feet are beginning to slide out from under me. And Leda is there.

Leda is there, reaching for me. I don't know if she is trying to save me or trying to kill me. And that dilemma is the essence of the nightmare.

This time it seems to be the good dream. Or is that Leda below me, hauling her tall form and considerable but well-structured weight over an impossibly difficult cornice?

I never find out, for the next thing I'm aware of, Jester, the turnkey with the permanent sneer, is shaking me awake. It seems as if he's simultaneously trying to bash in my skull on the metal flooring.

"Stop it, Jester!" I cry. "I'm awake. I'm awake. See my eyes. Open, right? Awake. Open means awake."

Finally, reluctantly, he stops shaking me, mutters in that voice that sounds like scree underfoot:

"You're wanted."

"Wanted?"

"Get up. Colonial warriors here to see you."

"Tell 'em I only receive visitors at teatime."

He pulls me to my feet and pushes me out of the cell. As we stroll down the free-channel, between the rows of grid-cells, I hear the various dream noises of those other prisoners who are in their cells and not on some laborious work detail somewhere. The moans and grunts seem to blend into a chant of hatred and despair.

Jester takes me, surprisingly, to a briefing room in the barge's executive quarters. The place is well laid out. Plush chairs, posh tables, decorated mirrors, bad but colorful paintings on the walls—the kind of paintings that provide the approved reality for idiots who don't know a painting from a picture.

Standing on one side of the room, as if they're disdaining the use of the luxurious furniture, are two tall colonial warriors—one white, one black, both formidable-looking. The black is clearly bright, he has the kind of questing eyes that tell you he hasn't learned it all yet and neither have you. The white's a handsome guy, clearly a ladies' man, yet tough, the kind on whom a dress-uniform cape looks molded. His body is strong and muscular, I can tell he's from the best breed of pilots. But his eyes, his eyes are deceptive. They say he can bluff and he knows how to call a bluff. There's a little bit of con man in them, a little bit of fool, a little bit of hero. Take your pick. I think I'd kind of like him, like both of them in fact, if they weren't rotten colonial warriors.

Well, they might not want to take advantage of the soft furniture, but I might not see anything like one of these overstuffed conference chairs again, not for a long time. Ignoring Jester, I stride to the seat that obviously belongs to the head of the table during meetings, plop down on it and put my legs up, like I'm ready to call the meeting to order and am merely waiting for the yes-man to quit shuffling his notes. Neither of the warriors shows much reaction to my audacity, but Jester, rushing toward me, is clearly furious. Before he can get to me, though, the black waves him away.

The white begins to speak, addressing his remarks to his companion, talking of me in the third person in that bureaucratic way I'm always encountering and always despising.

"Croft," he says, reading the information off the screen of a mini-computer he holds in his hand. "Commander of the Snow Garrison on the ice planet Kalpa. He and his gang raided a Cylon outpost."

"Nothing illegal about that," the other man says, a smidgen of irony in his voice.

Sharp guy, like I thought.

"Not a military operation," the white says. "Armed robbery. They plundered a Cylon platinum mine. Wouldn't surrender the bounty to their colonial commander."

Just like all the others, this one's treating our escapade like an act of piracy. It didn't feel like that at the time. Took me a long while to assemble just the right team to join me and Leda. Besides Wolfe and Thane, there were the four others, the ones whose names I can't remember anymore. Their deaths have interfered with my ability to remember what they were called.

And it was no picnic stealing into that Cylon sector undetected, climbing the steep north face of the mountain overlooking the Cylon encampment and the mine, trying to hammer pitons into rotten rock that would not accept them, losing two men while attempting the traverse across the verglas-surfaced slope just because Thane had been too late in shifting into the boot-ax belay that might have saved them. And then there was the rope descent to the encampment in the dead of night after glissading down half of the gradual-sloped south face of the mountain. Our ropes were securely anchored in a saddle, but we knew there was danger always present. Especially since the Cylon guns could pick us off at will if they spotted us. But they didn't spot us. We sneaked into the encampment, slaughtered all the Cylon warriors, lost two more of our own team. The rest of the Cylons, the workers, capitulated to us easily, and we got out with all the

platinum we could store inside the Cylon freighter whose
controls Wolfe knew as well as those in a viper cockpit.
After all that, that smug colonial commander, with his
aristocratic overbearing manner, tried to force us to heave
to (who were the pirates, them or us?) and surrender the
bounty. What right did he have to it?

"He didn't go in under the Cylon guns," I say to the two
men, "so he didn't deserve any part of it. Who are you? I
like to know the bilge rats I'm dealing with."

Both men stand tall and exchange a puzzled glance
before replying.

"Starbuck," says the white man. "Viper pilot. Blue
Squadron, Battlestar *Galactica*."

"Boomer. Commander Adama's Strike Wing."

Adama, eh? I should have known his ugly puss was
involved in this somehow. Adama was the colonial
commander who'd tried to appropriate my bounty from
me. His angular face with those icy but penetrating eyes
appears before me. I almost want to tell Starbuck and
Boomer to find a quick black hole and jump in, but I
decide to play a waiting game, see what they're up to.
Anything to stay out of that cell for a while.

"What's the drill?" I ask.

"You'll find out soon enough," Starbuck replies, then
motions toward the door. I look in the direction of his
gesture. Wolfe is now standing there, his bullish body
nearly filling the entranceway. Well, the lower half of the
entranceway anyhow. Wolfe's not very tall, but it doesn't
matter much, the way his body—with its low center of
gravity and muscular broad shoulders—is constructed.
His hair is as shaggy as ever, Wolfe and combs are natural
enemies, and his deepset eyes smolder with the usual rage,
some of it probably deriving from the sight of me sitting
comfortably in my plush briefing-room chair.

A guard pushes him forward into the room, and the
chains which are always required on a rebellious bull like
Wolfe clank against the metal flooring. Wolfe looks back
at his guard as if he'd take the man out right now if the
chains didn't inhibit his movements so much.

Starbuck mutters to Boomer, but loud enough so I can
hear:

"That computer sure knows how to pick 'em." He looks down at the mini-computer screen. "Wolfe. Climber. Muscle man. Snow Garrison. A one-man task force."

Wolfe says nothing, just stares with his rheumy hate-filled eyes. There are bruises all over his face. His jailers are using psychological methods to keep him in line, I see. A wisecrack comes to my lips but before I can send it in Wolfe's direction, my attention is diverted toward the doorway again. It's dark, but I know what's coming. I can always sense Thane when he's within a kilometer of me. Sure enough, his lean, graceful snow leopard of a body eases itself into the room as if there were no turnkey guiding his way. A chill runs up and down my spine, freezes all my vertebrae. Thane always strikes me this way. His colorless eyes remind me of ice, or perhaps verglas might be the better description. Verglas—the brittle thin covering of ice on a rock, a shiny and slippery veneer, dangerous. His hair, in direct contrast to Wolfe's, is close-cut, its ivory-white color almost invisible against the whiteness of his scalp and the prison pallor of his face. I wonder if he still hates me, still resents me as a figure of authority, however much my leadership qualifications have been diminished by my hitch in this stinking prison.

"Thane," Starbuck says, staring at the screen, "demolitions expert and specialist in alien environments."

Thane steps forward and speaks. His voice is as quiet as his movements—and, in a way, just as graceful.

"When people talk about me, I like to see their eyes."

Starbuck glances up from the mini-computer. Interpreting their look at each other is a job for an expert in facial language. What with the trickiness in Starbuck's active eyes and the distance in Thane's placid eyes, there seems no possible meeting ground for communication between the two. Ever.

"I work with breathing gear," Thane says, his voice as gentle as powdery snow. "Rare gases, chemical blends. I can take you through land, air, fire, and water."

"It says you're in for murder," Starbuck says.

"That, too," says Thane, mysteriously smiling.

Murder. I'd forgotten that. After our capture Thane

had gotten into a brawl with the arresting officers. He knocked four of them down. Two never got up. I shouldn't have been surprised. When we met, rumors of past killings performed skillfully by Thane had preceded him.

I stare at Wolfe and Thane, wondering what to say to them, or if I should remain mute in order to scout out the general terrain. I am about to make the mountaineering hand signal that means all's well, but a voice from the doorway nearly knocks me right out of my seat:

"Hello, Croft, you miserable scabby insect."

I don't want to look. With Wolfe and Thane already here, I should have expected Leda would be next. I don't want to look. I look.

I'm not surprised at what I see. There's no way these abominable jailers could subdue her spirit. She still looks stunning. A big-boned woman, she's a shade taller than me and, in my present debilitated condition, I'm sure she appears more powerful. She's cut her hair short, though it's not as close-cropped as Thane's—its reddish color still brings out the keenness of her lynx-eyed look. Her high cheekbones add to her slightly alien appearance. She hates me. I want, this moment, to take her in my arms and beg her to love me again.

It's hard to remember when things were good for us. We met so long ago, before the platinum-mine raid, before Kalpa—on our mutual home-world of Scorpia. I vaguely recall a time when we were so young that we romped and frolicked, when our love was predominant, more important than the petty drives that impelled us later. After the platinum raid, she blamed me for the deaths of the four men and women, but the real split between us had formed much earlier. The last happy time I can clearly recall was a mountain-climbing expedition in the difficult Caprican range. We were both on extended furlough, with added time for injuries resulting from some acts of combat that the military chose to deem heroic, and we climbed those mountains alone, refusing even to take communicators along so that the safety-conscious Mountain Control Squad could know our whereabouts. We could easily have been lost forever, crushed in the white death of an avalanche, dropped down into a crevasse. But we not only survived our foolhardy adventure, we conquered five summits, one of them previously unclimbed.

What forced us apart after that is a series of little mysteries. An argument over a matter of battle strategy resulted in a small rift—in the terms of mountaineering, a crack in otherwise sturdy rock. A petty domestic harangue perhaps increased the crack to a roughed-out hollow. More disagreements, more dissatisfactions, more suppressing of real emotion, led to the hollow becoming part of a gully, the gully growing into a ravine, the ravine finally—with the tragic end of the raid—becoming a deep crevasse separating us forever. Even now, the moraine, the rock and glacial debris, of our lives seems to lie around us. Well, I carry the comparison too far. Leda would say I carry *everything* too far.

"She looks like she could take us all on," Boomer whispers to Starbuck, clearly impressed by Leda's formidable appearance. "With or without chains. She'd beat us all."

"Leda," Starbuck says, consulting his computer again. "Medic first class. Expert in laser wounds. And arctic experienced. She's—"

"What's the mission?" Leda interrupts sharply.

"Commander Adama'll be briefing you," Boomer says.

Leda glances my way.

"Adama, huh? You buddy-buddy with Adama now, Croft?"

I laugh.

"Just like a carabiner snaplocked to a piton," I say.

Leda scoffs at the joke, then addresses Starbuck and Boomer:

"To have Croft and myself in the same place at the same time invites disaster. I suggest you return me to my cell. I'm better off with the rot there than with the likes of Croft."

Starbuck smiles. What in blazes is he so pleased about?

"I take it you don't like him," he says to Leda.

Leda smiles broadly, displaying her white even teeth.

"I'm married to him," she says. The smile goes away as

quickly as it came, and she speaks more softly: "And no, I don't like him."

"Hello, Leda," I say. "You're still prettier than a Libran—"

"Shut up, Croft!" she says loudly. "I'm not taking any more of your birdlime. None of us are."

Boomer examines the four of us, the old team now in irrevocable rift, and mutters to Starbuck:

"Cozy little group. This is one mission, Starbuck, I *know* you're not going to volunteer for."

I feel for you, Boomer, but I'll never be able to reach you.

"Let's get these . . . these gentlemen and lady out of here, Boomer," Starbuck says, as he folds up his mini-computer and slips it into a pocket of his flight jacket.

Boomer looks very disturbed as he orders Leda and Wolfe unchained and then herds us all out of the briefing room. I'm going to miss that chair, and I figure it's going to be a long time before I ease myself into one like it again.

CHAPTER FIVE

Apollo could almost feel the *Galactica*'s motionlessness, as if the ship had miraculously managed to brake to a complete stop, instead of just drifting at a point out of the laser cannon's range.

He made his knock on Adama's cabin door sound firm and determined. A touch on Adama's desk panel made the door slide open. Adama looked up, smiled.

"Come in, Apollo. You look troubled."

"Not troubled. Just angry."

Adama's eyes narrowed, and the smile disappeared.

"Go on," he said to his son.

"The computer search for members of the landing party..."

"What about it?"

"It was influenced. Contrived."

A flicker of anger in Adama's eyes as he said:

"That's a serious charge."

He was offering Apollo a chance to retreat. Apollo was not going to take it.

"I'm aware of that," Apollo said. "It *is* a serious charge." He struggled to keep his voice level. "You don't want me to go, do you?"

Adama swung his chair away from the desk, gave Apollo a stare that would have withered the average Galactican officer, and said:

"You think I'd spare a member of my own family?"

Apollo became aware that the recording device above the desk was now on, had been operative perhaps since he had made his charge. He spoke slowly, measuring his words:

"I'm suggesting the selection was biased, or I would have been chosen. I'm qualified in survival techniques. I'm single. I have the correct endurance rating, not only correct but the highest among *Galactica*'s personnel, officer and enlisted man. I also have the weapons capability, command factor, the ability to—"

"But," Adama interrupted, "you lack experience in subzero temperatures."

Apollo was prepared for this objection.

"None of our warriors have such training," he said.

Adama swung his chair back toward the desk.

"If the computer passed you over, it did so for a reason."

Apollo was equally prepared for this observation, and struggling to keep his voice official and controlled, he said:

"And I know *exactly* what that reason is. *You* are the sole judge of who is expendable and who isn't. And, according to Colonel Tigh, I'm rated as nonexpendable."

Adama sighed.

"You are the highest-rated combat experienced commander we have. It's imperative that we conserve—"

"Are you sure your feelings are not obscuring your objective judgment on this one, sir?"

Apollo moved toward his father. Adama remained silent, staring sightlessly at the surface of his desk.

"Don't you think I understand?" Apollo said, his voice gentler now. "You've lost so many members of the family. Zac. Mother..."

Both of them now lapsed into silence. Obviously his

father was remembering the same scenes that were obsessing Apollo. Zac being blown out of the skies by the Cylons. He and his father returning to Caprica to realize that Ila, too, was dead. The feelings these memories engendered could not be adequately spoken, even between father and son. Adama rubbed his eyes as if to remove the memories and said to Apollo:

"Don't ask me to—I won't reprogram the search."

"You don't have to. Just expand the party by one."

"Apollo, I—"

"If, as you said, I am your highest-rated commander, you *need* me on this mission. What difference does my expendability or lack of it make when you know we're going up against that death weapon? If this mission fails, we're all doomed, all due to be blasted to pieces. And you know it!"

The two men stared at each other for a long moment, each trying to cling to his own stubbornness. But finally Adama, assuming his command voice, relented.

"Tell Colonel Tigh it is so ordered," he said, and started to swing his chair back to his desk. Before he could do so, Apollo touched his hand, and returned his cold look with an affectionate one. A hint of a warming effect in the commander's steel-blue eyes appeared briefly. It was enough for Apollo. He nodded and then strode quickly out of the command cabin.

Athena, who'd been informed by Apollo of his plan to join the mission and had advised him against confronting their father, felt angry when she pulled out the new mission list from the computer and saw her brother's name added to it. She considered going to her father to complain, but knew that would do no good. Adama wouldn't appreciate being besieged by both his children arguing opposite sides of an issue. And, worse, now it was impossible for her to put in the request that she become a substitute on the mission—to replace the medic, Leda, who had expressed so much reluctance to join the expeditionary team.

Starbuck suddenly confronted her, his eyes fixed on the computer sheet she was holding.

"Is that the revised list for the mission?" he asked.

"Yes. Apollo is on it. I wanted to be on it, but the computers chose this . . . this Leda. She's a convict!"

"Hate to tell you, but they're *all* convicts, darling. Feel lucky you're not on the list. I'm just praying that Apollo makes it back intact. Looks to me like a one-way voyage. Sure glad Boomer and I didn't make it."

Starbuck could always get a rise out of Athena, and he was especially successful with his last little aside.

"Starbuck," Athena whispered angrily. "That's the side of you I can never understand, or accept. One moment you're offering Blue Squadron for a daredevil foolish assault, the next you're oozing about how glad you are to be off the mission. These people have a chance to save the entire fleet, I'd give my eyeteeth to—"

"Good for them. I say good for them, and more power forever. I personally have a very dangerous card game coming up. Here, let me have that readout. I'll take it to Commander Adama."

She looked at him puzzledly. What was he up to now?

"Look," he urged, "I have to be at the briefing anyway. I'm in charge of the prisoner detail until they accept the mission."

She hesitated. It was always best to hesitate when Starbuck *volunteered* for anything, large or small. He smiled at her, and she handed him the list.

"Hang around that briefing room as long as you can," she said. "Maybe a little bravery will rub off."

It was a cheap shot, she knew, especially when directed at a warrior whose battle record was so distinguished. She just wanted him to act like the hero he was, a role he seemed to resist with relish. Except under battle conditions.

No, she thought as she watched him walk briskly away from her, *I shouldn't've said that. Should not have angered him. Now we're on the outs again! When will I ever learn?*

CHAPTER SIX

Croft:

Galactica lousy Commander lousy Adama doesn't even recognize me. Angry, I remind him. Even after I remind him, he gives me a blank look. He says yes he remembers, but he really doesn't. It was just a passing moment in his lousy life, just a matter of duty. I've been able to visualize every feature of his face since our capture, and yet it's clear he wouldn't know me from a pile of daggit-meat. I hate him more than ever.

"Do you harbor any feelings toward me that would hamper your performance in the mission we've selected you for?" he asks.

This is my chance, I realize. I can express my contempt and get away, not have to do a job for a man whom I'd rather kill than serve. But resigning from the mission means returning to the grid-barge, climbing into that rotten cell, and being forgotten again, maybe for good this time. I don't want to go back to that cell. I'd do anything to keep away from it. Even embrace lousy Adama as a long-lost friend.

"My feelings never hamper my performance," I say.

"That's true enough," Leda says, and then laughs. The echo of her laugh bounces around the command bridge like an artillery shell gone crazy.

Adama screws up those fierce, almost cruel eyes and stares deeply into mine—discovering, I know, eyes crueller and fiercer than his.

"How is it a man of your abilities, a commander, is still confined to a prison ship?" he asks suddenly.

"You oughta know. You put me there."

"I don't mean that. After the prison ship managed its escape from the confinement base on Sagitara, all prisoners were offered a chance at rehabilitation. We need personnel too badly to worry about past sins. Only the criminally insane were denied freedom."

Involuntarily I glance toward Wolfe, wondering what his classification was and if he'd ever been offered rehab. If he had been, he would have taken it, so I suspect he hadn't. What had changed things so now, so that even Wolfe was useful?

"Most prisoners accepted the offer of Core Command to join the fleet as useful personnel. You refused. Why?"

I shrug.

"Well, I guess I'm just a romantic at heart."

He screws up his brow to match his screwed-up eyes.

"What does that mean?" he asks.

"I don't know. Just that rehabilitation meant swabbing down landing decks and repairing the rubber bands that power this lousy fleet. Garbage details. Like the flirtatious maid said to her overeager master, I don't do windows."

"I doubt you refused rehab because you're a romantic. Sounds more like pride to me."

"We'll match numbers on pride sometime. Sir."

Adama gets more businesslike in his manner and briefs me on his precious mission. It's simple and complicated at the same time. The layout's not too bad. The gun emplacement takes up most of the mountaintop because of its size. There's a small area for landing a ship, nothing else. Nothing except a jagged mountain that looks like it's got more death traps hidden in its terrain than easy pathways or slopes. In the foothills is a large encampment that appears to contain a full Cylon garrison. Beside the garrison is a large airfield that scanners show has several Cylon warships of different classes spread across it. Great! This all looks just like the platinum raid. They discover we're on the mountain, they can pick us off for target practice.

"And you want us to go up that?" I ask Adama.

"It's not so high," Captain Apollo interjects. Who is this guy anyway? He acts like he's somebody important.

"Shows how much you know about mountains. Be glad you don't have to climb it."

Apollo flushes, red to the gills. He's furious, trying to hold it in.

"I'll be part of the team," he says.

"God save us," I say. "Look, the worst thing you can do to sabotage this mission, Commander, is give me some green amateur who doesn't know a piton from a—"

"My son will join the mission," Adama says quietly. His son! Terrific. I got to drag his son along, break my back belaying him up cliffsides, toss him ahead of me over ridges, probably get jounced into a ravine because of one of his mistakes. And all because a commander wants to give his son an edge. This mission is shaping up just dandy.

"I have mountaineering experience," Apollo says to me, as if that alone justifies his presence on the team.

"Is that so? Then how could you make such a dumb remark? Take a good look at the geologic scan of this mountain. What did you say, it's not so high? Look, man, height's not a measure of difficulty when you're assaulting a mountain, especially when it's a mountain where there's been no recorded previous climbs to provide us information on possible routes. Ever hear of Mount Cyimklen, Captain Apollo?"

Apollo looks like he doesn't want to discuss mountains with me, but he responds anyway:

"Of course. It's on my home planet, Caprica."

"Well, Mount Cyimklen is the second-highest mountain on your home world. And you've probably climbed it, right?"

"As a matter of fact—"

"Everybody has. Nothing to it. Six-year-olds can conquer Cyimklen. Despite its height, it's composed of easy slopes, well-worn trails, practically stairs carved into the rock. There was a time when it was something of a challenge because of its extreme height, but that was a millennium ago. Once somebody had challenged it, and climbed it, discovered its secrets, the ascent of it became easy. Now, let me ask you another question. Ever hear of Mount Pannurana?"

"Well, yes—"

"And I'd bet my grid-barge chits that you've never climbed it."

"I tried. Once."

"Pannurana is just slightly more than half the height of Cyimklen. And it's only been scaled to the top five times. Twice by me. And why? Because it's a rattrap of a mountain, that's why. Rotten rock, lousy footholds, ice like sheet glass, a peak that rises straight up on all sides with nothing to grab hold of, air as thin as your common sense, Cap'n. More guys died on Pannurana than all the surrounding mountains combined. All the surrounding *higher* mountains. So don't look at this geologic scan and tell me this one's not so high, all right?"

Apollo looks quite embarrassed. Good. Guys like him I like to keep off balance. Maybe if he listens to reason he'll be able to perform as a member of the team instead of being a drag on the ropes. Still, I don't like the look of this mountain, no matter who's on the team.

"Okay," I say. "Let's establish this. It's no easy climb, no jaunt in the clear air for eager amateurs. Ignoring for the moment the fact that we can be wiped out in a millicenton if the helmet-heads detect our presence, I can't see a single good route up the mountain, at least not on the basis of this geologic scan. The north and west faces are clearly too tough to tackle under the conditions down there. East and south are better, but I don't like the look of the glacial material near the summit. Southeast looks most promising—which is to say not very. Given the fact that you won't allow us sufficient time to study the mountain closely so we can plan out a proper route—"

"There's no time, Croft," Adama says. "I know you

need it, but if the Cylons pincer us between the pursuit force and that cannon, we're finished."

"I appreciate that, Commander, but I'm not, shall we say, pleased. A good climb requires long preparation. This mission—you might as well climb it with your eyes closed. After settling your dispersion plans for your share of the pension fund, of course. Are you sure there're no alternatives?"

Adama appears irritated. Perhaps he doesn't like the way I'm taking over the briefing. Tough chute-waste, Commander.

"What alternatives are you suggesting, Croft?"

"I assume direct assault with aircraft is out of the question." He nods. "What about a route *inside* the mountain? I never knew a Cylon setup that didn't have some below-ground facilities. They seem buggy about underground passages. I'd bet my pass back to the grid-barge that there're tunnels inside the mountain, maybe even some sort of elevator system."

Adama studies my face for a moment before answering. He thinks he can read me.

"Perhaps, but all our close probe-scans end up jammed. We don't know what's down there, except for what I've already shown you. If an alternate route is discovered, it should be used, I agree. For now, we have to assume that the only route to the laser cannon, the only chance we have at destroying it, is—unfortunately—up the mountain."

He's a fair man, I'll say that for Adama. I wish I had him for backup work in place of his overzealous and inexperienced offspring. I'd still hate him, but at least I could rely on him.

"I appreciate your evaluation of the situation, Commander. I feel a part of our goal has to involve being opportunistic. We should look for any alternatives to climbing the mountain."

"And if there are none?"

I shrug.

"Then we climb."

Adama is pleased. Well, that's okay with me. Maybe if we can just pull off this stunt, I can come back to the

Galactica and strangle its commander. Insurmountable challenges are easier to take if you got a worthwhile goal to come back to.

Adama briefs us on equipment. They have most of what we need. Good. There are even a few molecular-binding pitons. Normally I don't like to use special equipment—too many second-rate climbers get to the top more through technology than effort—but in a climb with so many unknowns, a molecular-binding piton is a good tool. If the rock is good, this kind of tricked-up piton can be just pushed into it, while the binding effect makes it take hold. Two advantages to us: certain phases of the climb can be shortened simply because we won't have to waste time pounding the little buggers in, and the Cylons won't be able to detect us by hearing the sound of hammering. Our ropes are doctored, too. They're made of Aquarian hemp, the kind with the alterable tensile strength. When you need extremely flexible rope, you twist your end to the left and it becomes as manipulable as a snake. When you need it stiff and straight, a twist to the right makes it as inflexible as metal cable. Even though I detest specialization in an ascent, I'll make an exception for these tricky pitons and the magical rope this time.

Adama completes his briefing and introduces us grid-rats to the straights who'll compose the remainder of the task-force personnel.

"The shuttle will carry a snow vehicle, Ram-class armed with lasers. Sergeant Haals is senior gunnery master."

Haals nods. He's a tough-looking bunny rabbit. I wouldn't mess with him. Adama continues:

"Vickers is from a gun crew that helped to hold the rear guard in the last phase of the Battle of Caprica."

Vickers looks like he has a high opinion of himself. A definite hero type. Another daredevil like Apollo. Well, at least he's apparently good with a gun. That's worth something.

"You'll need a laser technician. Voight is chief of the weapons-repair section."

Voight's a no-nonsense type, I can see that. Tight-lipped but reliable on the job. Not much use in a fight with his fists, but you don't have to be when you know the mechanics of laser weaponry.

"You've met the Snow Garrison demolitions unit under Commander Croft."

That sets me right back on my heels. From the way Adama looks at me, I can tell that's just the reaction he wants from me.

"Commander? Am I reinstated at full rank?"

Adama takes a long pause before replying.

"Temporarily. Full reinstatement will depend on the outcome of the operation."

The strings have been attached. No matter. They're to be expected.

"Reinstatement on one hand," I say, "death on the other."

Thane and Wolfe glare at me. I can tell they don't like me being put in charge of them. Neither one ever liked being told what to do. Leda's look is neutral. She may hate me, but she knows my reinstatement improves the safety of them all.

"Croft," Adama says, "you and your fellow convicts are not all that different from us right now. We're all in a kind of prison put up by the Cylons."

Wolfe bellows with sarcastic laughter, and says:

"Yeah, Commander, our chains are exactly alike."

I don't know whether outsiders could receive his message as well as the rest of us, but I'm glad the stocky little bull said that. People on the outside of a prison barge never really feel the pain of being inside, in spite of their fancy philosophical analogies to their own prisons. For the moment, Adama's point is well taken enough, but guys like him forget the fancy talk once they're sprung from their traps. I decide to break the uncomfortable silence that follows Wolfe's sarcasm.

"Am I in full command?"

If there's any sense to life, I should be.

"Of the demolitions unit, yes. Of the expedition: no."

I knew there was no sense to life, anyway.

"Three warriors will command you and your team. The officer in full command will be Captain Apollo."

In my mind I throw up my hands in despair. That's the

final capper, Captain Apollo in full command. Not only is there no sense to life, its absurdity is a set of calculated cruelties.

Adama scrutinizes his list further. What more pleasant little surprises has he got to spring on me?

"*Supporting* your team will be two of my finest officers, Lieutenants Boomer and Starbuck."

Well, I can accept that anyway. You can depend on a guy like Boomer to perform well, and I'd bet on Starbuck, too. Apollo is amazed by his father's announcement.

"Starbuck and Boomer?" he cries.

Starbuck smiles and glances toward Boomer, who looks a tad confused.

"Guess it was that tour we pulled on that Aeriana Ice Station."

I edge toward the two lieutenants. Something tells me there's something to be learned by eavesdropping on them.

"We have picked up Cylon base ships approaching on long-range scan," Adama says. "They will reach us in eight to nine hundred centons. Whether you have destroyed the pulsar weapon or not, the fleet moves in exactly seven hundred." His grim look takes in all of us. "Good luck. To us all."

Neither Boomer nor Starbuck notices me standing behind them. Boomer whispers to Starbuck:

"We were never at any ice station on Aeriana."

"Computers don't lie," Starbuck says.

Boomer shakes his head—a bit distraught, I suspect, at this turn of events. He moves a couple of steps away from his buddy. I wonder if I should expose Starbuck's con, but decide not to. I'd still rather have him at my side, with or without ice-station experience, than hardheaded punks like Apollo.

Speaking of hardheaded punks, here comes the youthful captain himself, sidling up to Starbuck and whispering in a friendly voice:

"I know how you feel about Cree, about losing those cadets, but you don't belong on this mission."

Starbuck stands tall and takes his shot:

"That makes two of us, doesn't it, Captain?"

"Tampering with a computer readout is a serious offense," Apollo says.

"I imagine it is," replies Starbuck.

I'm surprised by the broadness of Apollo's smile. Apparently he's glad to have Starbuck with us, too. At least he's showing some good judgment there.

I'd feel a lot more comfortable about the mission generally, if Leda, Wolfe, and Thane would stop looking at me with such enmity in their eyes.

FROM THE ADAMA JOURNALS:

Communication is impossible. Communication is improbable. Communication is implausible.

I've often considered having a sampler made of those nine words, with each embroidered splendidly in gilt threads. I'd then hang it behind the desk in my official quarters.

When I'm particularly frustrated, I believe people can never reach an understanding. At best they attain a level of verbal exchange which they invest with the illusion of an understanding. In my particularly bleak moods I even believe that people cannot even reach a point of *communication*, much less understanding, especially one in which something that is really meaningful to both is exchanged at the same moment. So many things—factors, aspects, character traits, tics, timing, temporary obsessions, all the words we cloak intentions under—interfere frustratingly with human contact. For some people distinctions of class, race, and personality cannot really be overcome, except for the trading off of ordinary banalities, themselves substitutes for communication.

In military life, I've often found the obligations of rank to be obstacles in moments when I've vitally needed sufficient trust for a subordinate to speak openly. Aboard the *Galactica*, I have tried to establish the custom that the commander is open to all points of view. But I'm still the commander, and that interferes even when I'm dealing with outspoken crew members like Tigh and Starbuck. Even Apollo and Athena, who rankle at the formalities they have to employ to speak to me officially, seem to choke up a bit when expressing their ideas on the command bridge. At least they speak openly to me in private. No matter how much I try to put my officers and crew at their ease, there always seems to be a formality in the order of presentation that affects my response to the message. I have to allow that formality as part of the necessary discipline required to keep our fleet continuing on its desperate quest. And always the point of real understanding, the bridge to genuine communication, seems to hang between us, invoked but not traveled. Sometimes I wish I could hear the message in the manner—be it angry, pleading, arrogant, or obscene— that would be most comfortable to the speaker expressing it.

I showed the above part of this entry to Tigh, to get his thoughts on the subject. He smiled and said not to sweat it, all the communication *Galactica* can handle is going on regularly. Any more, and he'd apply for transfer to the Colonial Movers transport ship.

CHAPTER SEVEN

Boxey could not get Muffy to master sit-ups. No matter how much the daggit tried, it had too much bulk to bend comfortably at the waist—although, since it had been programmed to please the boy, it gave the exercise a good try. Boxey told it that it was all right to stop trying. Muffit responded by standing on its head.

Boxey looked toward the doorway. His father, Apollo, stood there, wearing a snow parka. When their eyes met, he smiled at the boy. Boxey noticed there seemed to be tears in Apollo's eyes, and he wondered why.

"You've got him trained well," Apollo said, nodding toward Muffit.

"Muffit's very intelligent. For a daggit."

Sometimes Boxey remembered the first Muffit, back on Caprica, the daggit he'd lost. He was not always sure that the second Muffit was quite as nice as the first one. The first Muffit had been more affectionate, especially in the way it had licked his face with its wet tongue. The new Muffit's tongue was scratchy and dry, and he'd had to tell it not to lick his face.

Apollo got down on his haunches to talk to the child.

"Boxey, I have to go away for a while."

Boxey did not like that one bit.

"We don't want you to leave us," he said.

"It won't be long. I promise."

Boxey realized there was some mysterious force that guided grown-ups into making decisions that they, or anybody else, could not like. He did not know whether that force was the god he'd been told to pray to every night, or whether grown-ups just obeyed rules that were like his Dad's instructions to him about eating or preparing himself to be a colonial warrior.

"Where are you going?" Boxey asked.

"Down to the ice planet. With Starbuck and Boomer."

Boxey did like the sound of that.

"An ice planet!" he cried. "Can Muffit and I come with you? We've never seen real snow."

"Not this time. See, it's a special project. To help the *Galactica*."

"But I'm a warrior."

Apollo smiled and squeezed Boxey's arm.

"I know," he said. "And as one you'll follow orders. Right?"

Boxey looked downcast.

"Yes, sir."

"Good. See, disappointment at being left off a mission roster is all part of your warrior training. When your qualifications meet the needs of a mission, why then you'll be picked. Do you see?"

"I suppose so."

"Okay." Apollo's voice became more military. "Your orders are to eat your primaries and go to bed when Commander Adama says it's time, and—"

"And say my prayers."

"Yes. Say your prayers."

Apollo called to Muffit, who scampered over and offered a metallically taloned paw. The captain shook it, then hugged Boxey. It seemed to the boy that his dad's hug was harder and longer than usual. Then, saying goodbye again, Apollo quickly left the room. Boxey stared at the doorway for a moment, then he said aloud:

"Remember, Muffy, when Dad showed us the shuttle as part of our training?"

The sensors inside the daggit picking up the questioning sound in the boy's rising tone of voice, Muffit nodded.

"Well, remember that hatchway that Dad said was an emergency exit?"

The daggit nodded again. Since this time the boy's question was more conspiratorial, the daggit's sensors transmitted the message that the droid should add a low growl, and Muffit growled quietly.

"Well, remember he told us the story of the time he'd saved a trapped squadron by using it as an entrance?"

The daggit-droid kept nodding.

"Well, I can eat my primaries and say my prayers on that ice planet, Muffy. Let's go try that hatchway."

Muffit, reacting to sensor-transmission, barked eagerly.

CHAPTER EIGHT

Croft:

Never seen it to fail. Everybody on a ship gets at least a little twitchy in those agonizing moments of waiting to launch. This shuttle's no exception. Wolfe's shifting his legs like there's still chains attached to them. Leda keeps fooling with a breather, examining its straps like she's never going to get the hang of them. Thane sits unmoving and straight. He looks calm. But Thane only gets *that* stiff just before he's ready to set an explosion, or to explode emotionally.

The shuttle is so crammed with gear it's hard to move around the compartment. I don't know what's in Adama's mind sending down this much junk, we'll never use half of it. I told him about traveling light. He just nodded like he understood. Guys like him always nod, then go by the book anyway.

The gun crew, who were down in the hold checking out the armored snow-ram vehicle we're going to use on the planet's surface, stumble into our compartment like a

bunch of drunks just back from a spree. Vickers trips over
Thane's feet and sprawls against Wolfe's barrel chest like
a swan out to achieve duckling status. Thane snarls at him
as Wolfe pushes him away:

"Watch who you're stepping on."

Vickers regains his balance and growls:

"Move your feet."

Thane gives him a disdainful look but doesn't move a
millimeter. Sergeant Haals bursts into the compartment,
his arms clutching a small arsenal. None of these guys
believes in traveling light, it seems.

"Clear the way," Haals says, "coming through."

"Not over me," Thane says.

"Out of the way," Haals says. He hands his weaponry
to Voight and grabs Thane by his shoulder harness. I
consider interceding, decide against it. Let them get all the
hostility out now. We've got to work as a team later.

"Take your hands off," Thane says quietly.

Vickers pipes up:

"Listen, you grid-rat, when a gunner tells you to clear
the way, you move your carcass on the double!"

I knew Vickers'd be real trouble. I'm going to have to
get into this mess. Wolfe's already sprung up to back
Thane's moves.

"Did you say grid-rat?" Wolfe shouts.

Turning toward Wolfe, Vickers—the idiot—says:

"Barge-louse would be more like it."

Wolfe slams Vickers into the nearest wall. For a
moment it looks like the gunner is going to go on clear
through the metal. In rushing to hold back Wolfe, I miss
Thane's move to his shirt pocket. Out of the corner of my
eye I can see him removing a small capsule. I should've
known. No matter where he is, Thane always manages to
find a supply of chemical commodities. He breaks the
ampule under Vickers' nose. Vickers' head jolts backward
and his body goes limp. Eyes glazed, he collapses to the
floor. Leda seizes Thane's hand as he thrusts the capsule
even closer to Vickers' face. Another dose and the
gunner's dead.

"You fool!" Leda whispers. "Our only chance to escape
is on the surface." So that's her game. And she looks at me

like I'm obviously going to agree to the escape. She turns back to Thane, whispers: "You want to get us thrown back to the grids?"

"No one steps on me," Thane says calmly, his hands fingering his shirt pocket as if he's ready to draw out another killer capsule. I want to tell him to lay off the chemicals, but the noise of scuffle behind me stops the words in my throat. Turning around, I see that Wolfe is now fighting Haals. Both can just barely swing a punch in this gear-filled compartment. On the other side of them, apparently attracted by all the noise, the three *Galactica* officers rush into the compartment.

"Haals! Wolfe!" Apollo shouts. "Break it off!"

I decide I better show some command-level initiative by backing up Apollo's play.

"Wolfe! Back off!"

Reluctantly Haals and Wolfe separate. Both of them look ready to go at it again in a minute. It's a fight that, under the proper conditions and with the proper space, I'd like to see. Haals looks big enough and tough enough to give Wolfe a good ride, though usually nobody beats Wolfe. I beat him once. That was in about five fights.

"How is he?" Apollo asks Leda, who's now stroking Vickers' throat with her strong but thin-fingered hands, helping him to breathe while Thane's chemical dosage is still in effect.

"He's all right. It's a short-span paralysis."

She's talking gently to Apollo. Why? Because she's attracted to him? Or because she wants him lulled so that she can put her escape plan into operation? Boomer gently removes a small electronic pack out of Thane's other jacket pocket. Delicately he holds it up for Apollo to see.

"Look at this."

Thane makes no move toward Boomer, but instead states calmly:

"Don't touch the switch. It's a hand mine."

You can see on Boomer's face he has no intention of touching the switch.

"You don't use the stuff on your own troops," Apollo says angrily.

Wolfe moves to Thane's side. They make a formidable pair: a thick-chested roughneck who'd be a giant if not for his height and the cool lean specter with death traps concealed all over his body.

"We're not barge-lice," Wolfe growls.

"Or grid-rats," Thane says softly, but with menace.

"Oh yes we are," I say, stepping between them and Apollo. "Lice and rats. Better yet, just bodies. We were picked for this drop because we're expendable."

"*Nobody's* expendable," Apollo says. I resist commenting, no, you probably aren't—as the commander's son you've probably already mapped a way out. Actually, Apollo's presence is comforting. So long as he's with us, and alive, we can be sure Adama'll dispatch a rescue force. Anything happens to him, the commander's not likely even to drop us rations. "You were picked," Apollo continues, "by a computer that didn't give an electronic damn about grid-barges, rats, lice, or warriors." Well, at least he's got us all neatly classified. "You're here to do a job on the Cylons"—he hands Thane back his kit; Thane replaces it in his pocket—"and not on each other. Stow your gear. And fasten your harness. We're on count-down."

A comforting rumble goes through the ship as we near launch point.

CHAPTER NINE

"Killer" Killian was not the type of colonial warrior who ever contemplated his own death in battle. A tough thick-muscled man, he looked like the grizzled veteran of many combats that he was. Nobody ever noticed the shrewdness in his eyes because his face was so dominated by a bushy mustache.

He pressed his shoulders back against his seat as he awaited the signal to launch his viper. If anyone had told him that this was his last launch and that in a few moments he would be dead, he would have just touched the end of his mustache with a stubby finger and shrugged. He might have commented that if his number was up, it was up, and then gripped his throttle a shade more tightly.

Over the commline the command came: "Let's fly!" Killian's viper, escort to the expedition shuttle, slammed down the launching tube with a great roar.

First Centurion Vulpa was beginning to doubt whether any information of value could be extracted from Cree.

So far the human vermin had been able to stand up to torture well, responding only with his name and an interminably large amount of numbers.

"Entry tracks," a technician announced.

"How many?" Vulpa asked.

"Two."

"Describe."

"One large. What the humans call a shuttlecraft. The other a fighting ship, a viper, flying escort for the shuttle, it appears."

"Any indications of their origin?"

"No."

Vulpa considered allowing the ships to land, but there were too many unknown factors. If the shuttle contained a rescue force or an assault team, the possibility of losses to his own understaffed garrison of troops was too strong. He would order the cannon to annihilate them, to wipe— no, that was impossible. Dr. Ravashol and a crew of his precious creations were up at the pulsar installation for repair and maintenance. It would be a mistake now to alert Ravashol to Vulpa's modifications of his invention, even though he suspected Ravashol already knew about them. No, better to destroy the intruders through more conventional means.

"Activate a destroyer shell-fighter with full warhead."

The shell-fighter was a variation of the new type of Cylon pilotless craft that could be guided by personnel in ordinary fighters. The difference in the warhead-equipped model was that it was constructed from the barest minimum of components. Since the entire ship exploded along with its target, there had been no need to waste material. When he had still been a member of Imperious Leader's general staff, Vulpa had ordered the development of the destroyer shell-fighter because of the heavy losses that were being sustained, losses that were out of all proportion to the firepower of their under-equipped human adversaries.

He ordered his command pilots to guide the warhead fighter toward the shuttle, while themselves engaging the escort viper and destroying it.

•　•　•

To Apollo the dense cloud cover of the planet below them looked spectral. Gray and smooth-surfaced, it seemed to conceal eerie mysteries. Its appearance only increased his natural caution. Looking over his shoulder, he crisply gave orders to Boomer:

"Get a navigational fix before we penetrate the cloud cover. We don't know what to expect on the surface. It could be pitch black, as it was when you and Starbuck went after Cree. No telling what the ground surface is like. Snow powder, pack ice, perhaps more di-ethene clouds than—"

Starbuck, in the copilot seat, interrupted:

"Cylons low on the starboard quarter!"

Apollo ordered a quick scan. There was a Cylon patrol formation just in back of another ship which the scanner indicated as unpiloted. The ship also lacked most of the familiar features of the normal Cylon fighter.

"What is it, do you think?" Apollo asked Boomer.

But the odd hollow sound of Thane's voice answered:

"It's not really a ship at all."

"Thane! How'd you get there?"

"I got tired of being harnessed back in that cabin. Thought I'd visit."

"You know you're not allowed—"

"This isn't the time to quote your stupid regulations at me, Captain. That ship out there, what your inefficient scanner describes as a ship, is actually a weapon. A guided device whose nose contains a solenite warhead, with sufficient power to blow this shuttle to bits. Tiny bits disintegrating to nothing. I would assume that its guidance system is set on a course for us."

Thane spoke all this so calmly, so dispassionately, that Apollo was not sure whether or not to believe him. He was describing their deaths, and he did not seem at all to care about the fact that he would die too.

"Employ evasion maneuver," Apollo ordered Starbuck, who immediately reset the shuttle's course.

"You can't evade that weapon," Thane said. "It's one of the Cylons' best technological achievements. I respect it. You can't evade it no matter how sophisticated your evasion procedures are."

"What do you suggest?"

"Destroy it before it destroys you."

Apollo wanted to ask Thane how he proposed to destroy a strange new weapon, but the man had disappeared as oddly as he had materialized.

Killian, alerted by Starbuck to the sudden attack, arced his viper into a long curve, heading on a line toward the trio of Cylon fighters that flew just behind the ghost ship with the lethal warhead. One of the Cylon ships peeled away from the tight formation and headed for Killian.

"Starbuck!" Killian shouted into his commline mike. "Dive for the cloud cover!"

"Won't work. They'll outrun us."

"Don't worry. I'll block for you."

Even as he said that, Killian pressed his firing button and placed a dozen quick laser shots in a small circle that first ripped off the rear section of the Cylon plane, then transformed it into a blazing fireball. In reaction to the loss of a ship, another Cylon fighter swerved toward Killian's viper.

Everybody in the shuttle was hurtled backward in their seats as Starbuck accelerated. The sound of the engines was, to Apollo, like a shriek of fright.

"Starbuck!" he yelled. "This isn't a fighter! You'll overrun the turbines!"

"Tell that to the Cylons," Starbuck yelled back.

The shuttle plunged into the cloud cover. The only light in the cockpit came from the scanner which displayed Killian's battle in the skies above them. They saw the second Cylon fighter shatter under Killian's cool and accurate firing. The last fighter and the warhead ship had altered course to pursue the shuttle. Starbuck tried to find more power in the shuttle's engines, but all that he could discover was a louder shriek.

Killian zeroed in on the last fighter but it evaded his fire and came in under his viper. His ship rocked as the Cylon's shot hit him amidship. He checked his scanner for damage report. The lousy Cylon had destroyed the lowside engine. Before Killian could pull out of the spin he was now in, the Cylon fired again and knocked a big chunk out of Killian's ship. Employing all the piloting instinct he had at his command, Killian pulled his viper out of the spin. Damage report showed a fuel line had been severed. The viper would blow up at any moment.

The Cylon fighter was streaking toward him. Killian tried to shoot at it, but his laser did not respond to the touch of the firing button. So that was out, too; it had been hit. Veering his ship to the right, he escaped the next burst of Cylon shots. But he knew that he could not evade for much longer. This time he had, after all, drawn his number.

Starbuck's voice came over the commline:

"I can't get this wreck going any faster. There's no way I can maneuver out of that warhead's way. There's no—"

"Shut up, Starbuck," Killian cried. "That thing's my job."

Evading the Cylon fighter one more time, Killian aimed his ship at the warhead-equipped shell. Engaging the turbos at full thrust of the remaining engines, he aimed his viper directly at the warhead ship. He shouted a curse that had a long-standing tradition aboard the *Galactica*. Killian's viper and the warhead ship collided just above the cloud cover of the ice planet. The explosion that resulted from the crash spread across the sky in a massive fireball that rushed toward the remaining Cylon fighter. The Cylon ship tried to curve away from it, but before it could complete the arc, it was sucked into and enveloped by the widening flame.

The shuttle lurched violently and Starbuck's gloved hand came off the throttle as if the device had suddenly turned red-hot.

"What is it?" Apollo screamed.

"Either we got hit by a stray shot or this speed's too much for the shuttle. I don't—"

"Captain Apollo!" Leda cried from the entranceway to the passenger compartment. "Everything's flying around back here. The wind's terrific! Something's split in the side of the ship, I think. Can't identify where in all the debris, but—"

"Try to hold control, Starbuck," Apollo cried. "I'll check this out."

"I'll try, but the ship's maneuvering like a balloon that's come untied."

Apollo rushed back to the passenger cabin. He spotted the dark split along the ship's side immediately.

"The skin's ruptured! Grab your breather gear!"

Everyone clamped on their breathers in quick motions—except for Croft, whose moves were methodical, and Thane, who attached his breather to his face slowly, looking as if he didn't care whether he wore it or not. Starbuck's voice came over the intercom:

"The ship won't respond. We're dropping down into a blizzard! Visibility zero. Surface coming up on all instruments. Counting down! Three! Two! One! Zero! Heads down!"

A loud rumble went through the ship, sounding like a warning that the shuttle was about to shatter into a thousand pieces. Buffeted by the violent winds, the shuttle went into a spin that made its passengers grasp at the air, looking for something solid to cling to. Suddenly Starbuck pulled the nose of the ship upward just before it made ground contact and skidded across the surface. Whirling snow created a fierce small blizzard inside the vehicle. The ship's sudden stop was thunderously loud, had all the bone-breaking power of a three-G force, and felt to the shuttle passengers like death.

The bridge crew of the *Galactica* fell silent as the monitoring screens blanked out suddenly. Adama, alerted by the silence, looked away from the reports of Cylon pursuit and into Tigh's tense eyes.

"We've lost signal from both ships," Tigh said.

Adama, recalling his conversation with Apollo about expendability, felt cold pain at the pit of his stomach.

"Any reception at all?" he asked.

"The viper channel is dead. No lights. Telemetry indicates total destruct."

"Who was it?"

"Killian."

Adama remembered the mustachioed officer vividly. His experience and combat instincts would be missed.

"And the shuttle?" he asked Tigh.

Tigh paused before answering:

"The emergency channel kicked in. All reds. Telemetry indicates heavy structural damage. We could reach for them on high band."

"No. Maintain silence."

"But—"

"I want to try to reach them as much as you do, Tigh. But we can't. We can't reveal our position."

If he could have talked to his son now, he would have told him that expendability or nonexpendability had nothing to do with the fact that Apollo had been programmed out of the mission computer search. It had more to do with the fear of having to deal with the exhausted emptiness of this moment.

Vulpa hovered over the communications panel, where his operator studied the action in the clouds above Tairac.

"One ship destroyed," the operator said. "One probable."

"The patrol with the warhead ship?" Vulpa asked.

"All contact lost. They may be destroyed."

"Contact Rearguard Patrol Leader."

"Garrison Command to Rearguard Patrol Leader."

Vulpa considered the possibility that the advance patrol had been completely destroyed. He did not like it. Because of what had been termed important matters relating to the war with the humans, he had been denied a full contingent for the garrison on Tairac. The general staff had argued that, after all, it was extremely unlikely that the humans would attempt to break through that particular defense perimeter. Now they were here. Not only that, but the general staff and its Imperious Leader had guided them here. Further, they expected Vulpa to counter any assault in spite of his understaffed situation. He wondered if they relied too much, perhaps, on the awesome power of the laser cannon with its annihilative strike capability. It was, naturally, true that the pulses from the cannon could easily destroy the *Galactica* and the ships of its fleet. However, before it could do that, those ships must be located.

The patrol leader reported in, and Vulpa addressed him:

"Tracking reports one invader destroyed. One probable."

"That agrees with what our instruments show. The probable dropped into cloud cover and spun out of control before our instruments lost contact with it. Sector Hekla."

Vulpa was annoyed that the shuttle's status remained probable.

"Search for wreckage!" he barked. "Leave no survivors."

"No survivors."

The shuttle *must* have crashed, Vulpa thought. If the humans were not dead, his task of destroying them became infinitely more complicated. The unstable weather conditions on Tairac's surface caused too much interference and distortion in the Cylons' monitoring equipment. Blizzards could hide the intruders, ragged terrain offered them places to crouch out of sight, darkness made visual discernment of them near to impossible. If there were any survivors, they must be discovered immediately, before they had a chance to become aware of the conditions that could be turned to their advantage.

CHAPTER TEN

Croft:

During the disoriented moment after the crash, I see stars and fire. That's dreadfully wrong, I tell myself. Doesn't jibe with the cold in my bones. I feel like a statue of ice. A statue to what? To my own stupidity at leaving my rotten-smelling, claustrophobic, painful—but warm, always warm—cell aboard the prison ship? I've felt cold before, even cold this intense. I've been on mountains whose violent cold winds nearly blew me away. Been inside a snow pile from an avalanche that took me centons to dig out of. Experienced wet-cold that caused cracks in my clothing, made ropes split unexpectedly, left corpses whose eyes still expressed a live disbelief in their own mortality.

When I come to, all I can see first is snow whipping around the passenger cabin. The temperature's dropped so fast I can't work the breather right. My eyes adjust and some of the snow subsides. We're all entangled. Supplies have tumbled upon us, we've tumbled upon each other.

Light. Apollo has a working lantern in his hand. The lamp shines on a gaping rent in the fuselage of the ship. Outside, a dense blizzard is howling around us. I don't want to go out there. I'll freeze to death here. Still, I want to choose here.

Starbuck crawls out of the front end of the ship, a thin trickle of blood seeping from a wound on his scalp.

"Just the kind of landing you dreamed of," he says. "No instruments, no engines, no field—"

Boomer, crawling out behind him and immediately standing up, says:

"Grab a light."

Starbuck staggers to his feet, grabs a light, and mutters:

"You did a great job, Starbuck, mastering an out-of-control shuttle, keeping us from crashing head-on. You're one fine pilot—"

"When you're through feeling unappreciated here," Apollo interrupts, "help check the wounded. We lost half the ship back there."

"Aye-aye, sir."

Apollo is being tough. Taking charge. I don't know how much of him taking charge I'm going to be able to stand.

Boomer claps a hand on Starbuck's shoulder and says:

"Don't feel too bad. Anyone else would have lost it all."

"Don't worry, I—" Starbuck says as he shoots an angry glance at his captain. I gather that Starbuck doesn't always see eye to eye with Apollo. "I'll be all right, Boomer."

Pushing a couple of heavy cartons aside, I make my way toward the rear of the shuttle, where I see what a real wreck looks like. Metal that used to be separated by intervening materiel is now securely interlocked. The materiel itself is unrecognizably crushed. Wolfe is leaning over Voight. Apollo moves toward them.

"How is he?" he asks Wolfe.

Wolfe looks for a moment like it's an imposition for him to answer any question, then he says:

"Just a rap on the head. He'll come around in half a centon."

"Apollo," Leda says from the other side of the passenger cabin. She's crouched over Vickers. "I can help them if you can find my case."

Apollo moves off, his eyes scanning the wreckage. I am about to join in the search, but I notice an odd body movement from Wolfe. He leans just slightly toward Voight's body, his hand grabs at something which he secretes in his parka, then he swaggers away. I decide to check Voight. The flap of his laser holster is unsnapped, the weapon is missing. Wolfe may have the pistol, then. Maybe not, but it's a darn good guess. I can't take it away from him. With Wolfe's volatile temper, I can't tell anybody he's got it either. If he has it, it'll be out and firing at any of us he happens to get mad at. I'll just have to sit tight on the information, see what I can do about Wolfe later.

Apollo is helping Leda. He's snatched the medical case from beneath a pile of debris.

"What's it look like?" he asks her.

"Broken arm and a couple of ribs." Her voice is cool and businesslike now. That's what I like about Leda, one of the things I loved once, perhaps love still. No matter what she feels about any of us, she can be trusted to do her job well. "Possible internal injuries." She looks around at the rest of us. "Anyone else hurt?"

"I am," Thane says softly.

She moves quickly to Thane's side.

"What's your problem?" she says, looking into her case.

Thane grins maliciously, edges his lean body toward hers, whispers just loudly enough so the rest of us can hear:

"I'm lonely."

That's Thane, all right. Even his little jokes come out with icicles hanging all over them. Leda, clearly furious with him, grabs her case and moves off, saying:

"Stay out of my way. I have work to do."

She settles down beside Vickers again.

"Don't waste your time on him," Thane says. "We'll have to leave him behind to die anyway."

Always the humanitarian, Thane. This time he arouses the ire of Apollo, who shouts:

"We're not leaving anyone behind!"

Thane looks coldly at Apollo. It's the look he gets just before he's ready to spring.

"We'll see, Captain. We'll see."

Apollo, busy seeing to Voight, doesn't hear Thane. I wish I hadn't. Thane's all coiled up inside. If that tension gets released, I don't know if I can handle it.

Boomer, directing his light toward another gash in the side of the shuttle, reports to Apollo:

"It isn't good. She'll never fly again."

Great!

"Worse," Apollo comments, "she can't sustain life inside. All of her systems are purged."

Terrific, even better!

"Looking on the brighter side," Boomer says, "I think the snow ram's operable."

"Let's get her out fast, then, so we can move the wounded into her."

Apollo takes a step toward the gash. Outside, the sound of a far-off aircraft becomes louder quickly. Apollo tries to look out the opening. The roar grows to a deafening scream as a Cylon fighter flies over us.

"He'll be back!" Apollo cries. "We better get everyone out of the shuttle. Boomer, Croft, help me get the snow ram."

The three of us crawl into the hold containing the snow-ram vehicle. Apollo climbs into it, and starts throwing switches. As I climb into the other side, I am startled out of my wits by a low growl. Apollo whirls in his seat and shines his light toward the rear of the snow ram. A child and a furry animal crouch there, huddled into a corner, obviously on the verge of becoming one youthful and one furry icicle.

"Boxey!" Apollo shouts, amazed. Apparently he knows the kid. Unless Boxey's the animal. The child crawls forward, attempts a smile that turns out painfully weak.

"Muffit wanted to see snow," he says. Muffit must be the animal. It sidles to the boy's side. It's not an animal. It's some sort of droid version of an animal. A copy of a daggit, I think, though I haven't seen a daggit since God knows when.

Apollo looks ready to bawl out the kid, but he reacts instead to the obvious fact that the kid is terribly cold and scared.

"Come here, son," Apollo says softly, affectionately. Did I hear right? The kid is Apollo's son? That's just perfect.

The kid hugs Apollo. Apollo hugs back. Cozy.

"I'm sorry," the kid says.

"It's all right," Apollo says soothingly. "It's all right."

I resist saying maybe it's all right with *you*, but what about the rest of us? The droid must be a mind reader. He looks my way and growls again.

I don't like this setup and I don't like the way it's going. Wolfe may have a gun, Thane is ready to cut throats, Leda—who knows what ever goes on in Leda's head? Apollo's trying to assert command over a bunch to whom command is a threat. We have no shuttle to return to the *Galactica* in. A Cylon fighter plane may be returning at any moment. The captain's kid is a stowaway. I've got to put up with his mechanical pet growling meanly at me. There's snow everywhere and it's colder than a Scorpion slumlord. We're expected to climb a mountain that might not even have a rock you can cling to without sliding off, knock off a weapon that can destroy a whole fleet, escape with our teeth intact. Nope, I don't like this setup one bit, and it's beginning to look like it's going to have to be me who makes it function at all.

CHAPTER ELEVEN

Cylon scout ships had once again detected a flaw in the camouflage force field of Battlestar *Galactica* and its ragtag fleet, and Imperious Leader was quite pleased to verify that the humans, their progress slowed almost to a standstill, had fallen right into his trap. It was obvious they were trying to stay out of the accuracy range of the laser cannon on Mount Hekla. It was time to prod Adama and his vile human forces. Turning to the ring of executive officers surrounding his high pedestal, he ordered:

"I wish to close in on the human fleet. Double our speed and inform our warriors to make ready. This will be the final battle. Send out one phalanx of the ghost ships to attack the fleet immediately. I want them frightened and aware we have discovered them."

Satisfied with his strategy, he dispatched the officers. The ghost-ship phalanx should serve to confuse Adama's fleet. The development of the pilotless warhead aircraft had been one of First Centurion Vulpa's finest ideas. If Vulpa did succeed to the position of Imperious Leader, his technologically innovative abilities should be vastly improved by the addition of the third brain.

He reviewed the details of his plan, satisfied with the general outline of squeezing the humans between the Cylon pursuit force and the Mount Hekla weapon. Although there was no apparent reason to doubt, he decided to consult the Starbuck simulation again. Turning to the simulator, which he had not yet sent away from his pedestal, he stared at the telepathy-template and requested the simulacrum of the arrogant human lieutenant.

"Hi, chum," the Starbuck simulacrum said after the outline of his body had solidified. Turning his attention back to the telepathy-template, the Leader ordered that the simulacrum have memory of their previous conversations.

"I'm still not going to help you," the Starbuck said.

"You can't avoid it. Your programming impels you to answer any question according to the knowledge we have accumulated about your real self."

"You can take all your programming strips and eat them for breakfast, bug-eyes. Better than primaries any day."

"Do you know about our pilotless aircraft?"

"Your ships are pilotless even when you guys are in them."

Suppressing his anger, Imperious Leader turned toward the template and ordered that knowledge of the ghost ships be added to the simulacrum's information. The Starbuck smiled as soon as the information was provided it.

"Trying to spook us, then. Nice play, I'll give you credit."

"Oh?"

"Sure. We humans have a natural tendency toward suspicion. Give us a force we can't explain, or a strange shape drifting through the darkness, and we all feel a clutching in our chest, a shiver up our spine, and the urge to run for the hills."

"Then the ghost ships will be a successful maneuver?"

The Starbuck appeared to think for a moment. The

simulator was searching its data banks for an appropriate human-language response.

"Doubt it," the Starbuck finally said.

"Why do you say that?"

"It's like this: Adama. You can't fool him with magic tricks. He ain't like the rest of us. Sometimes he's downright inhuman."

"Then you believe he might not be, to use your word, spooked by our pilotless aircraft?"

"You might spook him a little, but you won't scare him."

"What is the precise difference in terminology?"

"Spooking requires merely a feeling that the object is mysterious; scaring requires that the object come up, smack you in the face, and convince you it's out for your soul."

"I do not follow that completely."

"You never will, chum, you never will."

"I believe our strategy will succeed."

The Starbuck smiled.

"Best of luck," it said.

Imperious Leader was surprised.

"You wish me luck?"

"What do I care? I'm only a simulation."

Imperious Leader wondered for a moment if, since this simulacrum seemed quite insane, the real Starbuck was equally mad.

CHAPTER TWELVE

Croft:

Nothing's so bad it can't get worse if you apply a little human ingenuity to the situation. We could hear the Cylon fighter in the distance, swooping to ground level, then accelerating upward. There was a phantomlike quality to the sound. The fighter could locate us at any time, and all of us were too cold or injured to move out of its way with any speed.

Boomer tries to get things hopping:

"Okay, everybody out! Now!"

Wolfe scrambles for the hole leading outside, Thane strolls to it. Sorting through the smashed containers, I manage to liberate a number of ice axes, some of the molecular-binding pitons, other odds and ends of climbing equipment. They wouldn't be enough, perhaps, but we have to salvage as much as possible. Near the gaping hole, while still scrounging for materiel, I stumble across a large figure huddled in the dark. A face, angry, comes into the dim light. Leda.

"I might have expected you to trample me on your way out," she says.

"I wasn't on my way out. I was—never mind. I didn't see you there in the dark."

"You never did."

She glares at me, but in her eyes is some delight at scoring her point. Let her have her little triumph. Nothing gained by alienating her any further. If this operation is successful, maybe we can get back together, maybe—ah, it's no good fretting over futile wishes.

Boomer rushes past us, not seeing myself or Leda.

"I'll take Vickers," he says. "Starbuck!" Starbuck pokes his head through the entranceway to the forward cabin. "Give me a hand."

"I'm trying to remove the communicator," Starbuck protests. "We're going to need it."

"Sorry, you don't have the time. Captain Apollo thinks they've spotted us. That Cylon ship'll be back for another pass quick as a flash. Give me a hand with Vickers."

Starbuck comes into the passenger compartment and reaches for Vickers' feet while Boomer cradles the gunner's head and shoulders. I hustle toward the exit, immediately feel the harsh sting of fiercely blowing snow against that part of my face that's not covered by the breather. In spite of the snow and the darkness, the gray shape of the Cylon fighter is immediately visible hurtling toward us.

"Here he comes!" I shout.

The fighter dips into a strafing run. The fire from its lasers hisses and crackles across the ice field. I dive to the ground, feel the sharp smack of firm ice against my whole body. Behind me, I can hear the other members of the team scrambling out of the shuttle. Looking up, I'm just in time to watch the forward section of the shuttle burst into a bright yellow flame.

As the Cylon fighter slips upward in a loop designed to end in another strafing run, a deep rumble sounds from inside the shuttle. The snow ram kicking into life. With a loud roar, the vehicle smashes through the side of the shuttle, creating still another large hole. Its sleek black surface streaked by the glow of flames from the burning shuttle, the snow ram swerves furiously into defensive artillery position. Apollo sticks his head out the snow ram's portside window, hollers:

"Starbuck! Get up here!"

"Always in demand," Starbuck yells as he jumps up on the turret of the vehicle.

The Cylon ship, not expecting to encounter resistance, appears again and initiates its run. Starbuck extends the long barrel of the snow-ram gun, and spinning it around, takes aim on the enemy ship as it approaches. The Cylon fighter's guns, with their longer range, score a pair of hits on the snow ram. The cover flies off the vehicle's external battery. Starbuck seems not to notice. Holding back until the properly timed moment, he stares upward, sighting along the narrow barrel of the gun to the enlarging shadowy form of the advancing ship. Just as I'm about to yell at him to fire, he does. With an ear-splitting howl, he unloads at the swooping Cylon plane. The shots fly straight to their mark. The ship explodes like a meteor cracking apart. We all shield our eyes from the incandescent glare.

Turning the vehicle around, Apollo aligns it alongside the shuttle, whose fire has now dimmed. In the dying light we assemble, at least those of us still conscious do. The snow-ram engine coughs and shakes. Something's obviously wrong with it.

Suddenly the kid sticks his head out the highside hatchway of the snow ram and cries out:

"Great shooting, Starbuck!"

From the looks on the face of Starbuck and some of the others, I can tell Apollo and Boomer have forgotten to inform them of Boxey's presence. When they hear the droid inside start to bark, they all jump, startled at the abrupt sound.

Apollo, cutting off any queries about the presence of the kid and his mechanical pet, tells everyone to crowd around the snow vehicle. As we do, he lights a lamp. I become more aware of the ferocity of the wind as the fire in the shuttle finally flickers out.

"Light the other snow lamp," Apollo orders. "Keep them shielded."

Starbuck takes care of the other lamp.

"Crowd as many as possible inside," Apollo says. "We'll rotate riding on top. Haals and Wolfe go first."

Neither Haals nor Wolfe looks like he appreciates the privilege of being first. The wind's increasing in velocity, while the snow's back to mere blizzard level. Starbuck hands me his light and everybody starts loading the snow ram. When the job's just about done, I become conscious of Thane and Wolfe standing behind me. I turn and face them, after checking that everybody else is still busy with the loading.

"What is it?" I say as quietly and guardedly as I can across the roar of the blizzard.

"You're not going to guide them across to the mountain?" Thane says. Somehow his quiet voice manages to carry no matter what noise is raging around him.

"We can make it," I say.

"It's our chance to make a break."

Exactly what I suspected. They've been cooped up for too long. Their desire for escape has overcome their common sense, and they're not going to listen to me for long before attempting to flee from the core group.

"A break, eh? To where? We're stuck on this ball of ice."

Thane's obviously been thinking this all out. His answers are ready.

"We can hunt. Build shelter. We've been in a lot worse."

Wolfe moves in closer and whispers in his raspy voice:

"Maybe we can hijack a Cylon transport and make a run for a sun system."

"Yeah, and maybe we can clip off all the hair on your body, Wolfe, and get rich selling it as animal pelts." Wolfe looks like he'd rather clip me. "We're not going to run anywhere. We signed on to blow up that pulsar-type cannon or whatever it is."

Thane's eyes narrow, as much a show of emotion as I've ever seen him manage at one time.

"You sayin' you'd crawl up that mountain to get your rank back?"

I want to take that scrawny neck of his in my hands and
squeeze it until life comes back into his eyes.

"It's low-blow time, that right, Thane?"

"Low blows are for people who can fight back. They
broke you, Croft. You used to bite, but now you're
toothless. Okay, you stay and wear their choke chain.
We're cutting loose the first chance we get!"

I remember when these guys didn't used to be so stupid.
Thane says they broke me. I'm not sure who they broke.
Maybe he's right. Maybe I've lost my sense of loyalty, that
feeling of companionship we'd all experienced before the
platinum raid. But is it disloyal to rank a selfish desire for
escape and personal freedom over our duty to save the
fleet from certain disaster? It doesn't seem so to me, and
I'm about to tell Thane and Wolfe that, but out of the
corner of my eye I can see Apollo walking up to us, the
snow crunching under his heavy boots.

"Soon as you're finished loading," Apollo says, "we'll
go."

I glance at Thane and Wolfe. I'm pretty sure both of
them have given up on me. Maybe I can convince them
later.

"We're through," I say to Apollo, and walk off next to
the captain, feeling the two pairs of eyes of my former
cohorts staring deep craters into my back.

Next to the shuttle wreck, Leda is working furiously on
the injured Vickers and Voight. Haals comes out of the
shuttle, his arms sliding into the harnesses of a backpack.

"How are they?" Apollo says, crouching by Leda. The
look she gives him reminds me of a look she once used to
reserve for me. Since she wants so badly to escape, the
look is probably phony. Maybe it was always phony.

"They'll survive," Leda says, "if we can get them to
shelter."

"Put them inside the ram. There'll be enough room,
with Wolfe and Haals riding on top."

Wolfe now hovers over all of us, growling:

"I'm not freezing, just so—"

"I said you ride on top," Apollo says, standing. "That's
an order."

"I'm not letting any punk of a—"

Wolfe stops suddenly, shoots a dirty look my way. I try to convince him with a shrug that I'm staying out of it. He spins on his heel and strides off. I should warn Apollo, if he hasn't realized it already, that Wolfe in a belligerent mood is extremely dangerous. But then I'd have to inform on Wolfe about the stolen gun, and what good would telling Apollo anything do? The smug young captain would just mutter he could take care of it, like he always does. I hope someday he comes up against something he can't take care of. Soon.

We load the two injured men aboard the snow ram, and Apollo goes to the controls. As I climb into the interior of the vehicle, I can hear Wolfe and Haals as they scramble into position up top.

"Get over!" Wolfe bellows.

"It's frozen on that side," Haals complains.

"That's your problem."

Let Wolfe *be* Haals's problem for a while. I'm getting into the ram and huddling against somebody for warmth, preferably Leda.

Leda, however, has positioned herself between Starbuck and Boomer. She'd probably rather be positioned against the captain, but she's always smart enough to take pot luck.

We go some distance in silence. Even the garrulous Starbuck stares off into space without talking. Once in a while the kid whispers to the droid, but that's about all the conversation anybody can work up. We're all tense. If everything's been this bad so far, what's up ahead?—in one way or another, that's what we're all thinking, whether our goal is the mountain or escape or a warm place for our mechanized daggit that probably has no sensors for cold anyway.

Suddenly there is the noise of a scuffle above us, then a thump followed by a loud, sharp crackling noise. Without even a cough, the snow-ram engine kicks out, and the vehicle skids a bit across a stretch of ice field.

Apollo is out of his driver seat and outside as soon as the vehicle comes to a stop. I come out right after him, Leda just behind me.

A short distance behind the snow ram, Haals is lying in

the snow, his arms outflung. Wolfe leaps off the top, stumbles, and rolls in the snow. Leda runs to Haals's prone body, checks him out.

"He's in bad shape," she cries back. "Very bad. He might die, looks like."

"What happened?" Apollo roars at Wolfe.

Wolfe takes a deep breath before snarling his answer:

"He was bawling me out. I told him to get off my back, pushed him a little. He tried to fight back. His feet went out from under him, and he slipped. His torch made contact with that thing there"—Wolfe pointed to the coverless external battery—"then there were sparks all over the place and he fell off the vehicle as it stopped. Your clumsy warrior shorted out the power cells, I guess."

Starbuck, emerging from the snow-ram interior, seems about to leap on Wolfe.

"I'll bet he did!"

Apollo holds Starbuck back.

"Stop it! We've got enough problems."

Searching the terrain ahead of me, I see just what I'm afraid to see. I whirl on Apollo, saying:

"We're going to have more problems if we don't adjust our breathers to full protective power, and right away. There's a di-ethene wave building up in this storm."

"The ram's powerless without these batteries," Apollo says. "Do we have time to hide it?"

Finally. He's learning something, showing enough sense to ask my opinion.

"Do we have a choice!" I say. "Of course we hide it."

Apollo and I begin to dig into the snow to throw up a wall around the ram to hide it from Cylon eyes. Starbuck and Boomer help Leda carry back Haals to the vehicle. Wolfe sulks for a moment, then joins the digging. Even Thane comes out of his hiding place aboard the snow ram to make adjustment checks on the breathing gear. For a moment at least we're all working together, making like a team. For whatever that's worth.

After the snow wall's constructed we all huddle together inside the snow ram for warmth. For now there's no other course of action. Apollo holds the kid in his arms. The breather mask the kid's wearing looks too big for him, though Thane's rigged a couple of extra straps to make it fit better. But it doesn't look like it's working so good. At least when he keels over we'll get an indication of how long the rest of us'll last. No, that's an unworthy thought. Where did I become the type who'd let a kid die for any selfish advantage? I glance down at the daggit, huddled against the boy, giving warmth instead of taking it. It's lucky. It doesn't even have to wear a breather mask. When we've all popped off for good, it can scamper among our bodies.

"How do you feel, Boxey?" Apollo says.

"Just a little cold."

Apollo pulls the boy even closer to him. It's not bad seeing a little human affection, even briefly, when you consider the composition of this team. I look over at Leda, who's deep in some private thoughts of her own. I remember seeing her this way, some time long ago, while she was resting in the saddle of a mountain ridge. I don't remember where, I don't remember what took place before or after, I just remember her sitting like that and I remember how much I loved her at that moment. I want to reach over and touch her arm, ask her thoughts, have her nestle close to me—but I know that one move in her direction and she'll smash her fist into my face and break my jaw.

Starbuck crawls over to me, asks:

"What are our chances?"

Another invocation of my expertise from a *Galactica* officer. I'm sure gaining in stature around here. Too bad it's probably too late.

"Depends on how long this storm lasts," I say, "and if the atmosphere, under the influence of the di-ethene, starts descending to the critical point of the gases composing it. That's the point when, well, when you can't really see much distinction on the critical-temperature curve between the gaseous and liquid phases. For our purposes, the air outside turns to liquid. Some call it deathpoint, though the name's never made much sense to me, since normally you're pretty dead long before the critical point. That satisfy you?"

"Not much. But thanks anyway."

"Anytime."

He crawls away very slowly. The cold's beginning to affect his muscles. It's affecting all of us that way. I have to force myself to keep exercising what muscles I can in this cramped sitting position.

The droid suddenly springs away from the kid's side. Its furry ears point upward. It looks like it's heard something, though I don't know what it can possibly hear with that blizzard howling outside. It begins to bark furiously. The kid tells it: Shut up, daggit. Then it breaks for the door. With more strength than I could work up, it forces the door open and bounds out. Starbuck tries to go for the door, but can't make it.

"I . . . I can't move," he mutters.

"Muffit," the kid whines weakly. "Muffit! Come back."

Apollo pulls the kid even closer to him, saying:

"It's all right, son. Muffit isn't like us. He can survive di-ethene."

"Three cheers for Muffit," I say.

"Will he be back?" the kid says.

"He'll be back."

Apollo glances around, then mutters to no one in particular:

"I just hope he doesn't bring a Cylon patrol back with him."

I almost wish he does. What good is it huddled inside this broken-down vehicle? The Cylons might just let us have a warm cell before executing us. Be fitting for me, wouldn't it? Complete the cycle? From warm cell to warm cell. Welcome it. Though I don't feel so cold anymore. Feel numb. Drowsy. Hey! Stop feeling drowsy. Can't go to sleep now. Sleep's death. Won't let everything end this way. Can't let it. Won't. Can't. It's not right. Not fair. Not . . .

FROM THE ADAMA JOURNALS:

I wonder if, when we finally outrun or destroy the Cylons and find a planet to welcome us, we will be able to
reconstruct our lost legends, our destroyed books, our
currently unperformed entertainments. Some of these
are, of course, preserved in our computer banks, but not
all. Not all. Yesterday I requested a copy of the Caprican
story *Sharky Star-rover,* confident that it *had* to be
preserved somewhere in the fleet records. But the answer
returned, *scan negative.* For a moment I could not accept
the answer. A book that I'd read and reread years ago was
no longer available—was, in effect, lost to us. No one
would ever read it again, unless a frayed copy turned up in
somebody's locker or as an artifact on some deserted
planetary outpost. I nearly instigated a search.

Alone in my quarters, I tried to remember the story of
Sharky Star-rover. I thought I could remember it easily.
Perhaps I could renew the oral tradition, keep alive at
least the major part of a story I had so loved. But, I soon
discovered, I had few of the details of the story in my

mind, even less memory of the order in which it happened.

Sharky was just a boy, that much I recalled. A tough kid just past the hurdle of puberty. Trapped on an out-of-the-way military asteroid, where his disabled-veteran father coped with his combat record by becoming a hophead and his mother coped with the father by turning into a shrew, Sharky vowed to escape. I don't remember how he managed it, but he stole a supply shuttle, having learned simple piloting by watching the ship's pilot do the job. He headed the shuttle away from the complex of military asteroids, setting his course for an area that was considered unpopulated, although appealing rumors of sin cities and pleasure palaces had accrued around it. Somehow he teamed up with his new pal Jameson. I don't remember whether Jameson stowed away on the shuttle when Sharky stole it, or whether they met on one of the many settlements Sharky visited. Jameson was some kind of blob, a representative of an alien race that was quite unpopular in some sectors of the galaxy. There were times when Sharky had to hide Jameson away, but when it was necessary, he fought tooth and nail for his alien friend.

It's Sharky's friendship with Jameson that I really want to remember. They worked so well together in flying the shuttlecraft across the galaxy—I recall all kinds of clever exchanges, all sorts of moments in which a sly joke of Jameson's gave Sharky peculiar and valuable insights on life. There was a meditation of Sharky's in which he almost said he wished that a real love were possible between a human and a member of Jameson's race. He never really said he wanted to embrace Jameson—and, remember, Jameson couldn't be embraced, or even held onto, no matter how hard you tried—but it was clear that Sharky's fantasy would include a Jameson magically transformed to human shape and quite embraceable.

The adventures are even harder to recall than the impressions of character. The book was basically a collection of episodes about Sharky's adventures on the various planets he stopped at. At the more civilized settlements he found that his theft of the shuttle had been recorded and he was wanted as a criminal. He had to go through some pretty hairy times to escape and not be returned home. (The continuing to flee was an especially important feature of the book—it seemed to suggest that irresponsibility was a desirable way of life, and I find it funny that my responsible adult self remembers that theme so nostalgically.) He fell in with a group of criminals, pretended to go along with them, then thwarted their plan by getting Jameson to walk in on them at the moment of the crime. But what was the crime? Who were the criminals? Why don't I remember their characters? Once Sharky—who was only in his early teens, remember—almost successfully impersonated a star-cruiser captain, a disguise he was using to try to obtain a cargo hold of food when he and Jameson were starving. I can remember that episode pretty well. I used to read it to my children when they were growing up. Zac used to pretend to be Jameson, and crawl bloblike around the floor.

I can still feel the sadness of the end of the book, when Sharky and Jameson were finally apprehended. Sharky wanted Jameson to be returned home with him, but the rules wouldn't allow it. The officer in charge of the squad that captured them told Sharky that Jameson could not survive within any military installation. He would be a figure of scorn. The captain said that separating them was an act of compassion and not cruelty. Sharky said he saw the point, but I never felt he did, and neither, I suspect, did any readers of the book. Anybody who could read the scene of parting between Sharky and Jameson without crying had to have a sturdy hold on his emotions. I can't really remember Sharky's return to home, perhaps because I don't really want to. I remember it was sentimental. Perhaps his dad had gone off his habit and his mother had become a saint. It doesn't matter. Nobody I know who ever read it ever bothered much about believing its ending.

Clearly, *Sharky Star-rover* was a flawed book, and perhaps some misguided programmer librarian thought he/she had good reason for not including it in the *Galactica* computer library. That's too bad. Sharky's quest for a more adventurous life seems so similar to our quest for Earth. The story might give us hope when we need it. No matter how much of the book I can reconstruct, no matter how much eloquence I attempt in trying to retell the story to anyone, I'll never really have *Sharky* again. So much has been destroyed. So much.

CHAPTER THIRTEEN

Although the *Galactica* bridge might have seemed still and inactive to an outside observer, there was an abundance of human movement going on. Crew members' hands were testing dials and gauges whose information had remained stable for some time. Communications officers kept pressing their earpieces harder against their ears, trying to discover some encouraging sounds. Colonel Tigh sat at his post, rippling the corners of printouts he'd stopped examining centons earlier. Athena's eyes searched every horizontal scan line of her monitoring screen, and kept punching new combinations of the same data into her computer setup. Adama's large knobby hands gripped and ungripped the railing that ran along the starfield walkway.

Suddenly one of the bridge officers grumbled a curse and called to Colonel Tigh. Tigh rushed to the woman, Adama close behind him. She pointed to her long-range scanner. Tigh turned to Adama, saying:

"That scanner's picked up a Cylon fighter squadron."

"How many?" Adama asked.

"Looks like an attack phalanx. They're beginning to press."

Adama nodded.

"Order Blue Squadron to patrol the rear."

"Aye-aye, sir." Tigh flipped the nearest communication switch as activity around him on the bridge multiplied. "Scramble Blue Squadron! Patrol rear sectors Sigma through Omega!"

The claxons roared through the *Galactica*, and the bridge crew could almost physically detect the rush of pilots toward launching bays. On various screens, pilots could be seen swinging into action, flight crews readying the vipers, and the reverberations of the fighter ships themselves.

The squadron launched and achieved formation long before a visual contact with the Cylon attack phalanx was made. Positioned well to the rear of the fleet itself, the vipers were more than ready for the not-so-sneak attack of their enemy.

Aboard the *Galactica*, the bridge crew stood and sat at battle stations, their active eyes watching information screens and equipment. Adama ordered the picture being transmitted from Blue Leader One transferred to the main screen. Tensely, they all watched the distant points grow into blots and then take form as flat-looking but multileveled Cylon fighters. The first blast from a Cylon weapon was directed at Blue Leader One, and everyone on the bridge flinched and startled backward when the shot seemed to come right at them. Then the skies were filled with laser fire and the sudden bursting flames of direct hits. A pair of Cylon fighters broke through the Blue Squadron line of defense and headed for the fleet.

"Protect the freighters!" Adama ordered.

"*Galactica* to Blue Leader," transmitted a bridge officer. "Engage!"

A Blue Squadron viper peeled away from the squadron and in one long beautiful sweep fired at both of the attackers and transformed them into two masses of fire whose flames reached out toward each other, combined, fell together, and exploded further in a burst of bright light that, for a brief moment, illuminated the entire wide triangle of ships that was the present fleet formation.

"My God!" Athena gasped.

"Good shooting?" Adama, standing behind her, asked.

"Not only that. That double kill was accomplished by one of the *cadets*."

"As I said, good shooting."

Adama walked away from her, his face apparently expressionless, but Athena recognized a flicker of pleasure in his reaction to the heroism of a graduate of his makeshift flight academy.

The Cylon ships, quickly routed by the dizzying maneuvers of the Blue Squadron vipers, retreated into the distance, became points again. A flight officer approached Adama, and reported:

"Blue Squadron returning to base. Four Cylons destroyed, the rest are running."

"They'll be back," Adama commented. "In packs, like wolves. What do your reports show, Tigh?"

The colonel was scowling at a set of printouts that he gripped tightly in his hands. Something clearly disturbed him.

"We got ships again, but not Cylon *personnel*. The Cylons in the rearguard ships guided the others, as before. We lost one viper and one good pilot. They lost just the vehicles, if vehicles is the proper word. They're wearing us down with these empty ships. It's eerie."

"That may be what they want us to feel. If they come at us again, go for the rearguard ships. Station a few warriors on the slower freighters with heavy artillery to blast any of the pilotless aircraft that might get through next time."

"Aye-aye, sir."

Athena, eavesdropping on the conversation between her father and his aide, sidled up to Adama and whispered:

"Let me go."

"Go where?"

"Give me some heavy artillery, station me on a—"

"I told you. We need you here."

Adama's voice was firm. She should have immediately

returned to her station, but she decided to press her luck.

"Well, you're going to have to take a few warriors off the flight roster. Let me take up a viper the next attack. I can—"

"None of that. You stay here."

"I'm as well checked-out in a viper cockpit as any of those cadets you're rushing into battle."

Adama's shocked face cut off her little speech abruptly before she could get to the logical part.

"One of those *cadets*, as you so happily informed me moments ago, performed that skillful double kill, Athena."

"All right. I'm properly chastened, Commander. But one lucky cadet is just a rationalization for your keeping me stuck at a console on the command bridge. I want my chance at—"

Adama's stern expression softened.

"I promise I'll give you your chance, Athena. But right now, back to duty. You *are* needed."

"Yes, sir."

Tigh, the usual papers in his hand, returned to Adama's side, and said:

"Any estimate on time remaining until the landing party completes the mission?"

"It's irrelevant. We have to move forward in"—Adama glanced at his chronometer—"in four hundred and twenty centons regardless of whether they're successful or not."

Gradually the activity on command bridge had stopped, stalled. Only the nervous agitated hand movements remained.

CHAPTER FOURTEEN

Croft:

Clothes in pieces, shreds falling off my body. Ice-ax twisting and turning in the middle of a long slow bounce off a cornice. Bare feet getting number and number against the ice of the summit. Leda reaching for me. But without threat. Her outstretched hands are meant to comfort me. She wants to hold me. I slip and slide, trying to reach out to touch her. Her clothing's ragged, too. Flaps and rips all over it. Flecks of ice clinging to her face. The skin of her hand turning black, leprous. Her feet are going out from under her. No, Leda, *no*! Still reaching out, she's falling away from me. I start to fall, too, but grab an outcropping of ice and my body flaps like a flag in high winds. Twisting my neck, I look below me. Leda still stares up at me, her eyes pleading, her body gently spinning in a slow fall, doubling up as it hits the side of a ridge, then continues its descent. Beyond her, the ice-ax takes a high bounce off a serac. I am about to drop from the outcropping, dive after her, but I can't make my

fingers work, they seem glued into a permanent
handhold. I start to scream but I can't even hear myself
above the howling of the wind.

And then, suddenly, simply, noiselessly, I am awake.

Where am I? I seem still in a dream. My body feels so
numb, maybe I am. But why would I dream a place like
this? And so placidly? This place is the stuff of
nightmares. It's a cave, I can see that. Several entrances.
But what's that war junk on all the walls? There's a
hatchway from a Cylon aircraft. A stock from a laser stun
rifle. Bits and pieces of unidentifiable metal. Scanner
screens. A bunch of metallic Cylon uniforms. Signs in the
Cylon language. Half a control board. All this stuff is
hanging on the walls of the cave like casual decorations. I
get the name of their designer, I'm going to scratch him off
my fall list. The stove in the center of the cave is jerry-built
from a fuel tank. Stove! I've got to make my body work
and get near that stove. Even at this distance from it, I can
feel the side of my body facing it begin to thaw. But I can't
move yet. What's that on the lower part of the walls? Furs.
Mostly white and brown furs. There are animals
indigenous to this crummy planet? What's that junk in the
corner, piled so high? I can make out—what?—that looks
like snowshoes, and that like a mountain of skis, and I
suppose those're sleds, but they're so inefficiently
designed, so rough in construction, they might be a
sideline product of the guy that decorated the cave.

How did I get here? Last I remember, we were in the
snow ram and I was trying to get my fingers to work.
Looking around me now, I can see the other members of
our party, some of them still out, a couple beginning to
stir. Apollo springs up suddenly, looks around. At the
move, one of the fur bundles near the corner jumps up,
runs over, and begins to lick Apollo's face. It's the kid's
droid. From the other side of Apollo, the kid himself
jumps up, hugs his pet.

"Muffit. You came back."

Apollo puts an arm around the kid, says:

"Boxey..."

The kid smiles up at Apollo.

"You okay, Dad?"

Apollo's return smile is a bit weaker than the kid's eager one.

"I'm okay," he mumbles.

Others begin to stir. I can move now. I crawl toward the stove, try to lap up its heat like it's flowing water. As I stand up and turn around to warm my backside, I see an extremely large furry bundle that is definitely not Muffit standing beside an entranceway to this cave chamber. This is one big fellow! Taller than any of us, he's got that noble look that blond, blue-eyed types often have as a matter of course, even when they can't lick an intership postal stamp. Not that this guy is a coward. Not in any way. Muscles like that, he's a fighter. He looks almost superhuman. He's the kind of guy that, when you're assembling a team for mock hand-to-hand combat, you pick first for your side.

Everybody's noticed him now. When he speaks to us, his voice is so stentorian I'm not sure he's quite real:

"You are fortunate your daggit found our hunting party. You were on Deathpoint Plateau. Nothing survives there for long."

Well, he speaks our lingo, even down to such slang as deathpoint. It seems I was just talking about deathpoint to someone. But who? I can't remember. It's like my mind froze along with my body.

"We're grateful," Apollo says, moving forward, assuming his right of command in his usual smug way. "Who are you?"

"Simple hunters," the noble type answers.

"Then," Apollo says, glancing around the cave, "I assume you'll return our packs. And weapons. And that we are free to go."

That's it, Apollo. What a master strategist you are. Get to the point. Don't bother feeling out the intentions of the guys who rescue you, just start making demands. I consider pushing Apollo out of the way, taking over, employing a little smooth con on this fur-clad hunk, find out what's up.

"Go?" the hunter says. "Where would you go? The storm continues. The di-ethene has left you dehydrated. I will see that you receive liquids. Then, we can talk of your going."

With a regal turn, he leaves the cave through the nearest dark opening. Slowly, like wild animals circling a fire, the rest of the expeditionary team, except for the incapacitated wounded trio, comes to the stove. Starbuck is still looking back over his shoulder at the place where the hunter made his exit.

"I don't like the way he said that," Starbuck mutters.

Apollo, glancing around the cave interior, suspicion in his voice, says:

"Something's odd about this setup. Humans surviving on a Cylon outpost? I don't know anything about humans in this sector at all. Doesn't make sense."

"Something else doesn't make sense," I say. Both Starbuck and Apollo gawk at me. "They're not just hunters. Too heavily armed."

"And have you noticed the walls?" Boomer says. "They're studded with wreckage. Over there, that's Cylon armor."

Starbuck stares where Boomer points.

"With scorch marks from combat lasers," he says.

"I say we jump him and get outta here," Wolfe says.

Good old Wolfe, always right there with the sensible solution.

"I agree," Leda adds.

What's in *her* head?

"Wait a moment," Apollo says. "If it's the Cylons they fight, and those're mostly Cylon souvenirs all over those walls, then maybe they're on our side. We might be able to use their help."

"I'm thirsty," the kid says, and his lousy mechanical pet growls. We all turn toward the kid.

Behind Boxey, coming through an entirely different entranceway, the noble leader seems to have returned. He picks up a fur-covered pack, then stares over at us. Starbuck whispers:

"How'd he get behind us?"

Apollo approaches the hunter, puts on his best friendly voice:

"The water? Could we—"

"Silence," the hunter barks.

Starbuck rushes forward.

"Look," he says, "the boy and the wounded need water. You said—"

"I said, silence."

Apollo stares at the man, then remarks:

"Something's wrong."

Boomer, moving to Apollo's side, says softly:

"The hair on the back of my neck is starting to crawl, guys."

"Here is the liquid I promised, and some food," says the voice of the noble leader. But it's not the noble leader we're all looking at. We whirl around as one. The voice had come from the opening through which our hunter had originally exited. Now he's there again, holding packets of food and animal skins filled with water. Two other hunters are coming through two different cave openings.

"What the—" Boomer says.

"Didn't we just talk to that guy?" Starbuck says.

The two new hunters are exact duplicates of the guy carrying the rations. Apollo and I turn around again. The one at the far wall looks like the other three! They are all blond, blue-eyed, heroic-looking types. Apollo, stunned, whispers:

"They're clones!"

"Actually, we prefer the name Theta Class life forms," says a voice whose sultry softness in no way resembles the voices of the quartet of blond hunters. Through still another entranceway, one concealed by piles of fur, a woman has entered the cave chamber. And she is some impressive vision of a woman! Her lovely face slightly resembles the faces of the cloned men—at least she has the blue eyes and blond hair, but she looks more like a goddess than a huntress. Her snow parka and leather leggings, together with her arsenal of weapons (including a laser rifle slung over her shoulder), do not in any way conceal the superbly formed body underneath all that junk she's wearing. Starbuck stares at her as if one of his dreams has suddenly materialized.

"This mission is looking up!" he says to Boomer.

The first hunter who addressed us introduces himself as Ser 5-9, and the woman as Tenna 1. The others have similar names. Ser 5-9 distributes the food and water. We all fall on the stuff like a pack of ravaging monsters of prey. Ser 5-9 and Tenna take seats on a slightly raised platform and watch with interest our eager devouring of the rations. Ser 5-9 asks how we come to be on their planet. Apollo, before I can suggest to him that he use a little caution, gives them a quick briefing on our mission. He's apparently bought their act lock, stock, and barrel. I wish I could be so sure. Interrupting Apollo's statements, Ser 5-9 says:

"You came to destroy the Ravashol pulsaric-laser communication wave unit?"

"Ravashol?" Apollo asks.

"Dr. Ravashol," Tenna says. "He is human."

Starbuck, irritated, glances toward Tenna and says:

"Human, you said? A human created that monster up there for the use of Cylons?"

Tenna, though clearly on the defensive, shoots back: "If it were not for Ravashol, we would not exist."

"He is the father-creator," Ser 5-9 says reverently.

The kid, who's been taking all this in, pulls at Apollo's sleeve and asks:

"Is Ravashol God? I'd like to meet him."

Somehow Apollo's face manages to cross a half-smile with a whole frown.

"No, son," he says. "He's not God. Not if he's with the Cylons." He turns back to Ser 5-9. "Why does he work for the Cylons?"

None of the reverence leaves Ser 5-9's voice as he says:

"They let him live to experiment. To create."

"To create weapons that destroy other humans!" Starbuck says sardonically.

Tenna, addressing herself mainly to Starbuck, voices a warning:

"I would be careful what I said about the father-creator."

Ser 5-9 seems to come down from the clouds as he addresses Apollo:

"The pulsaric laser cannot be destroyed. The emplacement is guarded by Cylons. Still more Cylon soldiers are stationed in the garrison at the foothills to Mount Hekla. Even if you could get past them, the weapon itself is constructed of magna—practically indestructible."

"We have solenite," I interject quietly, then watch them for the reaction. They react as I expect, with a moment's silence to assimilate the information. When Ser 5-9 speaks again, it is with the same awe with which he speaks of Ravashol:

"Solenite. Ravashol explained solenite once."

It's always useful to use technical words when you're dealing with what appear to be primitive tribes. Well, the word "solenite" can give me a couple of shudders. I've used it before and I've found I can never feel quite calm about it. The name derives from the use of solenoid, the magnetic coiled wire that, when activated as the major part of the explosive's ignition system, clings to almost anything. Including magna. Easier to place around the objective than normal explosives requiring bore holes or the attachment of high-resistance wires by embedding them in plastic substances or through soldering, solenite need only be secured to the magna surfaces of the cannon and then connected to the equally magnetic base-charge materials at strategic points. (So long as you know where the strategic points are—which, come to think of it, we don't about this damn cannon.) Because of its high degree of water resistance, it is safe to carry solenite up the ice mountain, especially since its combination of chemical and plastic explosive substances is stable to lower temperatures than even humans can stand. Further, solenite has the most efficient pressure effect of any explosive I've ever used. Its density is such that its velocity of detonation is phenomenal. A good explosive's got to have shattering power; solenite's got that and then some. It blasts in all directions like an exploding star. That's why it's the safest and most dangerous explosive of all. Safe, because it's so transportable. Dangerous, because if you don't get out of its range pretty quick, you've had it. I can understand Ser 5-9's awe, because it's the natural reaction of anyone who's heard of solenite.

Ser 5-9 confers with Tenna for a moment. From his gestures I can tell he's informing her that our possession of solenite immeasurably increases our chances to get the weapon. When they regally turn their attention back to us, Ser 5-9 says:

"You can leave the injured members of your party here. They will be tended to. We will guide the rest of you to the village."

"And then?" Apollo asks

"You will see when we get there," Tenna says.

Apollo chews on this for a moment, then nods in agreement. The clones begin to assemble equipment for the trip.

Apollo, crouching by the injured threesome, says to Haals:

"I want you to stay here with Vickers and Voight."

Haals's eyes look like they're not quite functioning. I suspect that the dose of electricity he got on the snow ram still has some residual effects. He apparently doesn't think so, for he rises in protest and informs Apollo:

"Captain, I'm fine."

Apollo, rather than disputing the gunnery sergeant's bravado, gives him a tranquilizer of smooth talk:

"I know. I want someone here who can defend himself. Just in case. We'll be back for you."

Haals smiles.

"Right, skipper."

After Apollo and I check out the equipment, we join the clones and the rest of the party at an opening to the cave chamber. Starbuck is engaged in small talk with Tenna. Of course.

"I was hoping I'd have time to thaw out before we go out there again," he says.

"We'll find a living compartment in the village," she responds. "I can warm you up there."

"I'll bet you can."

Double that bet, Starbuck. Wish I could have some of the action myself.

Apollo asks if everybody's ready. We all nod and head out of the chamber. Ahead of us is a tunnel. From the blast of harsh wind and the flurries—like thin, streaky clouds—of snow, it's a good guess that it's a short trip to the outside. Muffit bounds ahead of us with his usual eagerness. I hang back, ready to take the point-man position outdoors, when I notice that Wolfe is deliberately hanging back with me.

"When do we break?" he whispers suddenly.

An interesting sign. He's still trusting enough to talk to me.

"Don't push it, Wolfe."

He glances around, making sure everybody else is ahead of us. From out of his jacket he takes a laser pistol. Must be the one he stole off Voight. Better I play dumb about it. I'll have to control him if he goes berserk.

"Just want you to know I'm ready," he whispers.

"Where'd you get that?"

"It doesn't matter where. I can use it on the Cylons. Or anyone else who gets in our way."

I can't argue with him. So long as he's got the gun, he's dangerous. I glance down at the weapon, gesture for him to put it away for the time being. He slips it inside his jacket and strides bullishly ahead to the others.

Outside, both the winds and snowfalls have subsided. No di-ethene clouds in sight anywhere. But the cold remains. My God, does the cold remain.

We proceed across the ice field very slowly. Packs weigh us down, our own weariness doubles the weight of the packs. Our walking boots, the best the *Galactica* quartermaster has been able to come up with, don't grip as well as I'd like. The scree caps at the heels don't provide the proper friction. Ah, well, just one small problem among many.

Apollo gestures me forward. He and Ser 5-9 are conferring. Ser 5-9 says to me:

"This is the edge of the ice field. We'll have to follow the ravines from here."

I agree, happy that the clone shows the kind of smarts I can trust. His people obviously know their way around mountains and ice fields. They may prove useful as guides.

We traverse the icy ravines, a tricky task. The three warriors from the *Galactica* have trouble maintaining their balance. I have to laugh a couple of times at their intricate slipping and sliding maneuvers. Ser 5–9 signals a stop, then explains:

"We are close to the village."

There is a wave of relief among our party. We're all cold, colder than Thane's eyes. Last time I felt this chilled was back on Kalpa, when we had to go in hand-to-hand combat across a series of snow bridges against a Cylon attacking force.

"The entry hatch is at the end of this ravine," Ser 5–9 says. "Wait here."

Edging his body away from the side of the ravine, Ser 5–9 descends a little ways, with Tenna following him. As I watch them go down, I feel a chill of suspicion go through my body. In spite of the irrational nature of that feeling, I have to ask Apollo:

"Think they're turning us in?"

Apollo clearly doesn't like that idea one bit.

"No," he says brusquely. "I don't know why I feel that way—but no."

"Well, you got all the command insights, Captain."

He gives me his harshest stare, as we start to follow Ser 5–9 and Tenna down the rather steep slope. Starbuck comes immediately behind us, then the ever-reliable Boomer. God, Boomer's hardly said a word since we settled down on this godforsaken planet, but I know I want him by my side if we get into any trouble.

Ahead of us, both Ser 5–9 and Tenna stop abruptly, crouch behind a large rock. They talk together, then Tenna comes climbing up back toward us. Starbuck passes Apollo and me, and welcomes her:

"I knew you missed me, but . . ."

Some things never seem to leave Starbuck's mind.

"Cylon patrol!" Tenna whispers, then points upward toward the rim of the ravine. "Pass the word."

We all quickly find hiding places. Along the top of the ravine, the Cylon patrol can be glimpsed at intervals, metallic shadows that almost blend in with the ice of the surface, the only interrupting color being those blasted red lights on their helmets, sliding so sinisterly from side to side. Fortunately, no red light seems directed

downward where we all crouch. Just as they are about out
of sight, the dumb daggit-droid begins to growl, and the
kid whispers:

"Sssshh . . . good daggit."

The droid shuts up. A Cylon seems to glance
downward, but apparently sees nothing. Good daggit.
When we've seen no Cylon for a while and are about to
become permanently ensconced ice statues honoring
caution, Ser 5-9 laboriously works his way back up to us
and says:

"The way is clear now."

I glance toward him. His eyes are bright, concerned.
All my doubts about him melt away.

"So you're not turning us in to the Cylons," I say.

"No," Tenna mutters angrily. "We hate the Cylons."

Ser 5-9 crawls closer to me. His staring wrath-filled
eyes alone could destroy me at this moment, I suspect.

"Pardon me," I say, "I'm not the most . . . not the most
trusting person in the universe."

"We are Theta Class life forms," Ser 5-9 says.
"Considered by the Cylons to be . . . to be subhuman."

The bitterness in his voice convinces me of his hatred
for the Cylons.

"We were created for slave labor," Tenna adds. "Most
of our brothers and sisters are still slaves in the village."

"But you revolted," Apollo says.

Both Tenna and Ser 5-9 appear to be embarrassed by
the implication of Apollo's statement.

"No," Ser 5-9 says, "I'm afraid we did not. Evidently
we are not perfect."

Apollo's smile contains a great deal of sadness.

"No," he says. "Just human."

Ser 5-9 and Tenna appear pleased by Apollo's
understanding. They smile broadly.

"Then," Apollo continues, "as *humans* you'll help us
destroy that pulsar cannon."

Both smiles fade quickly from the clones' faces.

"First we must get into the village," Ser 5-9 says.
"Come."

Moving with a speed we haven't been able to summon
since the launch of the shuttle from the pod decks of the

Galactica, we make our way down to the village entry hatch. Using a chipping tool, Ser 5-9 punches ice away from the hatch. Forcing the valve wheels, he pulls the hatch open. As it raises, there is the hissing sound of released pressure. Ser 5-9 takes us each by the arm and helps us down into the corridor below. Tenna takes over command of the expedition and hurries us along the subterranean tunnel corridor. Although the passageway glitters with frost, it seems much warmer than the outer surface of the planet. I am glad to be here.

CHAPTER FIFTEEN

After angrily receiving the report of his scouts that the Cylon patrol ship assigned to kill the human intruders had been itself shot down, First Centurion Vulpa sent out foot patrols, with orders to hunt down the humans and destroy them.

On one of the planets of the Cylon Alliance, there was a kind of insect—small, gray-bodied creatures with eight wirelike long legs and antennae that never ceased activity. They were not poisonous nor did they bite nor were they in any way destructive to the planet's ecological systems. Their only drawback was that they were irresistibly attracted to the shininess of the metal in Cylon uniforms. All Cylons stationed on that planet, as Vulpa had been for a long time, came to hate these insects, because they were ingenious in finding ways to penetrate the Cylon covering and implant themselves upon Cylon skin, sometimes even shorting out a wire or two embedded in the middle layer of the uniform. Once on Cylon skin they became that terrible annoyance, an itch that could not be scratched. If several of them penetrated the uniform, even a normally unemotional Cylon could be driven mad. This expeditionary team of humans, Vulpa thought, seemed composed of that revolting kind of insect. They were making him itch considerably, and he wanted them exterminated immediately, so that he could transfer his attention away from this minor futile mission and back to the major goal of eliminating the *Galactica* and its fleet.

"We found the wreckage of the humans' shuttle," a foot-patrol leader reported in. "The rest escaped in a snow ram. We found the vehicle, broken down and abandoned on the plateau."

"You hunted them down?" Vulpa asked hopefully.

"No. But humanoids cannot survive the plateau."

"I hope you are right."

Vulpa felt annoyed. The humans should be dead. Then why did he feel they were still skittering around like those insects beneath Cylon metal?

The corridor down which Ser 5-9 and the other clones guided the expedition team proved to be one part of a vast subterranean system of caves. Apollo sensed that the dwellings which were placed within depressions and cliffsides along the high walls would be of great interest to geologists and archaeologists of *Galactica*'s space fleet— if they only had time for research these days. The clone habitations were carved out of the relatively soft rock. To Apollo, they appeared quite primitive, with their unevenly balanced windows and entranceways, their mottled surfaces of stone and closely packed mud. Their rich brown coloration suggested the dwellings had been subjected to a sun. Since that was impossible, Apollo wondered if the colors and textures were natural, or perhaps the result of some special treatment applied to the surfaces of the dwellings.

Ser 5-9 halted the group, gestured that it should remain in the shadows.

"This passage leads to the bottom of the research station," he said.

"Research station?" Apollo said. "How is it—"

"Some time ago, a group of human scientists, fleeing

from the war with the Cylons, landed on this planet and established an experimental research station whose purpose was to develop inventions that could be used to bring and sustain peace. After the scientists' arduous work to build the station and begin their experiments, the Cylons came. They engaged the human group in battle, killed almost all of them, then took charge of this planet and powered it away from the sun system to which it had belonged. The ice formed, covered the caves, and even infiltrated areas of the research station itself. It is not used for scientific research any longer, but the planners meet there."

"Planners?"

"The father-creator made two types of Theta life forms. We are hunters, workers. The planners are thinkers. They will know best how to approach the pulsar weapon."

Ser 5–9 abruptly went to Tenna's side and talked with her again. Returning to Apollo, he announced:

"You come with me. Tenna will stay with your friends in the village."

"I don't know if we should separate."

"Too many of you at one time may frighten the planners. They are not . . . especially brave."

"I think I understand. Back at the fleet we have a group like that which we call the Council of the Twelve."

Apollo led Starbuck into a different set of shadows, saying:

"Our turn for a conference."

When sufficient distance from the others had been established, Apollo said softly:

"Anything happens to me, you're in command."

"All right, Captain. But remember command upsets my stomach, so don't stay away too long."

"You love command, and you know it."

"When you get back, be careful you're looking in the right place."

"What do you mean?"

Starbuck glanced over his shoulder, as if he expected attackers at any moment.

"Boomer and I have a wager going," he said.

"You surprise me."

"Which of our specialized team is going to jump us first."

Apollo stared at him questioningly.

"You really think they're going to go through with this mission?" Starbuck said caustically.

"I had been counting on it."

"Our lives are on the line."

"So are theirs."

"And so's their freedom. If we're successful, we go home. They go back into chains."

"Not necessarily. The commander might—"

"And you can stash that might in the deepest cargo hold of a straggler ship. Adama might be willing to take a chance on Croft, and maybe Leda, but do you see either Wolfe or Thane going the redeemed-hero route?"

"They don't have to be warriors."

"They're *always* warriors, they wouldn't know how to be anything else. No, they got to make their break. If not here, on this mission, then somewhere else on some other boondoggle. If I were them, I wouldn't be taking the chance..."

Apollo nodded, said:

"I see what you mean."

"I thought you would."

"Watch yourself, you hear?"

"Sure. Sure, skipper."

Tenna had assembled the rest of the group. Before taking leave of them, Apollo leaned close to Boxey and whispered:

"Boxey, stick close to Starbuck."

"Don't worry, Dad. I'll keep an eye on him for you."

Apollo tousled Boxey's hair, then gestured for Tenna to take over the group. He felt a clutch of fear as he watched the team walk off. *But why should I worry?* he thought. *Boxey's safe, so long as Starbuck and Boomer are there to protect him.* He nodded toward Ser 5-9, and the two tall men entered the passageway leading to the research station.

The planners looked nothing like hunters, although as clones they all looked like each other. Planners were thin and fragile, adding to the intellectuality of their appearance. Their faces were gaunt and dominated by high-bridged noses. They were dressed in thick robes, their faces almost obscured by large-fold cowls. Five of them sat at a primitive conference table underneath the emblem of the Experimental Research Station, a weathered holographic mural-photo of the father-creator. Planner One brought the meeting to order by informing the others:

"Worker Ser 5-9 is here, in the village!"

Planner Two, incensed, slammed his fist on the table and stood up, shouting:

"He was told to keep his marauders out of the village."

Planner Two's voice was pitched the same as Planner One's, but there was an added level of petulance in it. Planner Three, in a gentler version of the voice, urged him to sit down again, an invocation that Planner Two obeyed immediately.

"I object to calling Ser 5-9's hunters *marauders*," Planner Three said quietly. "They are guerrilla warriors fighting for liberation."

Planner Three's statement initiated an argument among all five planners. To an outsider, the sound of these clones would have been strange—like a person arguing with his five selves. Finally, Planner Five began rapping the table with a clublike gavel, screaming:

"Order! Order!"

The others subsided.

"Bring them in," Planner One said to a guard.

Apollo and Ser 5-9 were admitted. They strode forward boldly and stopped in front of the conference table.

"Members of the Planner Council," Ser 5-9 said. His voice had taken on the impressive stentorian resonance with which he had initially greeted the expeditionary team. "We seek your wisdom. I have brought with me Flight Captain Apollo...from Battlestar *Galactica*."

"The *Galactica*!" Planner Three said, awed. The other planners displayed a similar surprise.

"The Cylons have posted warnings against you throughout the star system!" Planner Five said.

"Every outpost is on permanent alert!" said Planner One.

"If he is discovered here, we're . . ." said Planner Two, his voice trembling with fright. "This must be reported!"

Ser 5-9 stepped forward, placed his huge hands flat on the conference table, his bare arms powerful with tightened muscles, and said:

"Nothing will be reported."

Planner Two, though clearly intimidated by Ser 5-9's physical authority, squawked:

"That is not for you to say."

"Apollo and his team can—"

"His team?" screamed Planner Four. "There are others!"

"Yes. They have come to destroy the Ravashol pulsaric weapon."

All of the planners paled simultaneously, the effect looking to Apollo like a five-sectioned mirror.

"Impossible!" Planner Two shrieked.

"Impossible or not . . . we're going to try," Apollo said.

None of the planners could respond. Instead they went into a huddle. Their discussion sounded like a covey of birds agitated by the suspicion of preying hunters. *And these're supposed to be the intellectuals,* Apollo thought. *I should never have consented to consult with these lunatics. Seems clear that Ser 5-9 and the other worker clones are making a mistake in trusting these planners. They couldn't even plan the menus for a madhouse.* Finally the huddle broke and Planner One said formally:

"We will discuss your request and give you our answer shortly."

Apollo, furious, came forward. His upper legs collided with the table.

"We don't have time for bureaucratic discussions!" he hollered. "The fleet will soon be within range of that grotesque weapon up there! It *must* be destroyed!"

Planner Three, in his best peacemaking voice, said softly:

"We cannot rush into this. Such matters must be discussed." He looked genuinely troubled, and seemed to Apollo the one planner with at least a degree of sense and compassion. "I am sorry."

However, apologetic or not, the planner's sad plea only made Apollo angrier.

"Let's get out of here," he said, with disgust, to Ser 5–9. The two tall men started for the door.

"We will give you our answer," called Planner Four after them. "In time."

Ser 5–9 whirled around and faced the quintet of planners. He could barely suppress his indignation.

"Just don't betray us," he said intensely, then strode out of the room, Apollo right behind him.

At Ser 5–9's advice, Apollo remained close to the corridor walls, moving from shadow to shadow, as they returned down the passageway. Once, when a worker clone passed, Ser 5–9 pushed Apollo into an alcove and they silently waited for the worker to pass.

"Wait a moment longer," Ser 5–9 said. After a short pause he spoke again: "I'm sorry, Captain. I thought the planners would help. I should have known better."

Ser 5–9's voice was filled with disgust. Apollo understood. To this worthy young clone, the planners must have seemed the height of mental achievement. He had now seen them for the muddle-headed cowards they were. It was a bitter lesson, and one that needed no reinforcement, so Apollo said soothingly:

"No time for that now. We have to get to the top of that mountain."

Once the object of their mission was again put into words, Apollo felt a shiver of apprehension. It was easy to say: Get to the top of that mountain. But Croft's caution—and he was an expert, after all—and the misfortunes in the mission so far had made Apollo realize what a formidable task they had undertaken. They were all experts in their fields, yes, but expertise was useless when frigid air was breaking off chunks of your fingers.

Also, that last talk with Starbuck had unnerved him. If Starbuck was right, and the four criminals were about to bolt, then there was no way the rest of them could get to the top. They needed Croft and his collection of misfits. It seemed that the fate of the *Galactica*, of the fleet, of all the remnants of the human race, was now suspended on a very thin stretched thread.

"But when we get to the mountaintop," he said to Ser 5-9, "I'm not sure what to do. That cannon, according to our scanner analyses, is a multistage energy pump. We're unsure of its design. I'd hate to blow the lens or focusing system, something that could be repaired."

Ser 5-9's bright blue eyes narrowed, as if he were trying to reduce the lens system in his own head.

"There is another who could help," he said.

"Who?"

Ser 5-9, for a moment, seemed reluctant to answer; then he said:

"The father-creator. Ravashol."

Apollo, amazed, asked:

"He's here? In the village?"

The tall hunter shook his head no.

"He lives at the base of Hekla near the Cylon command post."

There was a strange reluctance in the way the clone pushed out the words of his declaration.

"You're afraid of something," Apollo said.

"Yes."

"I find that hard to believe. What could you possibly be afraid of?"

"His home is sacred ground."

"But you'll take me to him?"

Ser 5-9's eyes almost shut. The power of his eyes, however, seemed only momentarily dimmed.

"To free my people, yes!"

Apollo smiled and clasped his hand on Ser 5-9's shoulder. It was lucky they were nearly the same height. For some people the hunter's shoulder would have been a difficult reach.

Athena kept silent as she watched her father and Colonel Tigh crouch, like observers at a spectator sport, over the scanner screen. Some Cylon craft had been detected toward the rear of the fleet.

"They're looking for a straggler to pick off," Adama commented. He turned to Athena and asked: "What's our fleet spacing?"

"Standard defense between each ship."

"Close the gaps to twenty-five," Adama said, and Tigh protested:

"Commander, some of our ships have cadets at the helm. The collision risk—"

"I know. It's a chance we'll have to take. I want to give our fighters a tighter grouping to defend."

Tigh seemed reluctant to give the order, but finally said "Yes, sir" and transmitted the command. Athena scrutinized her father's face. His eyes seemed focused in the distance, as if he could see all the way to the ice planet and its awesome weapon atop a mountain. He looked, Athena thought, very, very worried.

Cree had not been aware of even a thought in his mind for some time. For hundreds of centons, it seemed. His only awareness had been pain. Now his mind couldn't even call up a picture of a single Cylon torture device, and he knew they had used several. Vague memories remained. Wires with fine needles being injected into various bodily pressure points. Clamps bunching up the skin and pulsating it with electric charges. Something that expanded his brain like a balloon and made him think of nothing else but that it would break into flying pieces at any millimicron of a centon.

Pain. That was all. All he could remember. When it had started, he had vowed not to tell the Cylon leader anything. He hoped he had not. He could not be sure, but he could hope.

Now consciousness returned. Or something like consciousness—who could be sure? He seemed to be back in the Cylon control headquarters, but the room seemed distorted now. The distortion could be residual effect of the torture. The Cylon leader sat in his command chair, oblivious to Cree. Vulpa appeared uglier, more repulsive than ever. Cree, in long discussions with his friends Shields and Bow, had argued that the supposed ugliness of the Cylons was the result of conditioning, that they were supposed to view the Cylons that way in order to summon up the urge to kill. Now, watching the Cylon leader, feeling his stomach churn with hatred, Cree wouldn't be at all willing to argue that side.

A human dressed in religious robes slunk into the control headquarters, then stood behind Vulpa's chair, waiting to be acknowledged. It was a moment before Cree realized the astonishing fact that the new entrant *was* a human. What was a strange human doing here, in Cylon territory, standing obsequiously behind an ugly Cylon leader?

When Vulpa finally did acknowledge the human visitor, he said:

"Yes, let's see, you're Planner Two, are you not? What is it?"

Planner Two leaned down next to Vulpa's helmet and whispered. Cree could not make out what the cowled man was saying, but Vulpa reacted to it by bellowing:

"Apollo? From the *Galactica*?"

Cree felt a surge of joy. The invocation of the name of his flight commander and his home battlestar buoyed his spirits. But where was Apollo? It seemed unlikely that the captain would be here on a mission to rescue a cadet.

Vulpa turned to a nearby subordinate and said in a sneering voice:

"So humans cannot survive the plateau? Well, it seems that they have, centurion! Search the village. Every compartment. Find them!"

The subordinate exited quickly, taking some other Cylon warriors with him. Cree almost laughed, but it was too soon to attempt such an exhaustive labor.

As soon as Tenna increased the heat of the glowing light in the middle of the chamber, the team crowded around it, pulling in its warmth as if it could be gathered in tangible rays. Tenna touched Starbuck's arm and led him away from the group. Although he desired the warmth, he was interested in anything the attractive blond huntress had to say to him.

And what she said surprised him.

"I will warm you now."

He glanced at the others. Thane seemed to have

noticed the separation of Tenna and Starbuck from the group. Just like Thane to keep his cool unemotional eyes on everything!

"Ah," Starbuck whispered to Tenna, "isn't there someplace, well, someplace more private?"

"Private?" Tenna said, genuinely astonished.

"Somewhere we can be *alone*," he whispered.

Now they had caught the attention of the *entire* group. Everybody watched them, including Boxey, although the child's smile did not resemble the odd leers of the others. Again except for Thane, who, it seemed, never smiled.

"There is no such place in the village," Tenna said. "Why should we have to be *alone*?"

"Ah, well, um, then, I think I'm not so cold anymore. I'll just go right back to my friends and—"

"But you don't have to be cold. In fact, it's preferred if—"

"I get the idea. And it's a good idea, but . . . well, say, look, Tenna. See, ah—"

Apollo and Ser 5-9 entered the chamber. Starbuck let out a sigh of relief.

"Am I glad to see you!" he said to the captain, who seemed puzzled by Starbuck's welcoming enthusiasm. Boomer laughed.

"What did you find out?" Croft asked Apollo.

"There's only one man who can help us," Apollo said grimly. The group congregated around him as he told them about Ravashol. Then his voice dropped to a whisper. "If Ravashol won't help . . . well, then, we'll just have to take our chances."

"Maybe we'll get lucky," Croft muttered. Starbuck couldn't tell whether the wiry-muscled mountaineer was being sarcastic or sincere. Before he could consider that problem, another clone resembling Ser 5-9 rushed into the chamber.

"The Cylons are searching the village!"

"Be calm," Ser 5-9 said to his duplicate. "Explain."

"There're search patrols marching around everywhere. All through the village, the underground mall, everywhere. Pushing us aside, searching us, kicking any worker who stops to look at them. They're going into our living quarters, searching, ripping things, smashing furniture, scattering us everywhere. At the meeting hall they're overturning the benches, tearing aside wall hangings. They say they're searching for the landing party and they'll start killing us if we don't tell them where they're hidden. They—"

"Enough," Ser 5-9 ordered with an imperial gesture. "It must be the planners. One of them, or all of them, informed."

"What did you expect?" Apollo said sarcastically. "We've got to get to Ravashol, and *now*!"

"I agree." Ser 5-9 turned to Tenna, commanded: "Tenna! Take the others and hide them."

"But where?" Tenna asked.

Ser 5-9 hesitated. His keen eyes searched the ceiling as if trying to find a place of concealment up there. Then he sighed and said:

"With the children."

"Hear that, Muffit!" Boxey yelped. "There's children!"

Muffit barked and wagged its tail. Beneath the tufts of overhanging fur, the metal surrounding the opening from which the tail protruded was briefly evident.

"What's this about children?" said Boomer. "Nobody said anything about children before."

"We were thought to be sterile," Tenna said, smiling. "It was a Cylon prerequisite to maintain what they termed the purity of the Theta life form. But we have been bearing children."

"And hiding them?" Boomer asked.

"Yes."

The clone who was a match for Ser 5-9 said nervously: "Please, we must hurry!"

Standing by the entranceway, he motioned for the others to move quickly. Some of the expedition members seemed to linger behind, as if afraid to leave the rare spot of warmth.

In the corridor, they split into two groups. Apollo and Ser 5-9 headed in one direction. The others followed Tenna. To the children, Starbuck presumed.

Glimpsing a squad of Cylons passing in a cross-corridor up ahead, Tenna motioned the group into alcoves located along the walls of the corridor. Thane chose to hide in the same alcove as Leda. She had no doubt Thane's choice was calculated. She'd had trouble with him before. He kept his attention on her as she watched around the edge of the alcove for an all-clear signal from Tenna.

Suddenly, without a warning, without any emotion showing on his face, Thane put his arms around Leda. Squirming within his grasp, she turned on him, her eyes blazing with anger. Thane whispered:

"Scream if you want. Then they'll hear you and we'll all die. I don't care."

He leaned in, tried to kiss her, while at the same time forcing her body against the wall.

Leda worked a hand free and quickly brought it up to Thane's throat. He stopped forcing her as she gripped the throat and squeezed. Slowly, utilizing the powerful strength in her arm, she forced him back. What little color there was in his face left it. His arms dropped to his sides.

"Scream if you want," Leda whispered, aping his intonations.

Obviously Thane could not scream. Not even if he wanted to. She might not have let him go if the all-clear signal had not come from Tenna.

CHAPTER SIXTEEN

Croft:

The place is crawling with Cylons. When Starbuck says it's all right to leave our hiding place, I'm reluctant to go. Perhaps I could run to the Cylons, make a deal, offer them—but no, no deals can be completed with Cylons. They make deals, sure, but soon as they've got what they want, they renege. I'm better off trying to climb Mount Hekla blindfolded than making small talk with the red-lights.

As the group reassembles, I decide to take the point again. Ahead of me, Leda, her face red in the aftermath of anger, moves out of her hiding place. A short interval later, Thane slinks out of the same alcove. His eyes shift about. He doesn't notice me, or doesn't care. Instead of rejoining the group, he begins taking steps backward. What's he up to? God, Thane, this is no time to try an escape. But that looks like exactly what he's trying to do. I'm about to pursue him, but I'm afraid he'll deliberately create a disturbance. He has no instinct for his own survival. Let him go. Perhaps we're better off without him. I follow a couple of steps anyway. He disappears into another alcove. When he comes out, he's in one of the clone leather working uniforms. How in the twelve worlds did he find *that*? It doesn't fit his lean body very well. After all, these guys are man-mountains and Thane's got that ax handle of a body! Still, he goes off down the corridor, with all the confidence in his stride that he's pulling it off. I have to let him try. As a prisoner, it's his right to try to escape. I used to think of nothing else but crashing out when I was on the prison ship, but I wouldn't join Thane now on a bet.

I catch up to the group. Leda hangs back and whispers to me:

"Thane's not here!"

"I know. He's off somewhere looking for an exit."

"Crashing out?"

"You got it."

"That creep! Least he could do was take me with him. Guess he couldn't, not after..."

"After what?"

"Nothing I'm going to tell you about, Croft. But you and him deserve the same fate, believe me."

"Maybe. But it's a fool's play, trying to escape from down here. Where can he go? What can he do?"

"I don't know, but at least he's trying."

"I get your drift. You're saying that he's trying and I'm not."

"Believe what you want. I don't know why I'm talking to you. I think you really buy that line these colonial warriors spout. You want to be returned to rank, to—"

"Stop it, Leda. I'll never be returned to rank. It's back to the grid-barge for us after—"

"And you're still going to help these idiots?"

"I don't know what I'm going to do."

"Well, you're going to have to decide soon. I hope nobody needs to crank your brain for you."

"Leda, I..."

I stop, hating myself for almost saying what I almost said. Leda seems to understand anyway. She says:

"No, nothing can be like what it was before. Don't you

know the real truth that keeps us hustling—nothing is ever like what it was before."

"You didn't used to be so bitter."

"Maybe. You were always the bitter one, Croft. What a switch, huh?"

Tenna signals for us to be still. Leda seems relieved at the signal. I wish I could haul her into one of these alcoves and talk sense to her.

Tenna leads us to a compartment that is identical to the one she took us from, except for a row of clone worker uniforms hanging on the far wall. Starbuck stays behind in the corridor to guard the entrance. Another glowing warm light dominates the center of the room, like in the previous place. Standing next to the light, brilliantly illuminated by it, is another woman. I know it's *another* woman, because I can clearly see that our guide is still with us, standing next to Wolfe. The woman in the room must be a clone of the same series as Tenna. She is introduced to us, for convenience' sake, as Tenna II. She's so identical, she might as well be called "Tenna too."

"Quick," the first Tenna says to the second, "we must hide these humans."

"But—" Tenna II says.

"No time for planner-type talk. The planners'll talk us *all* into death. We need to put them with the children."

Tenna II nods and presses a button. A piece of wall slices open, revealing another compartment, a large chamber populated by several fair-haired blue-eyed children. The room is not like the others. It's brighter. More color on the walls and in the children's clothing. Rough-crafted toys are scattered around the rocky floor. At first I think the children must be more clones, but closer study shows some variation in feature, some difference in body type.

As soon as the daggit-droid sees the children, it barks stupidly. The children, who clearly have never before seen such an ugly ball of animated fur, cower at the noise of the daggit. The kid rushes forward, grabs his pet by the collar. He addresses the children:

"He won't hurt you. He's just a daggit. Come on, Muffit."

The kid and the daggit step into the children's chamber. For a moment it's a standoff; then the clone kids gather around the daggit and compete to stroke its fur.

I go quietly to the entranceway to the corridor and motion for Starbuck to abandon his guard post and come in. As soon as Starbuck sees the two Tennas standing gorgeously side by side, his face brightens and he says:

"This is really getting interesting."

"Yeah, and I'm sure they'll both be responsive to your charms on an equal basis."

"Don't I wish."

Boomer catches sight of us, and rushes up.

"Starbuck!" He notices where Starbuck's attention is riveted and pulls at him, saying: "Later." He glances around the chamber. "Where's Thane?"

"I don't know," Starbuck says. "Maybe he got separated in the passageway."

I decide not to let the two of them in on what I saw in the corridor. Thane deserves his chance, even if he is an imbecile for making his play now.

"What do you say, Croft?" Boomer says suddenly. "I think Thane's been looking for the chance to make a break."

"Nobody's ever sure what Thane's looking for," I say noncommittally.

"We'd better go look for him," Starbuck says.

"No," says one of the Tennas. The first one, I think. "Let *us* do it. We've got a better chance to find him. As you can see"—she gestures toward the other Tenna—"in our small world, strangers are rather easy to single out."

She herds the team into the children's chamber, then closes the door behind us. The kids are chattering, asking Boxey a lot of questions, giving the daggit a good rubdown. I find a comfortable spot against the thick fur on one wall. This is terrific! Apollo's off on his little escapade to catechize the father-creator, and we're all stuck in the nursery. Maybe I can do the mountain on a rocking horse.

CHAPTER SEVENTEEN

The entranceway to Ravashol's domed dwelling was
decorated with scrollwork that, Apollo assumed, must
have something to do with the religious hold he had on the
clone population. Ser 5-9 and Apollo entered Ravashol's
quarters through a small, cramped, obviously secret
passage, and emerged behind a pile of equipment cases.

Ravashol's living space was, Apollo noted, in definite
contrast to the primitive look of the rest of the village. A
libraryful of books lined the high walls, and far off in a
corner was an area crammed with research equipment,
both electronic and chemical.

Ravashol himself sat at an enormous flat worktable. A
single light shone down from a source high in the ceiling.
Apollo wondered if the effect was calculated to add a
religious aura to the image of the father-creator busy at
work. Added to the bright light was an eerie glow which
seemed to emanate by itself from walls not containing
books or scientific equipment. It was easy to see why the
clones held their creator in such awe. Clearly, Ravashol
wanted it that way.

At first Ravashol didn't notice his two visitors. As he scribbled busily on a piece of paper, his small eyes squinted and his doll-like hands pulled at his thin beard. His hair was graying and brushed back from his forehead. One deviation from his religious appearance was his clothing, which appeared old, dusty, and ruffled.

He suddenly became aware of his intruders and looked up, alarmed. His hands went to his papers as if they were more worth protecting than himself. As Ravashol reached for a warning button, Apollo noted that the little man's spine appeared to be subtly deformed, a slight twist that turned his torso a few degrees sideways from the lower portion of his body.

Ser 5-9 ran forward, pleading in a voice that sounded much like a supplicant's in prayer:

"Please, father-creator, don't call for help."

Ravashol drew back his hand, a bit calmed by recognizing one of his clone creations. He took a slow walk around the large worktable until he was standing before Ser 5-9. Ravashol was about half the height of the clone.

"You are not permitted here," Ravashol said. "Only planners. And workers are *never* allowed to use the secret passage."

"Father-creator, we are in need of your help."

"You are one of the Five series."

Ravashol seemed uncertain.

"Yes," Ser 5-9 said proudly. "Series five, Culture nine."

So that's where they derive their names, Apollo thought, *words and numbers, that's their identity.*

"But you..." Ravashol said to Apollo. His voice had become fearful. "You are not one of mine. You... you are human!"

"Flight Captain Apollo, from Battlestar *Galactica*."

Shocked, Ravashol backed away from Apollo as if he were tainted by something—disease or unbelief or the quality of being human.

"The *Galactica* is a vessel of war!" Ravashol yelled. "We came here, my colleagues and I, to escape war. I am opposed to war, to violence of any kind."

"You have a strange way of showing it!"

Ravashol seemed genuinely surprised by Apollo's angry declaration.

"What do you mean?" he asked.

"What do I mean? So you're opposed to war. Well, what do you call that monstrosity on the top of that mountain? A weapon of peace?"

Ravashol seemed confused, embarrassed. He was caught in a trap and he knew it, but he still was looking for a way to pull himself out, even if it meant cutting off a limb.

"It ... it ... is an energy lens system. Designed to transmit intelligence across galaxies."

"Your *energy lens system* has fried two of my fighters and is holding the colonial fleet at bay until Cylon battlestars can reach and destroy it."

Ravashol's eyes looked frantically around the room, at Apollo, at Ser 5-9, at the shelves of books, at the scientific equipment.

"Impossible!" he said. "My system is maintained by Series Five Theta life forms!"

The shiftiness of the father-creator's eyes led Apollo to suspect that the man was lying, trumping up quick excuses to justify himself before his intruder. Ser 5-9, towering over his creator, took a step forward and said to Ravashol:

"With all reverence, father-creator, the workers among the Series Five Theta life forms are whipped if they come near the pulsaric weapon, except at times when you are present."

Ravashol looked at Ser 5-9 as any god would at a subject who had rebelled, who was in danger of falling from grace.

"You are wrong!" Ravashol said sternly. "I ... I make adjustments. Repairs. I transmit, and my helpers are Series Five."

"Maybe so," Apollo said, "but right now your precious pulsar gun, or whatever euphemism you want to call it, is manned by Cylons! *And* as a weapon of war!"

Ravashol began to pace.

"But that's ..." he said. "I mean, it's ... there's no ..."

He took a deep breath and addressed Apollo: "Don't you see? That's only a temporary misuse of its true function. A temporary abuse of—"

"So you *do* know how it's being used," Apollo said.

Ravashol could no longer hold in his anger.

"I have no control over the use of my creations! I'm lucky I wasn't eliminated, that I still have the chance to create. Ultimately, my inventions will be used properly, for peaceful—"

"*Ultimately?!*" Apollo shouted. "How long can you wait to get around to your precious peacetime uses of it?"

"I've no control, I said, no responsibility."

"Then who does?"

Apollo's voice was quiet but intense. Ravashol started to speak again, but before he could get a word out, there was a thunderous pounding knock on the laboratory door.

"Cylons!" Ravashol said, checking a monitor beside the large heavy door. Springing quickly into combat position, Apollo and Ser 5-9 drew their lasers. Ravashol, clearly frightened by the appearance of the weapons and the men holding them, hesitated a moment, then said:

"Shooting now will just bring more Cylons. Hide behind the research stacks." He guided Ser 5-9 toward the stacks, telling him: "In the equipment cases . . . hide under the panels."

With Apollo safely behind the research-library tape cases, his body surrounded by cases and one over his head, Ser 5-9 chose to hide in an alcove near the bookshelves. Another knock resounded throughout the room. *Knocking before charging in isn't the usual Cylon style*, Apollo thought. The third Cylon knock had a sense of urgency about it. Still, Ravashol waited a couple of beats before responding in an annoyed businesslike voice that displayed no trace of tension:

"Enter!"

He pressed a button releasing the door lock. A Cylon foot patrol entered.

"Why did you keep us waiting?" its leader asked.

"Did I keep you waiting? I didn't notice. My work must occupy all my concentration. Would you prefer I ruin my experiments? These are delicate compounds."

"Search," the Cylon leader ordered his soldiers.

"The garrison commander will hear that you have interfered with my valuable time," Ravashol grumbled.

"We have orders to search."

The troops overturned a couple of packing cases situated very near Apollo's place of concealment. Apollo tensed his body, ready to jump out at the enemy if discovered. Another Cylon awkwardly brushed against a bookshelf, sent a few volumes tumbling to the floor.

"This is intolerable," Ravashol said.

"Our orders are to—" the leader said.

"We'll see about that." Ravashol activated a telecom beside his worktable. "This is Dr. Ravashol. I wish to speak to the command centurion."

The image of First Centurion Vulpa appeared on-screen.

"Dr. Ravashol," Vulpa said in a voice that sounded respectful and almost friendly.

"Why is my work being disrupted?" Ravashol complained. "There is a patrol here in my laboratory. In my *laboratory*. And they're—"

"We are searching for human invaders," Vulpa said politely.

"Humans? Here in the village? Are you sure?"

"We have one of their pilots as prisoner already. We are looking for others."

"I know nothing about humans. My experiment is waiting, so please order your centurions to leave and let me continue my work. I need to—"

"First Centurion Vulpa!" the patrol leader interrupted.

"Yes, centurion?"

"We have found a subhuman, a worker clone, hiding here."

At a gesture from their leader, a pair of Cylons brought Ser 5-9 forward.

"Wait," Ravashol said. "He's helping me."

"Only planners are permitted to visit you," Vulpa said coldly.

"He is here because I needed a strong back to move some equipment immediately."

"Nevertheless, Dr. Ravashol, the use of a worker clone by you without my express authority is a violation of our agree..." Vulpa stopped talking, as his attention was diverted by a command-room centurion.

"We have captured another human—in the corridors of the village," the warrior announced,

Vulpa returned his attention to Ravashol.

"You see, doctor? I can't allow any divergence from normal procedure, not now. Centurion?"

"Yes, Commander Vulpa?" said the patrol leader.

"Leave Dr. Ravashol to his research."

"Should we let the worker clone remain here, sir?"

Vulpa thought for a moment.

"No. I can't allow such laxity. Punish the worker clone."

The screen went abruptly dark as Ravashol protested:

"But he is here on my orders. You can't—"

Before the Cylons dragged him out, Ser 5-9 said in a calm, reverent voice:

"Please, father-creator, I am satisfied to be punished. It is correct. I should have obtained the necessary clearance before coming here."

"But—" Ravashol said. The door closed behind the Cylons and Ser 5-9.

"Did you see who they hold prisoner?" Apollo said, climbing over the wall of cases. "I think one of our cadets—"

"No," Ravashol said, his voice collapsing in agony. "No." The doctor's eyes, when he looked at Apollo, were deeply pained. "Why couldn't you have left us alone? If you and your battlestar had not intruded upon this quadrant, all would be peaceful."

"You harp on the word 'peaceful' as if it has some magical qualities. Peace isn't brought about by magic, or even magical thinking. We didn't have a choice about coming into this quadrant, Dr. Ravashol. Father-creator! The Cylons forced us here. They are out to exterminate every human in the universe." He searched for any remnants of mercy toward his fellow humanity that might remain in the scientist's eyes. "Eventually, doctor, even you will go."

Ravashol seemed surprised by that idea.

"They let me live! They could have killed me, but they let me live."

"And undoubtedly they'll preserve your life even longer, so long as you keep producing your little peace weapons for them!"

"Captain, I cannot abide—you mustn't—they are . . ." He paused, and when he spoke again, it was in a near-whisper. "Understand my work. All you want to do is destroy what I have created."

"Sir, with all due respect, I have to say that something's gone haywire in your mind. Your creation *deserves* destruction. It's an instrument of destruction."

"But it's capable of carrying communication units all the way across—"

"And maybe it will still be later, when the theory is refined, when the machine can no longer be adjusted for use as a weapon. Please, sir, we must act, and soon. Our people are being captured, yours are being punished for—"

Ravashol waved a hand for Apollo to stop.

"Before you came," he muttered, "everything was in its proper place. Planners to think. Workers to work."

"I've got a couple pieces of news for you, doctor. The order you revere is that of the Cylons, an order based on the extermination of all species that do not conform to their specifications. Secondly, your planners are such evolved thinkers they can no longer allow themselves to come to decisions. And your workers are thinking . . . and breeding."

"Impossible."

"Their children are hidden in the village."

Ravashol, stunned, started to pace again.

"Children!" he muttered over and over.

"If you won't help me to save the lives on the *Galactica* and the ships of the fleet, if our participation in a war not of our own making so repels you, then do it for the Thetas. In a sense, they are all your children."

As soon as he'd said it, Apollo felt embarrassed at using such a cheap sentimental tactic. But, sentimental or not, it reached the doctor with the twisted body.

"I . . . I used some cells from the members of our teams, the ones who were later slaughtered by the Cylons, used their cells in my first experiments. I altered the structure of the cells, yes, to try to develop a more perfect style of human being. None of my experiments really worked, I thought. The clones' appearance was right, but they've never seemed quite human. I never saw them as quite human. I adopted the Cylon line to comfort my own failure, saw my creations as subhuman. I was wrong. I ignored the occasional flash in their eyes, the infrequent move of a hand, that reminded me of my dead colleagues. You're right, Captain, in a way they are my children. And, more than that, they *are* human."

Moving faster than his body seemed capable of, Ravashol hastened to his worktable. He began to press buttons furiously on a small console beside it. On its screen, complex and intricate diagrams began forming. Ravashol explained that the picture depicted in blueprint style the installation atop Mount Hekla.

"There are two chambers on the mountain itself, one housing the pulsaric laser unit, the other a small garrison maintained there to guard and operate it. On the other side is a small airfield big enough for one ship. The ship occasionally brings up supplies that cannot be transported by the single elevator the Cylons have constructed inside the mountain."

"The elevator? Could we get to it, use it to get our team up to the cannon?"

Ravashol thought for a moment.

"I would recommend against that plan. Too risky. The elevator, besides being rather small, is heavily guarded. Even if you could get your team crowded into it, your presence would have been detected before you finished the long trip to the top. The Cylons would be picking off your people one by one as they got off the elevator."

"There may be some way we can use it. Go on. What about the supply ship? Can it be hijacked?"

Ravashol gave this idea as careful consideration as he'd given the earlier one.

"No. You could hijack it, yes, at the airfield below, but the landing strip is so narrow the ship has to be guided in from a control tower in the garrison. It's doubtful you could surprise the Cylons, and surprise is essential to make your plan work."

"You're right, doctor. Tell me more about the installation."

"What you really need to know is how to destroy it. Do you have solenite?"

"Yes."

"Then you can destroy it. Solenite's your best chance."

Apollo let out a sigh of relief as he realized that Ravashol was, after all, going to help them plan the actual destruction of the weapon.

"For total destruction of the pulsaric laser unit I suggest the jamming or reversing of the main pump. That can be accomplished by disintegrating the double turbo refractor. Here, on this diagram, that's the point you must reach, and you must allow yourself enough time to implant the solenite. It's not easy, but it can be done. Without the use of the internal elevator or a ship, you'll have to scale the mountain."

"We have the personnel for such an ascent."

"Skilled?"

"As skilled as we could pull off a prison barge."

Ravashol frowned but continued with his briefing of the young *Galactica* captain.

Starbuck kept an eye on Croft, Leda, and Wolfe. At the same time, he had the strange sense that each of them was keeping an eye on him, even though there was little actual eye contact achieved. Wolfe, especially, seemed agitated. Boomer eased next to Starbuck and whispered:

"Still think they might take off?"

"Don't know. Right now they're caged. They've been caged for a long time. This might get to them. Looks to me like Wolfe'd like to beat his way through the wall."

"Things're really switched around."

"Don't follow you, Boomer."

"Not sure what I mean, myself. But they've been imprisoned for a long time, each of them. Been under the thumb of jailers, and who knows who else. Now we need their skills. They've got the upper hand. We have to rely on them. It's like we're the prisoners now."

"The strain's getting to you, old buddy. Nobody can turn us into prisoners. Nobody. Get loose. Go play with the kids for a while."

Boomer laughed. Both men watched the children at

play. Boxey seemed to thrive on the attention of the clone children and especially their interest in Muffit and the daggit's extensive repertoire of tricks.

Suddenly the door to the secret chamber started to open. Both Starbuck and Boomer, on alert in case Cylons were on the other side of the sliding portal, sprang up. But when the opening was wide enough, Tenna ran in, exclaiming:

"The Cylons have captured one of your party."

"Thane!" Leda said. "The poor—"

She started running for the entranceway.

"Where do you think you're going?" Starbuck said, blocking her way.

"I'm going after him!"

Starbuck almost let her, then it occurred to him that Leda might just be using the opportunity to split away from the main group herself.

"You're not going anywhere," Starbuck ordered. "We need you for the ascent of the mountain. Boomer, I'll take a look. You're in charge. If I'm not back in ten centons..."

Boomer's brow furled.

"I don't know, Starbuck."

"I do."

Boxey came running up to Starbuck, Muffit scampering behind him.

"I'm going, too. Dad told me to keep an eye on you."

"Oh, Dad told you, did he?"

The boy nodded yes. Starbuck put on a worried look and said:

"Look, Boxey, I'm counting on you as a young colonial warrior to keep these children safe. Now, your father also told you to obey orders. Right?"

"I guess so."

"Then snap to it, cadet." Boxey managed the stance of attention. "And stay clear of those women...you're on duty. Back in a flash."

Boxey returned to the clone children as Starbuck followed Tenna out of the chamber. In the outer room Starbuck said to her:

"Can you take me to where they have Thane?"

"The Cylons will recognize you."

"Not if I look like a Theta."

Going to the wall, Starbuck grabbed one of the worker clone uniforms hanging there, put it on over his own clothing, then gestured to Tenna to lead the way.

After they had gone a few steps, they spied a pair of Cylons walking ahead of them in the corridor. Not wanting to test his disguise with one of the red-lights, Starbuck cautioned Tenna to stay back. They hid for a moment in one of the many alcoves along the passageway. The closeness of the attractive tall woman sent a few thoughts not related to the mission sailing through Starbuck's head. He leaned closer to Tenna and whispered:

"Look, when we get out of here, maybe in some hidden chamber somewhere, we can find some, you know, *privacy*. You know what I mean..."

"No."

"But you brought up the subject of privacy yourself..."

She smiled at him.

"No. I did not."

"Sure you did. Back at the—"

"I know what you mean. But whatever was said, it was not said by me. Or to me, for that matter."

"But—"

"You think I am the Tenna who brought you to the children's quarters?"

"Yes, I—"

"Well, I am not. Wait! The way is clear. Come!"

As they crept out of the alcove, Starbuck finally got the point—this was not the Tenna who'd proposed the provocative ideas of warmth and privacy. This was the other Tenna, the one they'd seen in the—or maybe it was still a third Tenna, or even—no, he didn't want to think about it now. It was too confusing to sort out. It made no difference how many Ser 5-9's there were—but the number of Tennas was a subject worthy of further research. Studying the tantalizing shape of the one guiding him now, he realized it might just be fun sorting all of them out later.

• • •

Vulpa maintained a steady monitoring of the center mall area. After it had been cleared of the clone populace who generally milled about there, the execution platform was raised. The worker clones, now suddenly aware what was to take place, began discussing it actively among themselves. They seemed excited. Good, Vulpa thought. The execution would be a lesson for them. It should prod them into revealing the whereabouts of any other humans who might be concealed in the clone village. In time these human insects engaged on their tiny futile mission would be flushed out and killed, and Vulpa could stop feeling the vague itch inside his metallic uniform.

He glanced at another screen which displayed the entire underground chamber. Gloomy snow torches set in the walls projected the main light, together with reflections from the ghostly stalactites that hung from the high ceiling.

A centurion entered the command post, informing Vulpa that the execution ceremony would be initiated at his order. Vulpa waved a hand, so ordering. He turned back to the monitoring screen, where in a moment he saw a troop of his warriors lead the bound-and-tied prisoner to the execution platform. Along the way, they pushed clones aside. The clones, cowering, gave the Cylons a wide path. The prisoner was marched up a set of steps, where an executioner stood by.

Vulpa beckoned to an aide to bring the other prisoner, Cree, to him. When Cree had been dragged forward, Vulpa pointed him toward the monitor, ordered that a close-up view of the new prisoner be placed on the main screen. He watched Cree for a reaction.

"Do you know him?" Vulpa asked.

Cree could barely keep his eyes opened, but he managed to focus on the screen.

"No, I've never seen him before."

"You are certain."

"Certain."

"For the last time, how many vipers are still operational?"

"My name is Cree, my rank cadet, my numbers are—"

"Quiet. Centurion! Remove him from my presence."

The centurion dragged Cree back to his corner of the command-post room. The cadet immediately slipped back to unconsciousness.

Onscreen the new prisoner was being given his final interrogation. He had been instructed by the Cylon officer in charge that he could save his life by answering questions in open forum—but of course, Vulpa thought, he would be executed no matter what information he provided. It was essential that the clones be given an object lesson in order to keep them contained at their subhuman level of subservience.

Vulpa studied the prisoner as he gave laconic responses to the Cylon officer's questioning. It seemed odd that the man had chosen to disguise himself as a clone. He was much, much too thin. His pale, gaunt face simply looked nothing like the healthy facial type that Ravashol had chosen for the male worker clones. Nor did he look at all subhuman. He did not look very human, either. There was something extrahuman in his blank eyes and nearly white hair.

"What is your purpose here?" the interrogator asked.

"Just visiting," the prisoner said in an eerily quiet voice.

The interrogator, who had been instructed not to react to the prisoner no matter what he might say, continued to his next question:

"How many of you are there?"

"I travel alone. I've always been a little . . . antisocial."

"You're from the *Galactica*, are you not?"

"Never heard of it."

All of the prisoner's answers were unemotional. The man must expect that he was going to die—why did he not show some fear?

"How many combat ships in the fleet?"

"Tough question. There are so many!"

"How many?"

The prisoner stared up at the interrogator. He leaned his chest forward, glanced down at a pocket of his jacket.

"In my inner pocket. You'll find a tape coder. The information you want is recorded in it."

The prisoner was going to cooperate? Vulpa thought. That was a surprise. The interrogator opened the prisoner's jacket and reached in. He removed from inside a small electronic pack.

"Just press that button," the prisoner said, his eyes still emotionless. The Cylon's gloved hand reached for the button the prisoner indicated. Vulpa realized too late what the box might be, and he dived at the monitor screen as if he could somehow reach in and snatch the box away from the interrogator.

Entering the mall, Starbuck was surprised at the crowds assembled there. In the center of the large chamber, on a raised platform, Thane knelt in chains, several Cylons standing around him. Starbuck felt an urge to push through the crowd, sweep Thane off the platform, and escape with him. But, no, that wouldn't work. If only Boomer were here to help, then the two of them might pull it off, but there was too much Cylon firepower between him and Thane. A Cylon questioned the prisoner. Starbuck had never heard of Cylons conducting public interrogations, but perhaps there was a strategic reason for it—you never knew with Cylons.

His Tenna pulled at his arm and pointed toward their left, where Ser 5-9 and the other Tenna, the first Tenna, stood away from the back fringe of the crowd. Starbuck pulled the fur hood more tightly around his face and followed his Tenna to them.

"Starbuck!" Ser 5-9 whispered, obviously surprised.

The hunter didn't look too good, Starbuck thought.

"You all right?" he asked.

Ser 5-9 started to claim he was in the best of health, but the first Tenna interrupted:

"He was captured by the Cylon beasts. They used their laser whip on him. I rubbed healing salve on his back, but it's badly—"

"Forget that, Tenna," Ser 5-9 said. "We've got to go back and get Captain Apollo."

"Apollo?" said Starbuck, bewildered. "Where is he?"

"He stayed with Ravashol. I left him in hiding."

"Can Ravashol be trusted?"

"He saved Ser 5-9 from the Cylons," Tenna said.

The two Tennas were now standing together. Because

he had not been watching them, Starbuck couldn't tell which one had just spoken to him. Both their faces shared the same concern.

"Saved?" Starbuck said, looking back at Ser 5-9. "Looks more to me like they caught you."

"They took me into custody, but they would have killed me if the father-creator had not interceded. He lied to save my life. In the long run, I prefer getting whipped to getting killed."

"All right. We'll have to get the team back together, listen to whatever Apollo brings back. What should we do about Thane?"

"Nothing we can do. They'll execute him."

"Execute him? Maybe we can get the team back here, save him from—"

"There's no time."

Starbuck looked toward the platform. Thane was gesturing with his head down toward his jacket. The Cylon took a box out of Thane's clothes. A small electronic packet. *Where've I seen that before?* Starbuck thought. Then he remembered where, and he shouted to the Tennas and Ser 5-9:

"We've got to get out of here."

Thane's soft voice filled the cavernous chamber as the crowd fell silent:

"Just press that button."

Leading the three clones into a corridor, Starbuck yelled back at them:

"It's a hand mine! Get down!"

The shock waves from the explosion made the ground beneath Starbuck's body rumble. The rumbling was accompanied by screams and the sound of falling rocks in the main chamber.

The sound of the explosion faded. Starbuck rolled over and looked back. The execution area was a shambles, rocks and debris nearly enveloping it. Some smoke still clung to the ground and the walls, but Cylons and clones could be seen stirring and moving about, perhaps searching out the dead.

"What happened?" asked one of the Tennas. Starbuck had no idea which one.

"God," he mumbled, not ready yet to answer a question straight. "Thane. I didn't think he had the—no, I should have known, those eyes, those—I took him for a coward, Tenna. I thought the cold look was all a fake to hide what a misfit he actually—"

"Starbuck," Tenna interrupted. "What did he do?"

"He carries packs. Chemicals, explosives. That box was a hand mine. I guess he decided to take some Cylons with him. And, unfortunately, some of your people. I'm sorry."

"He was your friend?"

"Friend? He could have been. Maybe. Maybe we weren't so different. Ah, this ain't my style of thinking. We better get back."

"That way," the voice of Tenna said, but it was not the Tenna he was looking at. He turned and saw the other one pointing at a nearby corridor.

I keep thinking about *Sharky Star-rover*. Last night I dreamt I had a copy of the book in my hands, but when I opened it, the print was blurred and I couldn't make out a single word, no matter how close I held the volume to my face.

There was this one scene in the book, set on a lushly landscaped planet. Sharky, having fallen exhausted from being chased by some fierce hirsute denizens of the land, looked up at a beautiful tree that seemed to lunge toward the sky from his prone vantage point. It had, I seem to recall, a jagged irregular bark that, in the planet's gloomy darkness, glowed luminescently in abstract bloblike patterns. One particular blob reminded him of Jameson, who'd been captured by the natives. The last sight Sharky had had of Jameson, it had looked to him like the captors were considering boiling him for their evening meal. (I can't remember whether Jameson was rescued by Sharky or fate—for some mysterious reason the really exciting adventures seem to have slipped my memory. I don't even think Jameson was edible.) Anyway, Sharky—saddened by thinking of Jameson—starts to consider this oddly barked tree in more detail. Far above him, on snakelike branches, its leaves were ugly, furry, and dripping with an oily liquid, drops of which fell like miniature deadly bombs around Sharky. He did nothing to try to avoid the drops, but none of them hit him and he thought they even curved in their downward flight as if to miss him intentionally.

He stared at the tree for a long time. He had never seen one like it. His mind contemplated all the trees, all the landscapes, all the natural phenomena he had seen on his travels. Before, it had all impressed him, reminded him of the vast scope of the universe. Now, he wondered if that impression was an illusion. The universe was not so darn gosh-awful big, he thought, we are just too small to appreciate its finitude. This tree might be the only one of its kind on this planet, it might be found nowhere else in the universe, but it was just a tree. Other planets had trees, some did not. He knew that, of kinds of trees, there was only a finite number existing in the universe. Whatever the number was, it was not often increased by one more. That thought made Sharky think of how small the universe was. Perhaps, he thought, people had always been wrong in contemplating their insignificance in the universe. They, too, represented merely a finite number in a finite universe. Insignificance was not the point, that was only investing the number with an unnecessary emotional aspect. If trees contemplated the varieties of human being, or even the varieties of sentient creatures in the universe, they could come to their own similar conclusions about the significance or insignificance of trees. Then he began to laugh. (I remember the scene of his laughter very vividly.) Significance or insignificance, finity or infinity, the tree was extremely beautiful at that moment. For him. Nobody else would ever experience this moment, he thought, no matter who rushed in and sprawled beneath this tree.

As I search the universe for a place to escape to, I often consider Sharky's momentary dilemma. Are our possibilities for escape so finite that we'll eventually have to climb into the nets of a Cylon trap? Or should we continue to consider them infinite, or at least as a high number—say, the number of kinds of trees in the universe—in order to invest those possibilities with hope?

CHAPTER EIGHTEEN

"I have reports now that your puny mission on the surface of the ice planet Tairac is failing," Imperious Leader said to the Starbuck, who seemed to be half-sitting and half-lying on his simulated chair.

"That right? You capture everybody?"

"Well, not everybody yet, but soon."

"How about me, am I on the mission? You capture me?"

"I do not know of your presence on the mission."

"I probably am. I manage to get myself in trouble in spite of myself. If you haven't captured me, the mission isn't failing."

"Do you think you make a significant difference?"

"Any one of us makes a significant difference as long as we're alive. But I've always got a little edge. Luck, we call it. You guys don't know how to utilize luck."

"If it is not a tangible factor, we will not apply it to our strategy."

"Your mistake. It's tangible but you'll never see it."

Imperious Leader chose not to pursue that line of thought.

"One of your people is to be executed, another will be eventually."

"Oh? What're their names?"

"Thane and Cree."

"I don't know them."

"But they are a part of the information we—"

"Recall that, when I was programmed, it was based on the most recent information. This reproduction of me doesn't know of Thane or Cree yet, because they were not part of your latest information from captured prisoners. Your data banks can't get milk from a daggit, after all."

Imperious Leader wondered if the simulator, perhaps forced into overload in maintaining the Starbuck figure, was now itself actually talking back to him.

First Centurion Vulpa hoped that news of the explosion had not somehow reached Imperious Leader. It had seemed uncanny to him how Imperious Leader sometimes knew what had happened even though no one had transmitted him information concerning the subject. Perhaps, Vulpa thought, that also was a function of the third brain that he so desired. The prisoner's suicide made no sense to him, and frightened him a bit. He could counter human acts that conformed with the knowledge Cylons had of the species, but an act like the prisoner's, suicidal sabotage, was beyond his ken. Vulpa also did not want Imperious Leader to know the extent of casualties, the depletion of his already understaffed garrison.

"Stand by for a message from the High Command," the communications officer announced.

Vulpa turned to his telecom screen. All the other Cylons stood in a rigid silence. As the contact was made, the image on the screen was first a scramble of dots and lines, and then it slowly resolved into the awesome many-eyed face of Imperious Leader. The face was not clear, because the Leader sat in shadow.

"First Centurion Vulpa!" Imperious Leader barked.

"By your command," Vulpa answered, according to the honored ritual.

"The time for our final attack is nearing. Our base ships are approaching the *Galactica* and its fleet. The major assault on them is imminent. They will be in full range of the pulsar cannon soon. What is the status of the installation on Mount Hekla?"

"Fully operative."

"Good. Initiate random firing. Sweep the entire corridor. You may be able to catch the *Galactica* when it first enters your sector. Begin at once."

"By your command."

"I expect no less than the annihilation of that battlestar and the entire fleet. The way will then be clear for your return to the executive-officer staff on the command-base ship, Vulpa."

"Yes, sir."

As Imperious Leader's image disintegrated into an array of swarming and swimming bits, Vulpa considered the meaning of the Leader's last statement. With the success of the operation Vulpa's days of exile on this dreadful ice planet were nearly over. He swung around in his command chair and ordered the officers still standing at attention:

"Transmit those orders to Summit Station. Program for automatic fire. Random sweeps covering the corridor. Tell the gunnery squad I will be joining them to guide the entire operation. I will take the supply ship up to the station. Alert the control tower there to prepare for my arrival."

"What about the human invasion force?" an officer asked.

"I doubt they're much danger anymore. But double the guard at all strategic points, at the garrison here and the command post, and send a whole platoon to guard the elevator accessway, should they get foolish and think they can use it."

Vulpa noticed Cree still lying unconscious in his corner.

"We have no further need of that one. Take him to a cold cell. I will examine his cortex later. Is the supply ship ready?"

"Yes, First Centurion."

Vulpa swaggered out of the room. Two of the remaining Cylons picked up Cree, his body still limp, and dragged him out of the command-post headquarters.

CHAPTER NINETEEN

Croft:

Apollo's only just had time to catch his breath, when the door behind him begins sliding open. He spins around with his laser drawn. The smiling face of Starbuck peeks in through the opening, saying:

"Is that any way to greet a fellow warrior?"

Apollo looks disgusted at Starbuck, says:

"I thought I left you in charge."

"I made a command decision to reconnoiter."

Starbuck edges into the room. He's wearing a clone worker outfit, and it's filthy with dust. Apollo reaches out and touches the fur, then examines the dirt that comes off on his fingers. Ser 5-9 and a couple of the Tennas follow Starbuck into the room, looking quite downcast.

"What happened?" Apollo asks.

"Didn't you hear?"

"I thought I heard something when I was rushing back here through the corridors, but—"

"It was a big explosion. Thane's work. He's dead."

I glance at Wolfe and Leda. None of us speak. The old code: never show emotion when you hear one of your kind's been killed. Apollo studies all our faces for reactions to Starbuck's news. I'm glad we don't show him anything. We all learned long ago you get no prizes for compassion.

Starbuck tells about the explosion. I have to say I'm impressed. I always knew Thane had no regard for human life, but I always thought he had some regard for his own. Still, he's dead by his own choice, and that's the kind of control he always demanded.

"One thing sure," Starbuck finishes, "he didn't betray us on the mission."

The mission. I almost forgot that part of it. I counted on Thane to help me lay the solenite. He knew more about the stuff than I do. Without him, that puts us all a couple of steps closer to our own deaths. In the mission plan Leda's backup to Thane in helping me with placing the demolitions. That should be cozy. Well, she may kill me while we're working together, but she does know something about laying down the solenite.

"We've got a problem," Apollo declares.

"Tell me something I—" Starbuck starts, but gets a mean look from Apollo and stops. "Yes, sir. A problem."

"Ravashol says our best chance is a—"

"The father-creator helped you!" Ser 5–9 blurts out, astonished and pleased.

"Yes. We've worked out a simultaneous-attack strategy. It's our best chance."

Using maps supplied by Ravashol, Apollo explains the layout at the top of Mount Hekla and at the foothills garrison. Then he gets down to brass tacks:

"There're three phases to the assault and they must be coordinated precisely. Croft, Wolfe, Leda, and myself will make the ascent up Hekla. After we reach the top, Croft and Leda will take care of planting the explosives. At the same time, Wolfe and I'll take on the small guard stationed there, and keep them out of the way of Croft and Leda, then—"

"You're taking Wolfe in with you, Captain?" Starbuck asks.

"That's right."

All of us look toward Wolfe. He looks as mean and surly and insubordinate as ever. I were Apollo, I wouldn't take him anywhere.

Starbuck doesn't know where to turn.

"But, Captain, respectfully, I think Wolfe should be assigned to another part of the assault. I'll go with you up the mountain."

"No, Starbuck, you're in charge of attacking the main garrison, so they can't respond to any calls and interrupt our little task on Hekla."

"But, Captain—"

"No more buts. Wolfe has extensive climbing experience, you don't. And don't hand me any of that bilge about you and Boomer being stationed on some ice planet somewhere. You and I both know how that little detail found its way into your records. This mission is too important for me to have to be crawling down crevasses to get you out. Your job will be to strike the garrison—with the help of Ser 5-9 and a contingent of his best fighters. You have to render any Cylon rescue teams inoperable, especially keep them from launching an attack on us from the airfield. Then, you have to get to the underground complex below the garrison, and get through the tunnel there and encounter the Cylon troops guarding the elevator. It's located at this point on the map. Our best escape route from the emplacement is down that elevator. If we try to go down the mountain, we'll more than likely be killed by the explosion or buried in its debris. I don't want any Cylons waiting for us by the elevator when we get down there. Okay, Starbuck?"

"We won't let you down."

"I'm counting on your success. The survival of the rest of us depends on your gaining control of that elevator."

Starbuck nods, but his face still shows concern. Can't say as I blame him. I don't even know if I could control Wolfe on a run-in like that. Apollo better keep all ten eyes on Wolfe.

Ser 5-9 steps forward and speaks in his formal voice:

"Captain. I can delegate someone to join the attack squad on the main garrison, and lead those troops of our

people. My real usefulness to you is on the mountain.
Tenna"—he points to the nearest Tenna—"and I have
considerable experience on that mountain. We can help
you cut your time in half."

"No, Ser 5-9, I don't want to risk you on the mountain.
Your people'll need your leadership and—"

"Captain Apollo," I interrupt, "we *do* need someone of
Ser 5-9's abilities on Hekla. Remember, we've never seen
it, never had a chance to scout the terrain up close. It's like
he said. He may know the trails, the chimneys, the easy
slopes—he can save us a lot of time."

Apollo lets all this bounce around inside his head for a
moment, then nods in agreement.

"All right," he says. "Let's set our timepieces."

We all look at the chronometers supplied us by the
Galactica quartermaster. I never could make out how to
use one, but I fake the synchronization anyway, and I
press my button when Apollo tells us to start timers. After
the synchronization ritual, Apollo gets grim, tightens his
mouth, and says:

"We'll reach the top and start our attack in exactly
eighty-five centons."

"Captain," I say, "it takes me eighty-five centons just to
lace my boots."

God, the look he gives me is so hard I couldn't drive a
piton into it.

"We must reach the top in eighty-five centons," he
says. "The *Galactica* will be moving forward after that."

"You say so, Captain," I say, then mutter to Ser 5-9:
"You guys don't know any shortcuts, you'll have to throw
us to the top."

Ser 5-9 smiles. A revelation: clones have a sense of
humor. I'm glad he's joining us.

"You're the key down here, Starbuck, you and
Boomer," Apollo says. "We can't get down the elevator,
we blow up with the gun. For all our sakes, Starbuck,
don't be late!"

Again Starbuck reacts to a mean look from the
captain; then he says:

"No, sir. We'll be there."

As I test all twelve points of each crampon before

attaching them to my climbing shoes, I feel the kind of fear I felt during my preparations for every tough climb I've had to make. It's a good sign.

Ser 5-9 brings us out a cave set in the foothills of the mountain. Surrounded by high boulders and snowdrifts, we can't be seen from the main Cylon garrison. I turn around and look up at Hekla. Although not a high mountain in the usual mountaineering judgment of height, it is still awesome, since it rises from a relative flatland, with no easy smaller mountains or hills to make the approach to it gradual.

Like the best mountains I've seen, Hekla looks designed. Its slopes and angles seem freshly handled by a master sculptor who'll never grow tired of altering the look of it. Although this mountain's surfaces do not change their colors with the seasons and the position of a sun in the sky, its dark gray cast is varied with mysterious, and mysteriously attractive, shadows. The howling winds and the irregular plumes of blowing snow make Hekla all the more mysterious and terrifying. As the bitter cold begins to penetrate the many layers of my clothing, I feel more confident about the whole escapade. Well, if not confident, at least more buoyant in spirits. Like all experienced cragsmen, I long for the challenge of a mountain such as Hekla. The pain it will cause, the imminence of sudden death, the possibility of exhaustion and defeat—they're all part of the challenge. My body begins to long for the pain, the exhaustion, the cold. Maybe even the death, since I'd rather die huddled in the niche of a mountain than spread out in the most luxurious cell a prison has to offer.

Silently we all work on readying the ropes and harnesses. I check out the pitons, carabiners, ice-axes. In spite of the clinging material of our parka hoods, intruding snow and ice start to form cliffs and overhangs on the geography of our faces. Breathers might have protected our faces more, but there was no evidence, or even likelihood, of di-ethene on the mountain, so I'd argued against them. Breathers could get too easily clogged in a mountainside blizzard. I remember long ago coming across a climber just resting against a rock, smothered because his breather had iced over.

The storm noise around is so loud I don't hear Wolfe and Leda approach me. When I glance up, the two are just standing there, examining me with looks that suggest they've already decided the answers to questions they haven't gotten around to asking yet.

Wolfe speaks first:

"One of the clones told me there's a supply ship at an airfield at the top of the mountain, behind the pulsar emplacement."

"Yeah," I say. "Apollo told me about that. He thought we might be able to make our escape in it but, since he didn't know whether it would be there or if we could operate it, he's put it in our plan only on a contingency basis."

"Well, I can pilot one of those Cylon crates. Remember, I learned for the platinum raid? I say, when we get to the top, we grab the ship."

"And go where? How long do you think it will be before the *Galactica* hunts us down?"

"The *Galactica* is the *hunted*. Adama's not going to waste a squadron trying to track down three escaped convicts."

"He knows that," Leda says contemptuously. "You also know that, if we bug out on the mission, the chances are the *Galactica*'s not going to be in any shape to hunt us down."

"We can't let them die, we can't—"

"Since when are your loyalties with your jailers?" Leda says. "The *Galactica* and the whole fleet are finished."

"They will be if we don't knock that weapon out."

Leda steps back, looks at me as if I'm a painting that she doesn't want to buy because its surface layer is cracking apart.

"That's right," she says, "they'll all be destroyed. And we'll be *free*. Don't give me any of that bilge about how this planet's too hostile an environment—anything's better so long as you're free. We'll find another planet. Starlos isn't all that far. We can pick up food, water, fuel. Go anywhere. C'mon, Croft, are you with us?"

All I can think is she really wants me to come with them. Maybe we can get together again. Maybe it'll be like the old days—the cheerfulness, the joking around, the love. Looking into her gelid eyes, it's hard to see any possibility of cheer, love, or jokes reviving there, but there's always a chance.

"Are you going to turn your back on freedom, Croft? Again?"

Her words go through me more fiercely than the piercing winds of the mountain. She's blaming me for my failure, my ineptitude during our confrontation with Adama's warriors right before our capture. I had had their pursuing ship in my sights and had not been able to fire.

"I couldn't shoot down colonial warriors," I say to Leda now. It was what I'd said to her then, too.

"I know," she says, hate in her voice. "The code. The bloodline. And for your compassion they chained you like an animal. Now's your chance. *Our* chance. One last time, my husband."

What can I say to her? She knows if I don't respond to that last plea, I'll never agree to their plan. And she's right, it is our chance. I thought I'd trade my soul to have Leda back. Now that the opportunity is here, and my soul isn't even on the line, I am no longer so sure. Or perhaps my soul *is* on the line and that's why I feel so empty.

Wolfe leans toward me, says:

"Are you with us?"

If I say yes, I win Leda back. If I say no, I not only lose her but we'll blow the mission—Leda and Wolfe'll make their move without me, Apollo and I'll wind up dead, and so much for saving the fleet from the damn laser gun. I can't say no at all, whether it's truthful or not. With a certain feeling of relief at postponing the real decision, I accede to their plan.

"I'm with you."

As I look again up the majestic sculpturesque slopes of the mountain, and consider how futile this mission seems, I realize that maybe I am telling Leda and Wolfe the truth.

CHAPTER TWENTY

"It's about time we moved out," Boomer said. "We haven't much time."

Starbuck, peering at his chronometer, nodded.

"I'll be ready," he said grimly.

Boomer frowned.

"What's on your mind, old buddy? You and Apollo've been about as tight-lipped as—"

"It's Cree," Starbuck said. "The Cylon commander told Ravashol they had a prisoner."

"Sure, Thane, but he's dead."

"No, this was before Thane was caught. They *already* had a prisoner. It's got to be Cree, couldn't be anybody else."

"You have any idea where they're holding him?"

"No. The maps Apollo brought back don't indicate any prisoner-detention areas. But I'm going to find Cree somehow."

Boomer sighed.

"Look, bucko, I know you're upset about losing those

cadets, but get it through your head it wasn't your fault. There's no reason to turn this job into a lousy crusade just for—"

"He's somewhere in the Cylon underground complex, Boom-boom. I'm sure of it."

"Well, let's keep an eye out for him, then. The both of us."

Starbuck smiled at Boomer.

"Thanks, old buddy."

"Forget the thanks. Let's get hopping."

"Right. As soon as I give our rear-force officer his instructions."

"Our rear—oh, I get you. I'll wait for you by the door."

Starbuck walked to Boxey and knelt beside him. Muffit tried to squeeze into the embrace the lieutenant gave the child.

"Okay, Boxey," Starbuck said, "as a colonial warrior, first class, I'm leaving you in charge of these children. They need somebody who knows the ropes. You and Muffit have to protect them by keeping them all together. Don't make a sound, no matter what you hear."

Boxey frowned.

"What will I hear?"

"We're going to be making some noise. Then we'll be back for you. For all of you."

Starbuck stood up, started for the door.

"Take care of my father," Boxey said.

"I'll do that."

In the corridor outside, they were joined by one of the Tennas—which one, Starbuck wasn't sure. He had seen so many of them now. When he'd dozed off once, he'd had a dream in which hundreds of Tennas seemed to be approaching him, all with their arms out, inviting him to love. This Tenna looked afraid.

"Something's bothering you," Starbuck said to her. "What is it?"

"I don't wish to betray my people."

"I was right then. Something *is* wrong. Are they bugging out of attacking the garrison?"

"No. They will help you destroy the Cylon garrison."

"Then what is it?"

She paused, seemed to wish she could disappear into one of the niches along the corridor, then let out her breath and said:

"The planners have been at them. Now they want to stop you and your team from destroying the pulsar weapon."

Starbuck nearly groaned in agony and despair. He had suffered the meddling interferences of bureaucrats before. They always seemed to come up with some reason for wavering from a goal; perhaps it was their specialty.

"How will they stop us?" Starbuck asked Tenna. "Apollo and the others will be setting the charges while we're taking the garrison and the elevator."

"I'm not sure. I think they plan on using the elevator themselves, after you get control, then going up and talking Apollo out of the destruction of the gun."

"Then they have a lousy sense of timing. They'll never be able to—"

"Maybe, maybe not. All I know is that they'll try to stop you by whatever means they can. Here, they're waiting in this chamber."

"Well, let's talk to them."

Starbuck's voice was grim, determined. The room into which Tenna took him and Boomer was wide and high. Nevertheless, it seemed packed with planners and worker clones. A worker clone who identified himself as Ser 7–12 stepped forward, his feet planted firmly apart, appearing ready to confront Starbuck. Starbuck asked for the group's attention and said:

"Before we rush into anything rash, let's understand what our objectives are."

"The Cylon garrison," Ser 7–12 said.

"That's right. We have to knock it out and gain control of the elevator area within twenty centons or the *Galactica* is lost. We have to rescue our team from blowing up with half the mountain."

Starbuck took a pause, giving Ser 7–12 a hard stare, challenging the clone leader to reveal his mutinous attitudes. Ser 7–12 replied in a cautious and quiet voice:

"We will help you attack the garrison, as we've agreed. Many of us here will be pleased to help you kill Cylons.

But the pulsar weapon belongs to us and should be preserved intact."

"Keep that gun, and the *Galactica* will be blown out of the sky."

Behind Ser 7-12, a group of the planners kept a watchful eye on the confrontation. Suddenly they parted their rank, and another man, an older man, was revealed standing behind them. The old man's attention seemed elsewhere. Starbuck wondered if he was some kind of older planner.

"If the gun is destroyed, so are we," Ser 7-12 said. "Once news of our revolt reaches a Cylon outpost or base ship, they will come here in their fighters to destroy us. Our only hope is in turning the weapon against them. You of the *Galactica* and its fleet will have accomplished your heroics and will be gone. What's left then to us? We will be here alone. Defenseless. Unless we have the pulsar cannon to repel them."

A deep faraway rumble seemed to shake the walls of the chamber.

"Can't you hear that?" Starbuck said. "That's the gun. It's firing automatically! A random shot could destroy the *Galactica*, even while the position of the ship is unknown. Once the *Galactica*'s position is discovered, one shot will take it out. Don't you understand? The *Galactica* is the last colonial battlestar. It *has* to survive. The fate of an entire *race* depends upon it."

"Perhaps. But we don't know your people. All we do know is that you are willing to sacrifice us for yourselves. Why should we care about you, then, if you don't care about us? You are not our concern..."

"But, Ser 7-12, they are *mine*," the older man announced, limping forward. Ser 7-12 and the others seemed astonished at the man's interference. "I am a member of that race that is fleeing from Cylon tyranny."

"Father-creator," Ser 7-12 said, frightened. *So that's who the old man is*, thought Starbuck, *the notorious Dr. Ravashol*. "Their battle isn't ours, sir. We must protect ourselves. We will not be subjugated again. We are not perfect, but—"

"But you are human," Ravashol said, reaching up to put a small hand on Ser 7-12's massive shoulders. "More human than I could have imagined." He laughed wryly. "I must review my notes to see where I went wrong."

Ravashol stepped back from the clone leader and addressed the entire group:

"Those are your brothers in trouble in space. In an odd mythic sense, they are your genuine ancestors, the race whose cells provided the raw materials for the creation of the series of what I so confidently thought were more perfect versions of a humankind I had hated too long and too bitterly. I see now that what I may have hated was not my fellow humans, but myself. And you, all of you, are the manifestations of that hatred. Well, I was wrong. We have to help them. Allow the pulsaric unit to be destroyed and"—Ravashol paused as he examined the puzzled faces staring at him—"and *I* will protect you." The clones did not seem quite yet willing to accept that comforting statement, in spite of the man it originated from. "Trust me, my children."

Starbuck advanced toward Ser 7–12 and said firmly:

"We're out of time. We go now or not at all."

Ser 7–12's answer came back just as firmly:

"We're with you."

As Ser 7–12 began assembling his troops, gathering them into squads and platoons, Boomer whispered to Starbuck:

"You give any thought to what we would have done if they'd said they *wouldn't* go?"

"Don't scare me with logic."

Starbuck avoided Boomer's next question by going to Ravashol and saying softly to the old man:

"Either that was some fine con or you've got something up your sleeve, doctor. How are you going to protect them?"

Ravashol's grimness dropped away like a mask, and he smiled.

"I'm not exactly the quivering traitor that you people think. I did not give the Cylons all my creations. Perhaps I knew there'd be a time when someone like your Captain Apollo would arrive here and challenge me out of my self-induced trance, I don't know. Anyway, do not fear. We will be safe."

Starbuck matched Ravashol's smile.

"Yeah, I got a feeling you will. Some people'd envy you."

"Oh? Why is that?"

"Well, your godlike sway over these creations of yours is the kind of thing that fulfills some people's fantasies."

Ravashol stopped smiling abruptly, narrowed his eyes.

"Godlike, eh? I suppose you're right. Father-creator and all that inanity. I shouldn't have allowed it. It was merely convenient. More than that, it just froze my creations into attitudes of mindless duty. Thank you, Lieutenant."

"Why thank me?"

"You've made me realize I may have to do strenuous battle . . . with a false god."

Starbuck felt the need to say something comforting, but couldn't think of anything. *Just as well,* he thought. *What do you say to comfort a fallen god?*

Ser 7–12 had his troops all organized and moving out of the chamber. With a casual salute Starbuck backed away from Ravashol and joined Boomer.

"We're gonna have to move fast," Boomer said. "I wish I knew how the captain and the others're doing. We might just liberate that elevator and find Cylons coming out at us when the doors open."

"True. With Croft and that gang of his with Apollo, they—God, I wish I'd talked Apollo into letting me go."

"Well, one thing at a time I guess. Let's go."

Boomer looked back at Ravashol.

"Funny," he said.

"You find something amusing in all this?"

"No. But look at him. He looks so small, so solitary, left behind there."

"Yeah, but I think he's thinking about five steps ahead of any of us, Boomer."

"Maybe."

Turning around, the two *Galactica* officers rushed out the doorway of the meeting chamber.

CHAPTER TWENTY-ONE

Croft:

I swear this mountain's living. It's out to get us. You can't go two steps without being enshrouded by blowing snow. Hard, icy snow looking to rip slices in your clothing. Every six or eight steps I have to tap ice off my crampons with my ax. Takes all my concentration to maintain friction on this jagged approach slope. Apollo keeps slipping and sliding. My legs aching already, I move up beside him, holler in his ear:

"Walk up straight!"

Some defiance in his eyes. He still doesn't like to take orders from me.

"Up straight! Try to keep the whole sole of your boot against the surface. You don't get good friction, you're going to collapse from exhaustion before we get anywhere near top."

He nods. I demonstrate a couple of steps. He picks it up from me. At least he's a good learner.

The two clones really know their way up the mountain,

although they don't climb with much style. I always said style meant nothing on the side of an icy mountain anyway. I'd rather have a clumsy person who knows the terrain than a stylist who thinks he can get by on good moves alone.

Wolfe and Leda keep exchanging meaningful glances with me. I don't know how they interpret the blank looks I return to them. Even if we do make it to Hekla's summit, I don't know how we're going to survive Wolfe and Leda.

The climb's getting more treacherous now. We're off the easy slopes. Up ahead I can see dim outlines of what we have to face. The castlelike configurations of such a mountain are even more pronounced from this vantage point. It seems a huge pile of battlements, turrets, steep walls that suggest hiding demons ready to push away ladders. I holler at Apollo:

"We need a rest, Captain!"

"There's not enough time. We can't rest now, not when—"

"Rest, hell, we need a bivouac. I know how much time we got and I know we can't rest long, but each moment of rest is worth several microns on the mountain. Sir."

"Croft, I—"

"Captain Apollo, a mountain's got to be climbed slow and steady. Out here, haste is the same word as death. Look, it's not just the danger of exhaustion I'm talking about. The atmosphere's getting thinner. You try to go up too fast, it's like getting the bends under water. Your internal organs are affected by height and rarefied atmosphere. Your perception of objects can go haywire, all your senses get dulled. You can easily reach a point where death seems better than taking another step. Believe me, Captain, going slow is going to save your precious fleet more than vain heroics."

Apollo glares at me for a moment, then reluctantly agrees. We choose a fairly level spot just ahead. I go up first, try to do a little site gardening to smooth it out, but it's no use—everything's solid and covered with ice. We fall into comfortable resting positions. Wolfe and Leda seem to purposely separate themselves from me. Apollo pulls himself beside me and asks:

"Any more advice?"

I am almost too surprised to answer. There's no sarcasm in his voice. He *really* wants to know. Perhaps we *can* pull together as a team, all of us. With the tenacity of the clones, the impulse toward escape of Wolfe and Leda, the willingness of Apollo to listen to reason—perhaps I can pull all this together, use their divergent motives to create the illusion of a team. Just for long enough to get us up to the gun emplacement. Then Wolfe and Leda will make their play, and I'll have to see where I stand—but no sense in worrying about *that* now.

"Advice, huh?" I say to Apollo. "Right now I couldn't give you the standard lecture. Either your instincts take hold or they don't. Just remember it's more important to climb with your feet and not with your hands. Hands are for leverage, for position, for balance, for keeping you on the side of the mountain. But you don't get a good hold, all the arm-strength you can summon isn't going to be much help in keeping you from falling and maybe taking the rest of us with you. Solid anchors, good holds, and remembering to keep your feet the best place you can, or the second-best place, or third, or any damn place that'll keep you steady—that's the most I can tell you right now, Captain."

Apollo nods and looks up the mountain. You can't see the top. All you can see are vague shadowy shapes, the snow plumes rising regularly from ridges—a sure sign of strong-wind areas—a low-hanging band of clouds in the distance. Even in the darkness of this ice asteroid, the suggestion of color in the surface of the mountain is impressive to me. Far away the ice veneer is a shadowy gray; closer there are streaks and blots of blue; nearby, in the meager light of our lanterns, I can make out a faint crystalline suggestion of purple, the same near-purple I've seen on the ice mountains of Caprica.

"What're the chances of avalanche?" Apollo asks suddenly.

"From what I can tell, no worse than usual. No guarantees I know of that they won't happen. Still, this mountain's less likely than some."

"Oh? Why?"

"Well, this's a dark planet. No sun to screw things up—melting surfaces, altering terrain so that weight pressures change and cause the kind of shifts that result in avalanches. Everything stays cold at about the same temperature, so there's no shifts of climate to get an icefall started. Terrain and climate here should combine to make the mountain relatively stable. But God, man, you never know. And there's always a good chance of a loose-snow avalanche, if there's any disturbance or one of us sets up a chain reaction that jars some snow away from someplace higher up and it starts charging down at us, gathering more snow to it. Creating an avalanche with a snowball effect, see? But, I were you, I wouldn't spend much time worrying about avalanches. There's lots more out there to get us. And we've had enough rest. It's time to move out, Captain."

I whisper the last as a hint so that the others can't hear. It's important to Apollo that he appear to be in control of the expedition. Any takeover from me would just cause resentment all around. I have to control this little foray with subtlety. Always good to employ subtlety on your superior officer if you want to get anything done.

The next stage of climbing is easier than I'd expected. In spite of the rough appearance of the terrain, there are plenty of holds. Ser 5–9, with his knowledge of the mountain, has saved us a great deal of time. We're able to cover a significant amount of distance just using pull holds to move our bodies up, and there's a good deal of friction to create an anchoring counterforce. Watching Apollo frequently check his chronometer, its faint illumination sending evil-looking shadows into his face, I begin to get hopeful. Maybe Hekla is one of those mountains that look rough but prove to be no real challenge to a good set of climbers.

Suddenly things get tougher, as we reach a glacial formation. Apollo wants to head straight up, but I counsel traversing the glacier as the best strategy. Ser 5–9 agrees. I take the lead, setting a slow pace, tapping and puncturing the snow-covered ground ahead of me with the point of my ax. It's important here to maintain the slow pace. Any point ahead of us can turn out to be a crevasse and plunge us all to sudden death.

Coming upon a wide crevasse, we cross over a snow bridge, each climber taking it alone and slowly. On the other side of the bridge, Apollo keeps peeking at that chronometer. He's obviously getting twitchy, but I refuse his suggestion that we cross the snow bridge in pairs. This is the wrong time to take that kind of chance.

Reaching a steep icefall, Ser 5-9 signals that it's the best and most direct way up. I agree. Using some of its jagged points to make my way a short distance upward, I start bringing out the pitons, which till now I've hoarded. They're in short supply and had to be saved for a difficult part of the ascent. I'm glad that they're molecular-binding, since I am afraid of excessive sound in this area of the mountain. One good solid echo, and who knows what's going to fall on you. I push the setting on the outer edge of the piton to *ice*, and push it in. It goes in with a sound that rises in pitch. A good sign. Whether hammer-driven or molecular-binding, the piton whose sound descends in pitch signifies that it is insecurely anchored. Being able to interpret the song of the piton is a lifesaving technique. Quickly the piton's shaft works its way all the way in, and only the oval eye at its end is visible. There's not enough time to loop ropes through the pitons, so we'll have to use them simply for direct-aid climbing.

Not thinking about our goals or the complications to them, I work slowly, pushing in one piton after another and forming a zigzag ladder up the icefall. I can sense the others climbing up behind me, but do not look down. I try never to look down. On a mountain there's no place you've been to that you are eager to see again right away. I just concentrate on setting the pitons in the right places and listening to the monotonous but comforting sound of their song.

The top of the icefall is narrow and slightly sloped but secure. Above it is an overhang that could give us trouble. Twisting the tricked-up rope so that it's slack, I sling it over the overhang. The other end floats down. Ser 5-9 and Wolfe each take an end of the rope and pull at it to make sure the rope is anchored and in a secure place. Then I twist the rope in the other direction, making it hard and stiff as a cable. Climbing quickly hand over hand, I make my way to the edge of the overhang, then laboriously pull myself onto it. Up farther is a more secure ledge. Telling Ser 5-9 and Wolfe to let go of the rope ends, I climb to the ledge, where I drive the shaft of my ax into the hard snow as far as I can. Far enough to serve as an anchor for a belay. The ice-ax shaft belay is the safest for the situation. I brace my right leg by kicking out a large step below the ax and setting my foot firmly into it. Supporting the ax with the upper knee of my left leg, I set the belay rope slack and feed it around the shaft of the ax with one hand in a round turn, low on the ax shaft, while holding onto the ax head with my other hand. Because of the slope, I also run the rope around the small of my back for further anchorage, then throw it back down to the others. Jerking on the rope, I alert them to finish their climb to this ledge. Gradually I watch each of them, Ser 5-9 and Tenna first, then Apollo, Leda, and Wolfe, come over the ledge.

At Ser 5-9's suggestion we rope together and work our way along the ledge, sometimes holding close to the wall of ice at spots where the ledge narrows, sometimes crunching down to creep beneath low-hanging cornices. We reach a point where a fairly gentle slope eases away from us to our left. I signal the others to hold back while I take a look, and edge myself forward gradually along the edge toward the slope. As I look up, some clouds above me part briefly and I think I see the outline of the gun emplacement, dark against darkness, not far above us. I turn to tell Apollo, but before I can say anything, there is a great shuddering explosion above me and the sky is briefly lit up brilliantly by a pulse from the gun. It's firing now. Maybe the *Galactica* is within range. The sound of the weapon is deafening. The mountain seems to shake. The thunder of the gun is joined by a rumble that seems to emanate from deep within the mountain. I look up. A huge crest of snow is coming down at me. I have just enough time to shout:

"Avalanche!"

Then the snow reaches me, and the ledge beneath me breaks off in a falling chunk. There is a brief jerk on my rope, then an abrupt sense of free fall. Apollo has acted quickly and sensibly. He's cut the rope to save the rest of the team. My face is briefly in the air outside, then I am completely enveloped by the snow. I seem to be falling more deeply into it, like a swimmer being pulled along by an unexpected fierce underwater current.

CHAPTER TWENTY-TWO

Landing his ship on the narrow airfield atop the mountain, Vulpa released it from the control of the guidance personnel, while a ground crew slung cables around it to secure it against the high winds. Snakelike, a tunnel emerged from the side of the gun-emplacement building and attached itself to the ship's exit hatch. Inside the tunnel, a gunnery master joined Vulpa and a moving runway carried them into Summit Station. The gun took up most of the space within the emplacement. It looked like a massive chunk of gray metal cut out of the mountain itself.

"Are you ready?" Vulpa asked the gunnery master, who turned to the chief gunner and said:

"Lens system aligned?"

"Aligned," the gunner replied.

"Pump system to speed?"

"Speed."

The master turned to Vulpa and announced:

"Ready."

Vulpa, feeling a moment's glow of satisfaction, ordered:

"Commence automatic fire."

The master pressed a button and the weapon shuddered into action. Vulpa could sense the energy gathering within the bore of the gun as it quickly built up the power to generate its pulses. The first pulse seemed to burst from the gun unexpectedly. As it blasted upward, the sky was briefly filled with a flaring light. For a very short time the asteroid seemed lighted by a returning sun; then the beam entered the cloud cover and darkness came back abruptly. Beneath them, the mountain seemed to shake, the usual reaction. Vulpa heard the sound of a small avalanche developing. Even though the foundation of the emplacement went deeply into the mountain, Vulpa sometimes worried that the entire structure could tumble from the mountain as the result of a massive avalanche. But the gun rumbled again and another sky-lighting flare burst forth from the mouth of the cannon.

Vulpa checked with his control room to see if the *Galactica* had yet been discovered within the sector. The report was negative. Still, Vulpa knew, one of these powerful beams from the pulsaric-laser-unit weapon could still find its way randomly to wherever the *Galactica* was. If that happened, even more glory would accrue to him, and Imperious Leader would be suitably impressed, Vulpa was sure. Vulpa's ambition was suddenly making sense again, and he looked forward to the successful outcome of this assignment—the termination of the human enemy and Vulpa's restoration from exile to full rank and responsibility.

Imperious Leader had to interrupt his dialogues with the Starbuck to direct the final phase of the assault upon the human fleet. His base ship had now arrived at the sector where the *Galactica* and its fleet drifted. He directed a Cylon task force to initiate attack upon the rear of the fleet, not a sneak attack this time but a full-fledged assault.

He would send wave after wave against the humans, enough warships to finally wear them down or push them

into the range of the Hekla weapon. It was a flawless plan.
To Imperious Leader the attack seemed already ended.
His active third brain was already contemplating post-
battle problems and matters upon Cylon-dominated
planets. Strange political factions seemed to be emerging
around the Cylon empire, and the members of these
nearly rebellious groups had not yet been located and
shunted off to the harmless classes of Cylon society.

He looked over at the Starbuck-simulacrum, which
was lounging in its usual arrogant way. Logic dictated
that the simulator be removed from the pedestal, but
Imperious Leader wanted the simulacrum to view the
final defeat of the race for which it was a representative
illusion. The Leader realized that, once the simulator was
deactivated, the simulacrum would no longer exist—that
any feeling of vengeance the Leader might achieve from
the Starbuck's reaction to the annihilation was merely a
response to information gathered from data banks and
presented in human form. The Starbuck would be
returned to nothingness, a collection of data bits that
would never form again. Imperious Leader wondered
what revenge he would gain by showing the Starbuck the
annihilation of the human race. His feeling of vengeance
would be as illusory as the Starbuck itself. Nevertheless, if
the Starbuck displayed any reaction—shock, anger,
disgust—it would be a satisfying coda to the moment of
victory. And Imperious Leader very much wanted to
observe the arrogance of the Starbuck collapse.

Adama watched the attack of the Cylon task force on a
series of screens above the communications console.
Colonial vipers were fiercely engaged in a running battle
with the front ranks of the Cylon force. On a central
screen, he could see a wave of Cylon fighters sweeping
into position and firing their lasers in a wide-arced
multiplaned pattern of fire. Two colonial vipers shattered
into fragments and disintegrated in a consuming fire.
Athena, standing beside Adama, cursed under her breath
and clenched her fists. But there were only communications screens to hit.

A quartet of vipers peeled off from the main group as if
to flee, then abruptly turned and fired furiously at the

right flank of the attacking force. Lines of laser fire crossed and intersected, forming a brief asymmetric network of fine-lined light. A pair of Cylon ships fell from the rank and blew up, then a third, and a fourth. With each destroyed Cylon ship, Athena whispered encouragement to the vipers that had knocked them out. In a moment the screens seemed filled with exploding Cylon ships.

Although the *Galactica* squadrons had turned back the first line of Cylon attack, there were more warships in the distance. Tigh silently handed Adama a report which showed that the Cylon base ship had now entered the sector and was bearing down on the ragtag fleet at high speed.

Adama looked up from the report just in time to see a massive spear of light stabbing into space ahead of the battlestar. It had passed by them and narrowed to a dim line in the distance before anyone on the *Galactica* had had time to react to it. Another beam of light followed it, at a different angle, farther away. A third seemed dangerously close.

"They're sweeping the entire corridor with that laser cannon," Adama said to Tigh.

"Blue Squadron coming in," Athena reported. "Nine destroyed vipers, seven of them piloted by cadets. Seventeen too damaged to go out again right away, perhaps a dozen ready for another battle. Red Squadron reports similar damages."

"What about the Cylon forces?" Adama asked her.

"They're retreating. But more Cylon warships have entered the quadrant. Base ship not far behind."

Adama looked at Tigh, who nodded in agreement to the question on the commander's face.

"Our time is up, Colonel," Adama said, then turned to the bridge officer and ordered: "Flank speed ahead. We're going right through."

Another spear of light was too far in the distance to be threatening, but it went through that part of the sector that was right on the *Galactica*'s course.

"The expedition must have failed," Tigh said, the suggestion of tears in his eyes.

Adama glanced at the console timer.

"They still have six centons left," he said.

"Six centons," Athena whispered, and tried not to think that Apollo and Starbuck might be already frozen dead upon the planet.

Starbuck, dodging blasts of laser fire from Cylons defending the entranceway to the underground complex, felt quite the opposite of frozen. Heated by the burning materials around him in the destroyed command post, he felt warmer than at any time since he'd descended to the ice planet.

Ravashol's clones, driven by the kind of hatred that accumulates from a long oppression, had easily gained the advantage on the Cylons guarding the command post. Approaching the headquarters in white and gray furs, the clones had so blended in with the landscape that they had caught the enemy by surprise. Boomer and Starbuck held back until combat had begun in earnest, then they entered the fray, laser pistols drawn and shooting. After disposing of the guards, Starbuck leaped down into the corridor leading to the main underground complex. Boomer remained right behind him.

As they ran down the passageway, one of the Tennas caught up with them. A Cylon lumbered out of a side corridor. Reacting quickly, Tenna fired at it. Sparks from the wired suit flew as the Cylon fell.

A group of Cylons at the end of the corridor began firing at them. Starbuck, Boomer, and Tenna plunged to the ground.

"We're trapped," Boomer yelled, looking behind him at the fight raging between the Cylon command-post guards, then ahead at their new attackers.

"Over there," Starbuck cried, pointing to a hatchway on his left. "What's on the other side of that?"

"The cold cells where the Cylons hold prisoners," whispered Tenna.

"Prisoners? I asked you before where the prisoners were kept, you told me you didn't know."

Tenna's eyes widened, in surprise, then in amusement.

"You didn't ask *me*. You—"

"I know, I know. One of the others in the Ten series. All right, all right. Can you open that hatch?"

Tenna crawled over to it, and slowly began to turn the valve which opened the hatch. There was a small surprising squeak, and Starbuck tensed himself for what might spring out, aiming his laser pistol directly at the hatchway.

"There's bound to be guards," Tenna said.

"I'll take them. They're probably not used to people breaking into a prison."

As Tenna slowly opened the hatch, Starbuck eased himself through the narrow opening. He motioned for Boomer to follow. A blast of cold air quickly dissipated all the warmth he'd accumulated in the battle.

Cree had been concentrating on moving his head from side to side for some time. It was the only movement of which he was capable. He seemed to have lost contact with the rest of his body long ago, right after the Cylon guards had roughly dragged him to this chamber and pushed him into a tubular frost-gray cold cell. At first he had tried to keep his fingers and toes moving, but when they had turned completely numb he had started to do the exercise with his head and neck. Now he felt like stopping that, too.

His eyes were just beginning to droop shut when he saw a quick flash of movement to his right. He had just enough strength to look that way. A man was firing at the two Cylons who were standing guard in front of the triple row of cold cells. A colonial warrior, from the look of the outfit. Starbuck. It was Starbuck. Who was Starbuck? He could barely remember, even though the name had just flashed into his mind.

First one Cylon fell, then the other, both dropped by the crouching Starbuck. The clang of their metallic uniforms against the floor echoed through the cold-cell chamber. There seemed to be more movement on the right, but Cree found he could no longer turn his neck in that direction. For a moment he lost consciousness.

Suddenly he was awake again. Starbuck had broken open the door to Cree's cell and was pulling him out.

"Can you move?" Starbuck asked.

"Is he alive?" asked an attractive woman who stood behind Starbuck.

"Unless those tears in his eyes are self-generating, he's still with us."

Cree tried to talk but couldn't. Starbuck picked him up delicately, as if he were an expensive art item, and took him out of the cold-cell chamber. A rush of what seemed to be warm air in the corridor brought back feeling in Cree's toes and fingers. He tried to tell Starbuck. Although sound emerged from Cree's frozen lips, Starbuck said he couldn't understand what the young cadet was saying.

Gradually Cree became aware that combat was raging all around them. He tried to force his hand to reach toward his holster to draw out his pistol, then remembered that the Cylons had disarmed him when he'd first been captured.

Starbuck left him leaning against a wall inside a dark niche, like a sculpture propped up in a dusty forgotten museum storeroom. As he listened to the sounds of battle outside, Cree became aware of the feeling coming back into his body. When he was aware of the blood flowing through his body again, he knew he would be all right.

Starbuck returned to the niche. The lieutenant's face was grimy with dirt.

"Can you walk?" he asked Cree.

"I can try."

"Well, you better, cadet. I leave you here, the Cylons we missed might get you. If we missed any. C'mon, we're going to liberate an elevator."

"An elevator? I don't—"

"Don't worry about it. I just need the manpower. Maybe if the Cylons see *you*, they'll drop their guns and surrender."

"Drop guns? Surrender? Lieutenant—"

Starbuck seized Cree and pulled him out of the dark niche.

Loud noises above and below frightened the clone children, made them gather together in tight little groups and crouch against walls, hide behind piles of fur. At each vibrating noise, Muffit ran toward the doorway and hopped up and down. It looked like it wanted to bark, but

Boxey had ordered it not to, and Muffit was nothing if not obedient.

The doorway slid open slowly. One of the pretty women came through it, and told the children to be especially quiet. Alerted by the action at the garrison headquarters, some Cylons were roaming the corridors, looking for the agitators. Afraid, all the children nodded they would be quiet, and the woman went out again.

Boxey got down on his haunches by the doorway and listened. At first he could hear nothing; then—after another of the loud rumbling noises—he could hear the gravelly mechanical nasality that he knew was a Cylon voice. They were in the outer chamber. One of them thumped accidentally against the doorway. The woman was saying something to them, something about not knowing what was happening and would they please not violate her privacy. Another thump on the door, and he thought he could hear a Cylon asking what was on the other side of that entranceway. Boxey signaled the other children to come to him. Reluctantly they approached the doorway and Boxey told them:

"We might got to get out of here. If that door opens, we got to run. Muffit?"

The daggit-droid pivoted its head toward Boxey.

"You lead the way, you hear, daggit?"

Muffit responded with the low growl that was his programmed vocal response to a whispered instruction. Boxey crouched by the doorway, wondering if his dad or Starbuck would be proud of the way he took command just like a colonial warrior should.

Suddenly the door was ripped open. All Boxey saw was a Cylon gloved hand at the edge of the door before he quickly sprang into action. Hollering, "Okay, Muffy, now!" he barreled through the doorway, gesturing to the clone children to follow him. Muffit leaped right at the legs of the Cylon who'd opened the door, and tripped him. The Cylon's metal suit was ripped open by the jagged boulder he fell upon. The other Cylons, astonished by the fact that it was children attacking them, made futile grabs at the small forms scampering past them. But Cylons, in their heavy metallic suits, tended to be awkward in movement, and not a single child was captured by the cumbersome giants.

In the corridor, Boxey ran left, shouting:

"This way!"

He knew that his father or Starbuck would have led their troops with a shouted command like that. The only trouble was, he didn't know where he was going. Muffit dashed ahead. The best bet, Boxey figured, was to follow the daggit.

Muffit led them through several corridors, stopping every once in a while when there were Cylons in the vicinity. The slightest noise that sounded like a Cylon patrol marching near them made the children crouch behind rocks and hide in the alcoves. The loud noises that shook the walls of the corridors and caused rains of dirt and small rocks kept sounding regularly.

Finally the daggit stopped beside a hatchway whose portal had been loosened by one of the jarring explosive noises. Very cold air seeped in through the tiny spaces around the hatchway edge.

"It's cold out there, Muffy," Boxey said.

The daggit-droid growled in response but edged toward the hatchway and pointed its snout a little way out.

"But you think it's our best chance. Right, Muffy?"

Muffy growled again.

"Okay, we'll try it. I guess everybody's warm enough." Boxey glanced around at his squad of clone children. All of them were securely wrapped in fur outfits like the clothing that one of the pretty women had put on Boxey. But it still might be too cold. Maybe they should just head down the corridor. Suddenly there was the sound of a marching Cylon patrol coming toward them. Obviously Muffy was right. They had to go outside. Boxey got two of the larger children to push open the hatchway so they could all get out; then he gestured his squad to leave the corridor for the surface of the ice world.

It *was* cold outside, but not as cold as it had been earlier, when the *Galactica* team had first arrived on the planet. Boxey didn't know where they should go now. A fire raged in the distance, across the ice field. It was the only light, so Boxey decided they should go toward it. A moment later, the sky itself suddenly lit up like a flare, and he could see the building where the fire was raging. It wasn't that far away. They could make it.

The trek across the ice field was harder than Boxey had expected. Muffit kept returning from his guide position ahead and herding the children together, prodding them forward. Just when Boxey felt he was getting too sleepy to go any farther, they reached the edge of a field that wasn't covered by ice. Much of the rock underneath was showing. Some of the rock surface had scorch marks on it. Boxey looked up. It was an airfield. Arranged in rows were several Cylon fighters. Beyond the ships, inside the Cylon command post, the fire was now blazing out of control. They couldn't go inside there, Boxey realized. He looked again at the Cylon ships, dark silhouettes against the background of the fire. They looked warm and inviting.

"Get inside the ships," Boxey ordered the children, and they began scrambling into the nearest fighters. One child reported back that they were indeed warm enough inside. Boxey went ahead farther, Muffit scampering at his heels. He chose a ship at the end of a line, where he would have a good vantage point if any Cylons came toward them. As he climbed into it, he was surprised at how empty it was inside, not at all like the complicated technological insides of a viper or of the holograms of Cylon ships that Apollo had shown him. It didn't seem real; it seemed like the ghost of a ship. But, unlike a ghost, it was warm, and that was what was important. Nestling his fur suit against Muffit's fur, he curled into a ball and tried to maintain a watchful eye out of a side porthole of the ship. He remembered that this was where the Cylon navigator sat. It was nice. Comfortable. Warm.

He felt sleepy.

He was asleep.

CHAPTER TWENTY-THREE

Croft:

At first all I can think of is how foolish I feel at having told Apollo there was almost no chance of an avalanche. Of course this is just the sort of avalanche I'd warned him about, loose snow set rolling by a loud explosive sound. What am I doing worrying about how foolish I might've looked? What'll Apollo care about that when he's examining my blackened, crushed corpse? What am I thinking about, corpse? He'll never come looking for me. I'll just go up with the laser cannon when it explodes. If it explodes. God, the laying of solenite's up to Leda now, and all that's on her mind is escape.

Why am I worrying about Leda and Apollo? Got to start worrying about *myself*. Already I'm moving my arms in a swimming motion, seeking the surface of this crush of snow. It's important not to panic. Hold my breath. Find an opening of air, find the surface. I shake my ice-ax off my arm, work the pack off my back to lighten myself, give me the lightness to swim to the top of the snow. Don't panic. Keep the arms and legs moving. Grab at anything for leverage upward. Clear breathing space in front of me with my hands, take quick breaths, keep going upward.

I can't do it. I must be too deep under. Can't do it. Must keep trying. Keep trying until I die. It's that simple. Death, simple when you get the hang of it. Keep the arms going, thrusting upward, reaching for life, reaching for anything I can grab, reaching. My hand breaks the surface. I make my arms work even harder. My head doesn't seem able to get there. It should be there by now, should break clear. Why isn't it breaking clear?

Suddenly I realize I have broken the surface, perhaps for some time, and I take a breath.

Everything around me is still; then the sky lights up with another pulse from the laser gun. Now at least I'm oriented. I haven't fallen far. I'm lucky. I should be halfway down the mountain.

"Croft!"

That's Apollo's voice. Where is he? By the light of another pulse I see that he's a short distance above me, descending by rope from the ledge I fell from.

Working my legs slowly and steadily, I pull my whole body to the snow surface. Apollo, belayed by Leda back on the ledge, is laboriously making his way toward me, testing the surface in front of him with touches of his ice-ax. I pull myself into a semicrouch, enough to dig my crampons into the loose surface. God, how I wish now this planet had some kind of sun. It'd be wonderful to feel the brittle kind of surface that comes from a sun melting ice and the ice then reforming. More friction for the crampons. Still I make my way toward Apollo. He reaches a gloved hand toward me. Reaching up, I can just about touch him. One more tough step, then . . . Got him! With a fierce jerk of his arm he pulls me toward him, and I grab onto the rope. My eyes search the line of rope all the way up to Leda's belay. It looks all right.

"Slack," I holler up to Leda. She lets out more rope.

"You all right?" I ask Apollo.

"Was about to ask you the same thing."

"I'm fine. I'm surprised you came down to get me. What'll this do to the timing of the mission?"

Apollo smiles.

"We need you to lay the explosives, Croft. Had to come get you."

"Sorry, didn't mean to take a cheap shot at you. You're doing all right, Apollo. That was quick thinking back there, cutting the rope. You might've all been dragged down with me."

"Just did what you taught me."

"Well, it was good. You probably should've left me under the snow, but thanks."

"Just get that gun for me, okay?"

For a moment, I'm amused by the moral ambiguity of my position. I've told Wolfe and Leda I'm with them in their escape plan, even if I didn't know for sure whether I was. Now I tell Apollo I'll get the damn gun, even though I'm still inclined to take off with Wolfe and Leda. When we get to the top of Hekla, if we get to the top of Hekla, I may even be surprised by my own decision. Pulling at the rope, I yell up to Leda:

"Climbing!"

"Climb!" Leda yells back. And slowly Apollo and I ascend to the ledge.

Ser 5–9 and Tenna seem glad to see me alive. Wolfe's not so sure, I think. Leda's eyes are as blank as Thane's ever were. Does she really mean it when she hints we can get back together? Or is that just a ploy to gain my help? Ploy or not, Leda can be depended on to fulfill her promises. Should I care whether or not she does it willingly or just to complete a bargain? It would be easier if I didn't care, but—unfortunately—I do.

The rest of the climb presents few problems. The avalanche seems to have made it easier. There are hundreds of small ledges, footholds and handholds, that allow us to make it to the level of the gun emplacement in free climbing. Intermittently, the gun fires and its light shows us the route ahead. In a sense, the pulses from the gun are helping us to make up the time we lost, aiding us in its own destruction.

In the last stages, as if driven toward it, Wolfe and Leda lead the way to the gun emplacement itself. Then they turn, their figures ill-defined in the shadows. It is a moment before I realize that Wolfe has his laser drawn and is pointing it at the rest of us.

"If we go," he says to Leda, "it has to be now."

"I'm with you," she says, moving to his side and staring at me, looking for my response. I stop climbing and Apollo passes me as if he doesn't know there's a laser pistol pointed at his head. Pulling himself up to the level of the gun emplacement and standing up a short distance away from Wolfe, Apollo says:

"There's nowhere you can go, Wolfe."

"You didn't look careful enough, Captain, or you would've seen the Cylon ship anchored just over there."

He gestures to the left. Sure enough, the ship rests there, held down by electronic anchoring rays that give off occasional sparkles in the dim mountain light. I start climbing directly at Wolfe.

"We're getting off this piece of ice, Captain," Wolfe says, "and flying right out of—"

"There isn't *time*," Apollo says. "Don't you understand"—he points to his chronometer—"the *Galactica* is passing through the quadrant right *now*. We've got to silence that gun."

"You got a one-track mind, Captain." Wolfe's smile is grim, sinister. "You think I care about what happens to the *Galactica*?"

Apollo takes a step toward Wolfe. I keep climbing, my eye on Wolfe.

"The *Galactica* is the only ship that can protect you. *All* of you." He looks desperately at Wolfe and Leda, squints down at me. "Without us, you're finished."

Leda smiles. In the dim light, there's a lot of evil in that smile.

"You don't seem to realize who is finished here, Captain," she says. "Your mission. Your battlestar. Yourself."

I keep climbing.

"The Cylons won't rest until every one of us is put to death," Apollo says. "Every one of *you*."

"Don't worry about us," Wolfe says. "We're going to make it. We've been through just as tough. We'll make it."

"To where?"

Wolfe's voice drops, is just barely audible:

"Well, now, that isn't really going to matter a whole lot to you."

I'm up to the ledge now. I pull myself onto it, next to Leda, on the other side of Wolfe and Apollo.

"The Ice Gang's together again," Leda mutters. "What's left of it, anyway."

I nod.

"Glad you're with us, Croft. I wanted you back on my side."

When she says this, I am so tempted to be with Leda again that I almost grab the gun from Wolfe to shoot down Apollo myself. Apollo is clearly shocked seeing me stand up with my former gang.

"I should've expected this from you, Croft," he says. Looking down at Ser 5-9 and Tenna, who are still on the mountainside but slowly ascending, he says, "Stay back."

"Should I drop him, Croft?" Wolfe says, aiming his pistol toward Apollo's chest. I am surprised. It's been a long time since Wolfe last treated me as a leader. I almost like it.

"No," I say to Wolfe. "Give these people a fair chance. We'll just get to the Cylon ship and—"

"Fair chance?" Leda says. "That's still your trouble, isn't it, Croft? Always the humanitarian. Okay, so be it, let's—"

Above us, the pulsar gun roars. The sound is thunderous, feels like it's loud enough to kill. The vibration makes Wolfe lose footing for a brief moment, and he steadies himself by holding onto the emplacement wall with his free hand. It's my chance. I jump at Wolfe, getting a boot behind one of his stubby legs and tripping him up. He falls to the ground next to me. Inadvertently he fires the pistol, and its ray goes upward, looking strangely feeble against the bright light of the pulse shooting toward the cloud cover. I slam his arm against the emplacement wall. The pistol goes flying. Apollo picks it up. Knowing I'm at a disadvantage in fighting Wolfe, I spring away from him, go to Apollo's side.

"Your play, Captain," I say.

"For a moment there, Croft, I believed you."

"Believed myself. For a moment."

Apollo smiles.

"Even after all that, I still don't know whether or not to trust you."

"Better for you if you don't, Captain. I wouldn't."

Wolfe pulls himself up slowly, glaring at me. His hatred of me seems to have doubled, if that's possible. I'd hate to have to compute the degree to which Leda's hatred has grown.

"Croft!" she says. "That was our chance! We had to take it! And you, you—"

"Leda," I say, "I don't know how to make you understand. You can blame it on humanitarianism if you like, although I doubt if most straights'd care to call me that. But, look, we're here on a mission. When I accepted the mission, and you came with me, you were accepting it, too. I don't know what's got into you, but think: this is a mission to save what's left of the human race, what's left of a civilization that prospered for millennia on the twelve worlds. We can't let the remnants of the race die for our own selfish goals. So we're going to do this. You understand that, both of you? This mission is going *through*! And the two of you are going to help, understand?"

"A pretty speech, Croft," Leda says, "but I'm sitting here and watching. You can't make me do any—"

"All right. We're not a team anymore, Leda, okay. I guess the break in that came long ago, and it was probably my fault. All right. Deals. Both of you understand deals. Once we get the explosives planted, the timer set, and the Cylons effectively out of action, you two can have that ship, go anywhere you want, be *free*."

"Croft, I don't—" Apollo says.

"That's the way we'll do it, Apollo. You get your gun blown up, Leda and Wolfe get the ship. It's the only way everybody gets what they want. You can forget about the warbook fighting codes up here."

"And you, Croft," Leda says, stepping forward. "Where do you go? What do you do? What do you get?"

I want to tell her that I want her, but it's no good. You can't get Leda to give herself, no matter what deal you offer. She needs to be free, all right, I'll give her that.

"I stay with Apollo, with him and Ser 5-9 and Tenna. We'll take the elevator out of there. While we're on the way down, you two'll have plenty of time to take off and go...go wherever you can find that pleases you."

I look away from her piercing gaze and survey the panorama below us. There is nothing exceptional to see, nothing worth climbing this mountain for. Under normal conditions, with ample time for planning, it's an easy mountain, an easy climb, not worth the effort. The ice planet itself is ugly. Nothing on it is as beautiful as where we stand now, at the top of the mountain, next to an awesome weapon which we plan to blow to pieces moments from now.

"Come with *us*," Leda says, her voice offering nothing more than the trip.

I almost throw out all my fancy reasons and say yes anyway.

"Nope, Leda."

"Why not, Croft?"

"Can't say. Something about being responsible. Something about knocking out this weapon for whatever you want to call it, the common good or the salvation of—"

"Shut up, Croft. You just want to play hero, be he-man, copy this scanner-screen image of a warrior here..." She points to Apollo, who shows no reaction. "Well, okay. Just don't give me any of your he-man speeches. We do the job because we're professionals; don't mouth off about anything else. We do it because we're the ones who can do it. You can have the glory of humankind and sprinkle it on your crops as fertilizer. We accept your deal. Okay, Wolfe?"

Wolfe sullenly agrees.

"All right, then," Leda says. "Let's get to it."

Apollo steps forward, says:

"The *Galactica*'s time is running out."

As if to punctuate his remark, another pulse—perhaps the one destined to turn the *Galactica* into space ash—is emitted from the bore of the laser cannon.

"Get the explosives together," I say. "Then we get moving."

Apollo—who, after all, has taken a lot of bilge from me in the past few moments—hesitates, then nods.

"Okay," he says. "You're in charge, Croft. Get us into that pulsar station."

"You got it, Captain."

Working silently, we get the stuff together, each taking his assigned load, Leda and I splitting what Thane would have carried. Thane. I'd almost forgotten about him. What difference would it have made to the cause of Leda and Wolfe if he'd been there? What difference would it have made for my own decision? I had always really been afraid of Thane. One thing sure. Thane wouldn't have listened to reason, and he would have given the Ice Gang the edge they needed to succeed in their escape. Perhaps I couldn't have so easily stood on this godforsaken ledge and made my noble speeches and swung them to Apollo's side. If Thane had been there, perhaps I'd have gone with them. Well, no use worrying about that now, not with the job waiting to be done.

Circling around the emplacement, we arrive at the entrance to the intake tube. It opens onto a dark tunnel.

"This intake tube opens into the cooling system," I say to the rest. "The laser is inside. We've got to place the solenite just right. Our supply's a bit depleted, my fault. I let some of it go, sorry. Back in the avalanche when I released my pack. Matter of priorities. I put saving myself over preserving the solenite."

"You're prone to *mistakes* like that," Leda says, with the first smile I've seen from her in some time.

"According to Ravashol's geogram," Apollo says, "the key element is the energy-exchange pump. If we can wreck it, the cannon will overload and blow itself up."

"Sounds good to me. You and Wolfe and the clones hold off the Cylons, and Leda and I can lay the wire, set the timer. Let's take a look."

We crawl inside the intake-tube tunnel. It's narrow and we have to crouch down. I feel like an insect eating my way through insulation. Suddenly the walls of the tunnel begin to tremble as the laser sweep of the gun gathers intensity.

"Hang on!" Apollo shouts. "They're using the intake."

As the wind pulls through the tunnel, it's like being

outside in a mountain blizzard. Holding onto the side
walls, we are able to continue on. A sweep of vapor passes
us, and I hold my breath, not knowing what it's composed
of. When the laser emits its next pulse, the sound seems to
reverberate in the tunnel for an eternity, threatening to
diminish only when deafness has set in. But it stops after
the firing.

Up ahead is a grid that must be used as an entrance for
maintenance purposes. We crawl to it and Apollo pushes
it open. On the other side we can see the immensity of the
laser station's interior. The weapon, a mammoth dark
gray cylinder, dominates the center of the chamber.
Spreading down from its base is a central control shaft
around which several Cylons are working. Huge pillars
support domes in which the energy sources are apparently
collected. In the Cylon manner of illumination, lights
along the high castlelike walls shift irregularly in
intensity. It looks like a room in which nightmares are
stored.

A group of officers gather around some kind of
console, directing the action of the gun. Beyond them is
another officer, looking very much like them, except he's
got a lot more bands of black decorating his silver-
metallic uniform. The decoration, if I remember
correctly, identifies him as a first centurion. He's the chief
honcho, then, the one especially to watch out for. Apollo
leans toward me and whispers:

"The firing station in the center . . ."

"Yeah."

"It controls the energy pump."

"That's our target, then," Leda says grimly.

"Right," Apollo says.

"If I get you right, Apollo," I say, "we blow that and the
whole system overloads. I don't know if you realize it, but
it's also going to tear off the top of the mountain. Before I
set the timer, you better have that escape elevator secured.
I don't want to have to wait for it to arrive from the first
floor, buddy."

Apollo closes the grid and gawks at his ever-present
timepiece. The wrist device glows in the dark, and flickers
a bit as its coordinates change.

"Three centons," he whispers. "I hope Starbuck and Boomer are at the elevator by now, or else we'll have to take the fighter."

"Listen, Apollo, I promised the ship to Wolfe and—"

"If it means survival, all promises are off. Don't worry. I'll let your friends have the ship as soon as we're off the mountain. What's the matter?"

"I been worrying about how much trust you can have in me. I forgot to worry about whether or not I could trust you."

"You can't."

"I realize that now. You make a good member of the Ice Gang, Apollo."

"Thanks, I think."

The chief honcho barks something in that typical Cylon voice that sounds like a series of electric shorts. The other officers react and work some devices in their respective equipment. A surge of power resounds through the room.

"They're stepping up the rate of pulses," Apollo whispers. "They must know the *Galactica*'s entered the quadrant, maybe even know its coordinates."

"We're ready when you are, Captain."

Gently Apollo lifts the grid. Gesturing to Wolfe, Ser 5-9, and Tenna to follow him, he slips out the opening. Wolfe pushes Ser 5-9 aside. Once the combat's begun, Wolfe's always extra-eager to get into the fray, no matter whose side he thinks he's on. The two clones follow Wolfe out, and for a moment Leda and I are alone. Leda is carefully not looking at me. She adjusts her grip on the coil of solenite wire and waits, like me, for the shooting to start. I lean toward her and whisper:

"I'd go with you, Leda, but—"

"I don't want to hear about it."

And that about defines our relationship at the moment. This is the point toward which the years of love and working together were heading. It all comes to this. I want to say it, and you don't want to hear it. If you wanted to hear it, I wouldn't have to say it.

With a series of sudden hisses, the shooting begins in the emplacement-gun chamber. I jump through the grid

opening, Leda right behind me. Out of the corner of my
eye I can see Apollo blasting away from behind one of the
pillars. He drops a couple of Cylons with a pair of perfect
shots. Although I can't see them, I can figure where the
others are by the three pillars from which the other laser
fire is coming. The Cylon gunners and warriors guarding
them are trying to assemble into some order. Staying
close to the wall, Leda and I seem to have escaped their
notice. A communications device near us suddenly
explodes from being hit by a stray Cylon shot, and Leda
and I dive to the floor. Leda crawls by me, directly to the
base of the energy-exchange pump. Efficiently, without a
look at the battle raging around her, she begins to lay the
wire. I scamper to the other side of the pump and begin
putting down my wire, but I sense a movement to my
right. Glancing up, I see a Cylon coming at me, his
weapon drawn. Twisting around slightly, I bring out my
laser pistol and drop him. Like most Cylons, he falls with
a clumsy-sounding thump. No other Cylon seems to have
detected my presence. Good. I can't allow them to have
too much time while we're escaping. Solenite wire sticks
to the side of metal without even a loop of air showing in
it, and it's virtually uncuttable by normal means—but I
don't know what equipment these creeps might have. If
they're able to disconnect the wires, or enough of them,
the gun won't go up. But if we can hold them off until the
timer's set, then it's unlikely they'll be able to move fast
enough to save the gun.

I return to my work, feeling an odd glow of satisfaction
from the professional way I lay down the wire.
Everything's working out well. At least on our part. I
haven't time to check out how Apollo's attack is working
out. There are sufficient notches and outjuttings to wrap
the wire around, enough concave area in which to plant
the explosive charges. The wire adheres easily to the flat
surfaces of the pump.

Crawling underneath the pump through an arched
tunnel that leads to an energy feeder, I begin to attach the
timer there. Leda crawls into the tunnel from her side and
methodically leads her wire toward the timer. While I
manipulate the switches of the timer, she attaches the ends
of her wires to it.

"How's it going on your side?" I ask her.

"Good. Apollo and Wolfe're dropping the creatures left and right. A couple of them seemed to see what we were up to, but they were dropped before they got near to me."

"Okay. Everything's set. Look out and see if Apollo's got the elevator ready."

She crawls out and is back right away.

"He's doing something with the controls beside the doorway. But it's not open yet."

"Then we wait."

I glance over at her. Her face is now tense.

"You and Wolfe'll be in the air in a couple of microns. Maybe we'll all meet again sometime, in some exotic out-planet bar or—"

"I'll look again."

She comes back and says the way to the elevator is clear. Nodding, I flick the switch that irrevocably sets the timer. Now the Cylons can tear at the solenite all they wish. There's nothing they can do. The gun's going to go.

FROM THE ADAMA JOURNALS:

Ila and I used to enjoy going to the theater at least once or twice during each of my rare furloughs. She recognized my need for escape and usually selected comedies or musical entertainments. But once in a while, to satisfy Ila, we went to a tragedy.

Caprican tragedy contained one significant variation over the tragedies created in the rest of the twelve worlds—the added feature of the alternative ending. The alternative ending was intended as a kind of release following the emotional drain of the sad or awesome events of the play proper. Some audience members didn't stay around for it, claiming that the proper reaction to the fate of the tragic hero or heroine was to purge ourselves by participating emotionally in the tragedy. But I always enjoyed the alternative endings, bizarre as some of them were. Generally, they showed what the lives of their hero or heroine would have been like if they had surmounted or survived the dramatic events that had propelled them toward their disaster. Often their lives were shown as serene, their experiences having brought them emotional and intellectual growth as human beings. Because of what seemed to me a forced optimism in such an ending, I much preferred the other traditional alternative, in which the playwright generally showed that the complications of life (and, by implication, drama) continued to affect or plague the characters, although usually in not as nobly tragic a way as the main drama. I liked that. I liked the idea that we were all expected to continue the drama of our own lives past major crisis points, and had to renew our hopes, fears, and mysterious expectations on a regular basis.

Ila said such a reaction suited me, since after the pleasant intervals of furlough I always had to return to my own continuing tragedy, the war with the Cylons. She preferred the meaningful single crisis, the test of nobility or even merely of the dimensions of character, over the uncertain extensions of the alternative ending. She may have had something there. Whatever, she's dead now, away from suffering—while I have to confront one major crisis after another. I sometimes consider alternative endings—ones where the Cylons give up, or we finally destroy them, or a mysterious third force interferes and decides the outcome for us. Even more, I would rather not consider tragedy at all. Ila, I needed you here now, I needed that particular alternative ending.

CHAPTER TWENTY-FOUR

When he was informed that contact with the command post in the Hekla foothills had been lost, Vulpa was disturbed but not worried. Abrupt storms on the mountainside frequently interfered with communication between headquarters and summit station. Nevertheless, the interference was inconvenient at this moment. Just before communications were interrupted, Vulpa had been informed that objects appearing to be a battlestar and a number of smaller ships had entered the quadrant. A preliminary fix had been established, and Vulpa had directed that the weapon be set to send pulses toward that fix. There was a good chance the *Galactica* had already been destroyed. He ordered the emplacement communications officer to continue attempts to contact headquarters, and asked the gunnery master for more power and a faster pulse rate from the gun itself.

As he listened to the satisfying thunder of the laser-gun-pulse releases, Vulpa considered how he would return in triumph to Imperious Leader's base ship. He would have to be decorated, another thin-lined black band around the shoulder, or perhaps the more prestigious award of a thicker band at waist level....

He very nearly missed the beginning of the humans' attack. There was a brief flash of movement near an intake tube, and Vulpa turned to see a human leaping from behind an energy pillar, his laser pistol drawn and already firing. A Cylon gunner fell. Another human jumped out of the intake tube and fired. A trio of Cylon officers, Vulpa's bodyguard, gathered around him and almost blocked his line of sight toward the attackers. Two more figures jumped out of the grid opening. Vulpa could not believe what he saw. Unless they were humans in disguise, these were two of Ravashol's clones. And they were helping the human attackers!

The chamber was quickly filled with the blazing light and floating steam of the attack. Fire and crossfire obscured any sensible view of the action for Vulpa. To his left, one of his guards fell, his uniform on fire. For a moment Vulpa was fascinated with the corpse, clearly dead but with the red light in his helmet still actively piercing the layers of smoke. The humans, always more agile than Cylons, seemed to be leaping everywhere, taking up new positions behind new pillars. Gunners and warriors were falling at a rate near that of the now accelerated pulse rate of the laser cannon. The reserve squad of warriors from the garrison rooms joined the battle.

Vulpa's center bodyguard fell. The remaining guard pushed his commander back against the wall and started firing at anything that moved toward him, as if he did not care whether his target was human or Cylon as long as they did not endanger the commander. But a line of laser fire hit the last bodyguard at neck level. Sparks shot out from the wiring leading to his helmet and he tried to get off one more shot before dropping heavily to the floor. Vulpa, clinging to the wall, started easing his way along it, toward the elevator.

The smoke cleared momentarily and he saw that three of the humans were now gathered around the elevator, fending off attackers. Vulpa, drawing his pistol, tried to take aim on the tall young man who was the apparent leader, but one of his own warriors got in the way. Vulpa had to retreat. This was no time to get into the battle. His ship, he must get to his ship, alert the rest of the garrison at the command post, bring them back here to repel this strange quartet of human attackers. What were they doing here anyway? he thought as he ran toward the tube leading to his aircraft. Why did they want to destroy the small number of Cylons at the gun? The gun! Were they going to try to do something to the gun? They could not stop it so long as it was set on automatic. Only Vulpa or the gunnery master could do that. And the gun could not be destroyed—Ravashol had stated firmly that the material composing the gun was indestructible. The mechanism was too complex for them to tamper with in any way. Ravashol had provided the factor that allowed only specially imprinted gloved Cylon hands to operate the shut-off plate which would stop the gun's automatic steady firing. Ravashol had vowed that—but Ravashol was also responsible for the clones. He had been their protector, in fact, when the Cylons had wanted all batches destroyed. And now two of Ravashol's clones were involved in this sneak attack! If he had lied about the clones, then perhaps he had lied about the gun.

Vulpa felt an impulse to protect the gun, but the battle raging behind him was too fierce. He risked too much—his squadrons of warriors, the gun emplacement, himself, his ambition—to chance getting killed checking out such a suspicion. The important goal was to board his ship and gather troops to return here and vanquish the humans.

He looked back. How could only four attackers do so much damage? Cylons had fallen everywhere, it seemed. Smoke and fluttering sparks flew up from their bodies. Their red lights dimmed and went out. But this was no time to mourn the fallen. The official mourning would come later, in proper organized ceremonies. Vulpa turned to run through the gangway tunnel to his ship.

And found a short stocky human blocking his way and aiming a laser pistol at him. Vulpa threw himself against the wall as the human fired.

•   •   •

The light-spears were now coming toward the fleet with shorter time intervals between them. A supply ship had been hit and apparently swallowed up by the powerful beam. By quick alterations of course, the *Galactica* had missed being hit twice.

Athena studied her father's grim face. He stood at his post, gripping the railing that ran in front of him, and seemed stymied by the laser cannon's fierce attacks.

"Is there anything we can do to counter the force of the pulses?" he asked Tigh. The aide shook his head no.

"We've analyzed them from every angle, looked for some way to anticipate them, but we simply don't have sufficient data. If only the expedition had been able to—"

"Don't give up hope yet. The expedition may still be functioning."

Tigh seemed about to protest, but instead returned to duty. Athena knew that the colonel, knowing the efficiency with which Apollo worked, did not expect her brother to stretch out the mission time to the last possible micron. She hoped Tigh was wrong. But she could not help but feel despair over the mission. If they were going to destroy the cannon, they should have done it by now, they should—

Her thoughts on the subject were rudely interrupted by a light-spear that passed so near the *Galactica* that Athena was certain that, if she had time go out and check the superstructure surface, she'd discover singe marks there.

Imperious Leader was pleased with the progress of the attack. The trap was just about sprung. The *Galactica* had been forced into the quadrant where the pulses from the laser weapon would be most effective. He had ordered that the coordinates of the *Galactica* be transmitted regularly to Vulpa on the ice planet, then had continued the pursuit of his own fleet after the human ships.

Just after the coordinates had been transmitted, the Cylon fleet had lost contact with the garrison on Tairac. That was an annoyance, but a slight one. The *Galactica* was definitely trapped between the pursuit force and the ultimate weapon. There was no way it could escape.

Why was the Starbuck simulacrum, who had been informed of each phase of the action, and had to know that annihilation was imminent, grinning and keeping so quiet?

CHAPTER TWENTY-FIVE

Croft:

I don't expect what I see when I crawl out of the tunnel under the gun. Dead Cylons are lying all over the place. Apollo is gesturing toward the elevator. I start running toward it. Leda splits off away from me, toward the tunnel to the Cylon ship. I try not to look at her go. Then she stops running and yells:

"Croft!"

By the entrance to the tunnel, Wolfe is struggling with a Cylon. It's the officer, the chief honcho with all the decorations on his uniform. A section of his black-banded sleeve is sizzling—Wolfe's obviously fired at him, but missed. Now the Cylon creep's all over him. Wolfe still has his pistol, but it's pointing futilely upward toward the ceiling. He fires it once, and I hear the crackling of a destroyed light source above me. The Cylon picks Wolfe up, holds him with his feet dangling above the floor. My God! I never knew a Cylon could be that strong. He's Wolfe's match all the way. Leda tries to leap at the Cylon,

but the louse seems to anticipate her move and slides out
of her way while still clutching Wolfe. I start running
toward them, laser drawn and pointed in the Cylon's
direction, waiting for a clear shot at him. The Cylon's
holding Wolfe in front of him now. If I shoot I'm more
likely to get Wolfe. Leda, in better position, grips the
handle of her pistol to get a steady aim, but the Cylon
moves Wolfe's body a bit to the right toward her, blocking
her line of shot. He's using Wolfe as a shield.

Backing into a tunnel, he keeps his attention on both
Leda and me. Picking up Wolfe even higher, he squeezes
him in a fierce one-armed embrace. I can hear bones crack
inside Wolfe's body. The Cylon forces his other gloved
hand between himself and Wolfe's head. He pushes
Wolfe's head backward, breaking his neck. Then he tosses
Wolfe toward Leda, as if the body were a light bundle.
For a moment, my reflexes go bad on me; I can't really
comprehend what the Cylon officer has done. I never
could beat Wolfe in a fight, except for that once. This
Cylon creep has disposed of him in an instant. I start
chasing after the Cylon finally, firing wildly. Ahead in the
tunnel, the Cylon doesn't even look back. He's in his ship
and the tunnel's closed off before I can squeeze off a shot
at the ship's fueling area. The tunnel rumbles and
detaches from the ship. I feel the floor slipping out from
under me. I scramble backward, reach the main chamber
just in time. I would've slid downward through the
gangway tunnel and found myself back on the mountain
with nothing to do but kill time and wait for the explosion
to kill me.

Leda is kneeling beside Wolfe, trying to find some
miracle in her medical training she can use to restore him.
I grab her arm, try to pull her away. She resists, and I can't
budge her.

"He's dead, Leda."

"I know."

"Let's go."

She stands up, looks down at the corpse briefly, sadly.

"He was a killer, Leda, just a—"

"I know, and he was such a rotten bilge-rat I don't
know why I'm sad, why—let's get out of here."

We run to the elevator. Apollo pushes us inside, then he and Ser 5-9 back in, firing furiously at the few remaining Cylons. Tenna, firing off a few shots to the side, runs in just after them, and the doors close behind her. All of the technology on the elevator is of Cylon manufacture, but Apollo apparently knows something about it, because he pushes the right plates and we begin descending.

"How are we for time?" I ask Apollo.

"I'm not sure. Lost a little there at the last moment."

"Won't the blast cut the cable if we don't reach the lower level in time?"

"It might. We'll find out."

I'll say one thing for the Cylons, they sure know how to build elevators. This one moves downward so smoothly, it's impossible to tell what our descent speed is. I hope it's fast, I surely do. Leda has folded her tall broad body into a back corner of the elevator car. Her eyes are vacant, her mouth slack. Tenna whispers to her, evidently trying to say something comforting, but Leda isn't having any, and she regally gestures Tenna away. Taking off her gloves, she wipes her forehead with the back of her hand, dabs at her cheeks. Sweat is running off her. Running off all of us, in fact.

Apollo keeps his gaze fixed on the old chronometer. I try to interpret the strange flashes of light on the hexagons of the elevator control board. There's no way of telling whether or not we'll make it to the bottom in time.

"How much time?" I ask Apollo.

Without taking his eyes off his timepiece, he says: "Ten microns."

"You have any idea whether this elevator's out of range of the blast?"

"Can't say. Maybe."

"Hopeful, anyway."

"Eight microns."

Copying Apollo, I set my jaw at grim. The only sound in the elevator car is Apollo's whispering countdown. He reaches one, and we all tense. There is a long silence.

"Maybe I did something wrong with the—" I say.

But I am interrupted by the explosion. It's a deep

rumbling blast followed by a series of increasingly louder ones. The chain-reaction effect of the solenite is proceeding according to plan. I can interpret the sounds of solenite as precisely as an average person can detect changes in a melody.

At the loudest explosion, the elevator stops abruptly. My legs feel like they're being pushed through the floor. Ser 5–9 does fall, knocking against Apollo and Tenna. Apollo grabs at the control panel and steadies himself.

The explosions stop. We all take a simultaneous deep breath and I seem to feel the floor of the elevator swaying beneath me.

"Are we falling?" I ask Apollo.

"No. But something's loose somewhere. I don't know if—"

"Captain Apolllloooo!" cries a voice below us. The sound is faint but clear. Apollo, amazed, looks at me.

"That's Starbuck's voice," he says, then crouches down near the doorway and shouts downward, "We're up here, Starbuck. Can you hear me?"

"Pretty good, Captain. Think I can see you. You're about fifty meters above us. Looks to me like there's a maintenance ledge about...about twenty meters below you. If you can get to that, there's a sort of ladder."

"Okay, Starbuck, thanks. We'll be right down. Keep your people out of the way."

Apollo stands.

"Okay, Croft, what do you suggest?"

"Blast a hole in the flooring first, then we'll descend by rope. I mean, rope we got in abundance, right?"

"Just about my idea, too. Stand back, everybody."

Aiming his laser pistol at a section of flooring, he quickly carves out a rough circle of metal. Holstering the laser, he then taps that part of the flooring with his ice-ax. It gives way easily and falls down the shaft. We hear the clank of it hitting the bottom even sooner than we'd hoped.

"Okay," Apollo says to me. "Who should handle the belay?"

"No need for a belay, Captain. I still have some of the fancy pitons."

"I don't understand. How are you going to get out there into the shaft and push them into the rock, how—"

"They hold in metal, too. Watch."

I set the molecular-binding scale on the top of the piton to *metal*. Kneeling down, I drive them into the thick flooring in a semicircle. Going in, they sound good. They should hold. Leda, thinking ahead of me, has rope ready and attaches it to five carabiners, then snap-locks them to the five pitons. I test that each carabiner is securely locked to each piton and satisfy myself that they should hold the rope.

"Good work," Apollo says. "Okay, I'll go first, test the holding power of the rope and—"

"No, Captain," Leda interrupts. "We appreciate your bravado but—"

"It's not bravado, it's common sense, as the leader of—"

"It's hardly common sense. You showed us on the mountainside how experienced you were when it came to climbing. All due apologies, but the same goes for descending, Captain. Croft and I have better experience, more training. We'll go first. Is that all right with you, Croft?"

"Of course it's all right."

I have to struggle to keep joy out of my voice. Leda's asked me to team up with her again, even if only for this one task. Of course it's all right.

"Ready, Croft?" Leda says, as she flings the coil of rope through the hole, then sets it for the stiff cablelike tensility.

Leda seems normal again, like in the old days. Efficient, steady, eager to attack a task without pause.

"Should we rope together?" I ask her.

"No. Better to descend one person at a time. Safer that way, in case the conditions on the mountain affected the rope at any point."

"Shall we toss for who goes first?"

"No. I'm going first."

"Leda, I'll—"

"Croft, it's my play."

She's appealing to my sense of leadership. If I tell her not to go first, she'll defer to me. But, on the other hand, she's telling me she's not only got the right to go first, but she has the best shot at doing it right. She's angling for an unselfish command decision. I have to give it to her.

"All right, Leda. Take care."

She smiles.

"Sure thing," she says, and has grabbed the stiff rope and started descending before I can come up with a clever good-bye. I lie prone by the hole and watch her descend in the dim light cast by our lanterns and the interior illumination of the elevator. A crack of light can be seen crossing the bottom of the shaft. It's not a long descent to the bottom at all.

"It's an easy rappel," Leda hollers up to us. "Easy. All of you, just dig your crampons in the wall and let your legs do the work. I have to. I forgot to wear my gloves, they're probably up there on the floor somewhere, and this rope's as rough as a rasp file. My hands're gonna be as raw as daggit-meat."

"The rock jutting out below you, Leda, it looks loose," I holler.

"Right. I see it. Thanks, Croft."

Bouncing her feet off the wall sometimes, at other times digging the crampons in for a few careful steps, she slowly makes her way down the rope.

"I think you're just about there, Leda."

"Yeah. About another half meter."

When she reaches the ledge, she gives a good kick at the side of the shaft wall and lands, clumsily but firmly, on the ledge.

"All right, Croft," she hollers up. "Nothing to it. Come on down. I can anchor the rope from down here, so it'll be even easier for you, cragsman."

Reacting quickly, I grab a section of the rope and ease myself out of the floor hole. Leda is right. The rappel is easy. Having watched her rappel, I can do it even faster. The rock I shove my crampons into is firm and I get good friction all the way down.

I am about three meters from the ledge when I hear a reverberating rumble above me.

"What's that?" Leda calls.

"Another explosion. Or one big avalanche or quake on the mountain."

I start scrambling down the rope. When I am near level with the ledge, the shaft starts trembling in reaction to the blast. Some rocks fall right by my head.

"Swing yourself this way, Croft," Leda yells.

I swing toward her. She grabs my leg, eases me down toward the ledge. The noise in the shaft grows louder. More rocks break loose from the shaft wall. Leda grabs my left hand with her right. My right is still on the rope. As my foot touches the surface of the ledge, there is another frightening rumble and I feel the ledge breaking away beneath my feet. Clinging to the rope, I try to tighten my grip on Leda's hand. She tries to do the same, but neither of us can quite coordinate. Her hand, raw and bleeding, slips a bit in my glove, but she manages to hold on. She flings out her feet, trying to get them onto the piece of ledge that's left. I try to get leverage to help her swing, but can't. My arm feels stretched, hanging from the rope. Another try by Leda for the ledge fails, although her foot briefly touches its edge. Now she's hanging below me. Dangling.

"Grab a piece of the rope!" I holler.

She reaches toward it with her left hand, puts her fingers around it, seems to grip it.

"Don't let go of me yet!" I cry, but she is already letting go. I don't know whether she intends to grab the stiff rope with both hands or whether her right hand, too raw to hold on, just slips out of my glove. Whatever, she has also lost her grip on the rope. She begins to slide downward. She makes a grab at the rope with her free hand, but misses. Then both hands are off the rope and she is falling.

I remember her falling away from me in my nightmare. This fall is nothing like the one in the dream. It is quick, and her scream echoes through the shaft even after her body has struck the bottom.

CHAPTER TWENTY-SIX

Athena brought Mount Hekla into focus on the monitor screen. This was the first scan they'd been able to make of the ice planet's surface in some time. Now, for a moment at least, the mountain could be seen clearly. She called Tigh over. He nodded grimly.

"Then they didn't get it," he said, pointing to the laser weapon on top of the mountain, which responded to his point by letting out another pulsing blast.

Athena and Tigh stared at the screen as if it were playing an entertainment cassette. For both of them, the apparent stillness on the planet's surface seemed to, once and for all, signal defeat for the *Galactica*.

"I thought for certain they'd—" Athena muttered, but was interrupted by an intensely bright flash of light from the top of the mountain. At first she thought it was just another pulse from the gun; then she saw the barrel of the cannon turn bright red, then white, just before the whole emplacement exploded outward. The whole summit of the mountain seemed to erupt and form a small cloud above where the gun emplacement had been. Debris was still flying outward when she turned to Tigh and yelled:

"They did it! They did it!"

"Commander," Tigh shouted. "The laser cannon's been destroyed. It—"

The *Galactica* was rocked by a pulse from the laser gun, passing closer to the battlestar than any previous pulse had. A warning light flashed on, signifying a fire in a cargo hold. Adama ordered a fire crew dispatched.

"Was that the last pulse from the gun before it—?" he said to Tigh.

"I hope so. I certainly hope so."

Tensely, everyone on the bridge waited, each person dreading the eerie thought of being wiped out by a weapon that had been already destroyed.

"That's it," Athena finally said, looking up from her scanner. "It was definitely the last one."

A sense of relief passed across the bridge, and several crew members managed a weak but emotion-filled cheer.

"They've done it!" Adama said, smiling for the first time since the attacks had begun. More crew members supplemented the growing cheer.

"Send down a rescue unit with full fighter escort," Adama ordered. "Athena can pilot the rescue ship. I'm sure she'd enjoy that."

Athena almost hadn't heard her father's last orders. Then they exchanged affectionate smiles, as she escaped from her communications console and headed for the launching deck.

Vulpa was nearing the headquarters airfield when the explosion above him sent his ship rocking, nearly into a spin. Climbing out of the spin, he saw the massive final blast that destroyed the laser weapon. He did not have much time to think about it, for the shock waves from the blast caused his ship to go out of control again. Vulpa tried to restore a steady course, but he could not stop the plunge downward. He managed to level the ship off just before striking ground, and it skidded to a stop in the ice field, a few meters away from headquarters.

Fearing a systems failure that would set the ship afire,

Vulpa scrambled clumsily out of the cockpit and staggered a few steps away. His arm, grazed by the shot from the stocky human's gun, began to hurt again. He looked back at his ship. Much of its underside had ripped away, and it was no longer flyable, but it did not catch fire.

Turning, he started walking toward the command-post building. For the first time he saw the dying fire inside its portals. Suddenly he understood everything. While the bomb-planting team had attacked the summit station, another group of humans, perhaps also aided by Ravashol's deceptive clones, had attacked the command post and probably the underground complex. That was why the Cylons at the gun had lost communication contact with the headquarters in the Hekla foothills.

Vulpa wanted to run wild with rage. Running wild was a rarity among Cylons, but not unknown. For the first time Vulpa understood what rage was all about. This infernal small group of humans had not only wrecked his garrison and blown up his gun, they had also exploded his life. There was no more point to his ambition. He would never return to Imperious Leader's base ship. He would be shifted from one exile post to another. He would never succeed Imperious Leader. His life had become as useless as a street poet's on the home planets of the Alliance.

Inside the command post, he surveyed the damage. The humans had almost totally wrecked the place. Their attack and the subsequent fire had transformed everything into smoldering wreckage. He touched the activation button of the transmitter, hoping to see the shape of Imperious Leader form bit by bit on the cracked screen, but there was no response to his pressing of the button. The only piece of furniture still intact in the room was his command chair. He slumped into it.

Using the meditative factor of his second brain, he was able to put himself into a kind of trance that not only calmed him, but mercifully removed awareness of his surroundings. He did not know how long he remained in this state. When he came to, he was immediately aware of danger. He looked out the command-post window. A large ship had just come out of the clouds, followed by an escort of fighters. Vipers. Human ships. What were they doing here? To rescue their invasion force? Or complete the destruction of his unit here? No matter. What did he care what the humans' motives were anymore? The only instinct left in him said to destroy them, any of them. He would start with this rescue force.

Slipping out of the command-post structure, he made his way to the airfield without being blocked by any of the enemy. The first ship he came to was one of the Cylon fighters that were equipped to guide the ghost ships that were positioned in the front ranks of the airfield. He could control five ghost ships from this guidance craft. It was just what he needed. The humans would think an entire Cylon squad was attacking them, when it was only Vulpa and a quintet of ghost ships. He looked up at the human ships. There might be too many of them, but he would give them a good battle before going down.

Pressing a control-panel plate so that the imprint of the glove on his right hand was recognized by the scanning equipment, he brought the fuel-activation level to full power. To his left, he saw some children, reacting perhaps to the sudden noise of his aircraft, crawling out of the fighter next to him. Children? What would children be doing in a Cylon fighter, especially children who vaguely resembled Ravashol's cursed clones? Everything, it seemed, was going crazy around him. No matter. The destruction of human ships would bring back his sanity. He pressed the plates that powered the ghost ships. Ahead of him, five ships stirred quickly to life.

Starbuck helped Apollo climb out of the elevator shaft. A meter and a half below, on the floor of the shaft, Croft still knelt by the body of Leda. The man just sat there, as if he were willing to wait through eternity for a flicker of movement from her. Starbuck considered going down there, convincing him to leave her, telling him that they could arrange a proper disposition of the body, burial or flames, later. But he decided to leave Croft alone with his sorrow for a couple of moments longer.

"She did a good job up there," Starbuck muttered.

"Both of them did," Apollo said. "By the way, thanks for being here."

"Told you not to worry about my timing. Though the

Cylon guards put up so much resistance, *they* darn near were your welcoming committee, Captain."

"Any Cylons left in the garrison?"

"No," Boomer said. "They seem to be wiped out."

"We'll have to regroup now. Boomer, you go back and get Haals and the wounded, bring them back here. Take a squad of Ser 5-9's people to help you."

"Yo," Boomer said. He turned militarily and strode away.

"Starbuck, you go get Boxey and the children."

"Right, Captain. Hey, Cadet Cree, come with me."

Cree—or at least a gaunt version of the formerly cocksure cadet—appeared from a shadowy niche and weakly saluted Apollo, who returned the courtesy.

"I didn't expect to see you, Cree."

"Never said a word to them, sir."

"Well, that might earn you a bit of metal, Cree."

"A . . . bit . . . of metal?"

"An award, Cree, a medal."

"Oh, yes, sir."

"Go help Starbuck."

Apollo went back to the elevator shaft and descended to Croft.

"We've got to go now," he whispered. "I'll send someone back for Leda."

"I should have saved her, shouldn't have let her drop, shouldn't—"

"Take it easy, Croft. We have to go."

Croft stood up, looked down at Leda's body.

"I wanted to get back together with her," he said. "I was thinking of that, back on the elevator. Well, that was probably just so much bilge. She'd never've come back to me. But there were so many things I—"

"Let's go."

"Right."

They climbed out of the shaft, Apollo giving Croft the final hand up. Ser 5-9 approached them, saying:

"Dr. Ravashol told me to tell you that he's established contact with the *Galactica*. They're sending down a rescue unit. It should arrive anytime now."

Apollo told Ser 5-9 to take him to Ravashol. With

Croft following, they made their way through labyrinthine corridors to Ravashol's quarters. Ravashol smiled when he saw Apollo.

"Your rescue ship's just outside the cloud cover now. It should be coming through momentarily. Are you all right?"

Apollo glanced at Croft, whose eyes seemed vacant.

"Well enough," Apollo said.

"My clones have been conducting a celebration in the main hall. Look."

Ravashol pointed toward the telecom screen. Apollo looked. The clones were, indeed, making merry, he thought.

"Emotion has been alien to them," Ravashol commented. "It is good to hear it again."

"The Cylons will come back," Apollo said.

"We will be ready for them. You have saved us. You've saved my children."

"I might suggest you stop calling them children, sir. You may be having a little trouble with them from now on. They seem to be getting more and more human."

"I am glad."

The handshake between Apollo and Ravashol was interrupted by Starbuck bursting into the room.

"Captain! Boxey and the children. They aren't there! One of the Tennas told me the Cylons came, and the children ran away in the confusion."

"Send everyone you can to search the corridors," Apollo commanded. "You come with me, Croft. You, too, Ser 5–9. I'll need your help getting around out there."

Croft followed Apollo and Ser 5–9 out of the room and down a long corridor. Finally catching up to them, Croft said to Apollo:

"Where we going?"

"To the airfield. The children might be wandering around out on the surface. The cold or the di-ethene could kill them!"

"But why the airfield?"

"We're going to hot-wire a Cylon ship and go off looking for them."

"Oh."

"That all right?"

"Sure. I just thought you wanted us to do something difficult."

Boxey had been awakened briefly by the sound of loud explosions and the lighting up of the sky. Muffit had barked. Boxey had told the daggit to be quiet and gone back to sleep.

Now he was awakened by the lurch of the ship in which he slept. A rumble from the front of the ship sent tremors through its walls.

"We better get out of here, daggit," Boxey said, but he had trouble getting his body to move. It felt numb all the way through.

"Go get Dad, Muffit . . . or Starbuck!"

The daggit barked again, seemed to hesitate, then shoved its snout against the exit hatch of the ship. It came open narrowly, and Muffit squeezed out. The hatch slammed shut behind it. Boxey could hear Muffy's barking outside. He tried to force his body toward the hatch. It was no use. He couldn't move fast enough. Just as he'd reached the hatch by crawling, the ship started throbbing and Boxey could feel it lift off the ground.

Boxey didn't know whether to be thrilled or scared. He'd always wanted a ride in a Cylon ship, he just wasn't sure now was the time.

Athena steadied the rescue shuttle just below the cloud cover and ordered a crewman to establish contact with the expedition. After a brief colloquy with a strange-looking man named Ravashol, who told her that Apollo, Starbuck, and Boomer were safe, she set the crew to their proper tasks. The medical officer reported ready. The pilot who'd be driving the snow ram reported ready. The warrior contingent, brought here in case any Cylons attacked during the rescue operation, reported ready. As she was about to set the rescue mission going, the communications officer reported:

"Activity on the airfield below. Cylon ships revving up."

"Are you sure it's Cylons? Ravashol said the garrison was wiped out."

"I can't tell who's piloting the ships. It looks like nobody's in some of them, from the scanner probe."

"Ghost ships! Equipped with warheads maybe. Alert the escort force but tell them to hold fire until intent of attack is established."

Athena's brow furled. She tightened her grip on the controls of the rescue shuttle.

Five of the Cylon ships on the airfield below lifted off simultaneously, followed quickly by a sixth ship from a rear rank. Athena asked for a further scanner probe, and was told that the rear ship contained personnel; outline indicated a lone Cylon. The other ships were definitely of the designation ghost ship, and were warhead-equipped.

"Any hint of hostile activity?" Athena asked.

"Not yet."

A moment later one of the Cylon ships gave a sign of hostile activity. It flew right at a colonial escort viper. Reacting rapidly to Athena's hasty order of "Fire!" the viper shot at the ghost ship. Hitting it head-on, the viper's fire caused the Cylon ship to burst into flame and plunge toward the planet's surface. It exploded before hitting the ground.

"The other Cylon ships are maneuvering into attack positions," the communications officer said.

"Blast them out of the skies!" Athena ordered.

Vulpa had put the first ghost ship into operation too hastily. He should not have sent it up against one of the vipers. The human craft was too maneuverable, could evade the ghost ship too easily, explode its warhead before it could do any damage. Clearly, the better strategy, if he were to get any revenge at all, was to destroy the larger, less maneuverable rescue ship. Fiddling with the controls, he set the guidance system for an attack on the human rescue shuttle by two of the remaining ghost ships.

Boxey, feeling warmer now from the exertion, pulled himself forward into the cockpit of the Cylon ship. He realized his ship was part of a line of ships. Up ahead was what looked like a shuttle from the *Galactica*. He hoped it was from the *Galactica*.

Next to him one of the other ships flew forward with a loud surge of power. It ran right at what Boxey recognized as a colonial viper, the kind he hoped to fly someday. It looked like the fighter was going to crash right into the viper.

"No, don't," Boxey cried aloud. "Shoot it down, warrior!"

Which the pilot of the viper promptly did.

"Good shooting!" Boxey yelled, then watched two other ships pull out of the line and head toward the formation of *Galactica* spacecraft.

Athena recognized the move of the two ghost ships immediately. One would loop up and attack the rescue shuttle from above, while the other would zero in from below.

"Intercept!" she ordered.

Two vipers intruded themselves between the lower attacker and the rescue shuttle. Catching the ghost ship between two lines of fire, they set it aflame. Another shot and they got the warhead. The ghost ship exploded. The shock wave rocked the shuttle, and Athena was able to level it off again with extreme difficulty and quick reflex responses. She wished she were in one of the vipers. Any ship lighter and more maneuverable than this rescue shuttle.

"The other ghost ship!" her communications officer said. "It got two vipers. Blew itself and them right out of the skies. It's horrible." He turned to the console. "There's a message coming in. It's Dr. Ravashol again."

Ravashol's voice sounded strained, desperate. He asked to speak to the officer in command.

"What is it?" Athena said.

"The ships attacking you. They are nonpersonnel guidance-system craft that—"

"Yes, I know all that. Don't worry. Three of them are already destroyed. We'll get the others, then—"

"No, you can't! One of them may have one of your people on it. A boy. A—"

"Boxey?"

Ravashol briefly conferred with a tall muscular blond

man dressed in thick furs. Turning back to face the screen, he said:

"Yes, that's the right name. Somehow he got on one of the Cylon ships. Captain Apollo's on his way up in a Cylon fighter."

"All right, doctor." She turned to the communications officer and said: "Report."

"The other two ghost ships are closing in together. Looks like they're ready for attack. The ship in the rear is definitely guiding them."

"Can you tell which ship Boxey's in?"

"No. Scanner probe's not come up with that information."

"All right. God, we might have killed—we'll have to execute evasive action until we're sure whether or not Boxey's in one of those two ships! Tell the fighter escort to pull away. They are officially out of combat."

"But—"

"I can't have one of them going off half-cocked and shooting down the ship Boxey's in. As soon as one of the ghost ships makes a move at us, we're just going to have to evade it. Those are your orders."

"We can send one of the vipers after the guidance ship, then—"

"No. That's risky. The guidance ship just might be able to explode the warheads on the ghost ships by remote. I don't even know if the lousy Cylon's aware of Boxey being in that ship."

Feeling her body tense, she gripped the controls as she heard the communications officer shout:

"One of them, it's coming right at us!"

CHAPTER TWENTY-SEVEN

Croft:

The way Apollo skims across the fields of ice, you'd never think he just got done climbing a mountain and attacking a laser station a short time ago. He's even still wearing half his climbing equipment. An ice-ax in holster bumps against the side of his hip as he runs. Ser 5-9, keeping up with him and giving him directions, is even more loaded down than Apollo. The clone still has a full pack and *all* his equipment.

Anyway, how do I know it's only been a short time since we got off the mountain? I haven't been keeping track. I don't know how long I sat by Leda's body. It could have been centons. Leda. I don't want to think of her. I don't want to think of that. At every step I take, I seem to think Leda's dead, Leda's dead, Leda's—I've got to stop it. She knew the risk she was taking, she accepted it. I would've been the same. But Leda's dead. And I'm not. I should be. Leda's...

I try to take my mind off it. Looking up, I can see the

rescue ship hovering beneath the cloud cover. Dimly outlined in the darkness, it seems like a somber queen bee, with the smaller vipercraft buzzing around it like drones.

I have to put on an extra rush to catch up to Apollo and Ser 5-9. Just ahead of us is the Cylon airfield, next to the wrecked command post. A group of the clone children are gathering at the edge of it. Apollo runs up to them, shouting:

"Where's Boxey?"

There's a desperation in his voice I've never heard before. A child answers:

"We don't know. He told us to hide in the ships. He went on ahead there."

The child points to the front rank of Cylon aircraft. Suddenly a fighter behind us starts throbbing with power. Ahead of us five ships in the front rank rev up. Apollo runs toward them, Ser 5-9 and I following a few steps behind. As we get near the five ships in front, the hatch of one of them squeezes open and what comes out of it but the kid's daggit-droid! The hatch springs shut behind it, as it scampers up to Apollo, barking loudly. Apollo seems to understand the bloody droid-animal.

"What is it?" I ask Apollo.

"Boxey's in there, I think. He must be, if Muffit was. In that ship. It's a ghost ship."

"What's a—"

Before I can finish the question, Apollo whirls around and starts running toward the ghost ship—just as it begins to lift off the ground. We're all forced backward by the swirling tornado in its wake.

I'm recovering my balance as Apollo grabs my arm and starts pulling me toward the nearest Cylon fighter. All of the ghost ships are in the air now. Stopping by the fighter, he turns to Ser 5-9, yells:

"Throw your mountaineering equipment aboard, then get to Ravashol! Have him send a message to that shuttle that Boxey's in one of the ghost ships. Hurry!"

Ser 5-9, reacting immediately, is hurling mountaineering equipment aboard the Cylon ship before Apollo finishes his orders. First there's his pack, then his ice-ax, then a whole package of pitons—he must have been hoarding them. Apollo, after dumping his climbing material onto the pile, pulls me onto the fighter. Ser 5-9's coil of rope follows me aboard; then the clone turns on his heels and sprints off. He is surprisingly agile for a big man running on an ice surface.

Apollo is busy monkeying with some wires beneath the control panel of the Cylon craft.

"You can really fly one of these things?" I yell.

"In theory."

"In theory! You mean you've never—"

"No."

I glance around me. The insides of the ship are weird, all pinwheels and improbably rounded gears, and other things I can't begin to make out. I turn back and stare at Apollo, trying to keep my mouth from hanging open.

"There," he says, getting up and taking the pilot seat.

"There what?"

"The controls are easy, but they're keyed to imprints of electronic wiring inside Cylon gloves. Fixing those wires should inform the monitoring devices that I'm a Cylon."

"Listen, Apollo, you're so alien to me right now, you're beginning to look like a Cylon."

He doesn't bother to respond, but fingers a couple of buttons and levers. The fighter kicks into action. I find myself falling into a copilot seat at the upward thrust of the ship.

Above us, I can see a ghost ship in the middle of blowing up. I glance over at Apollo. The strange controls are keeping him busy; he hasn't time to comment. I wonder what I'm doing here, and why he'd insisted on shoving me into this ship. His eyes look insane with desperation. What in bloody Scorpia is he planning? I think I don't want to know.

As we zoom upward, I watch two ghost ships, apparently guided by the fighter that's staying to the rear, suddenly zero in on the rescue shuttle, one from above, the other from below. The one going after the shuttle's underbelly is knocked out by a pair of vipers, but the other one very nearly succeeds in blowing up the rescue ship. It's stopped by two vipers, who are themselves caught and destroyed by the subsequent explosion. Other vipers seem on course to attack the remaining two ghost ships.

"No, don't, don't . . ." Apollo mutters.

Suddenly all the vipers peel away from the shuttle.

"Ser 5-9 got through to Ravashol," Apollo shouts. "They know Boxey's in one of those last two ships."

I almost don't want to say it, but I do:

"How do you know Boxey wasn't in one of the ships that went down?"

"I've kept track of the markings on the ship he was in. It's the one up there on the right."

I look where he points. That particular ship has left the other one now and is heading right toward the rescue shuttle. For a moment it looks like it's going to crash right into the front of the shuttle, but at the last moment the shuttle dips and flies under the ghost ship. The ghost ship flies up into the cloud cover. Just before it enters the clouds, its course is already being redirected by the guidance ship.

"Okay, good," Apollo says. "Whoever's flying the shuttle's an expert. That was precision flying!"

"I'm sure it was. But what good's it going to do? If I get you right, that Cylon thing's got a warhead and it's not going to stop searching out the—"

"We're going to have to stop it. We're going to have to get Boxey out of there."

Did I hear what I heard?

"Just how do you propose to—"

"Tell ya in a flash. Just let me take care of that other ghost ship before it gets the shuttle."

Manipulating the strange controls with a tense efficiency, Apollo heads for the other ghost ship, which is now bearing down on the shuttle. The shuttle has just pulled out of its dive, but it manages to veer off rightward to evade the attack of the warhead-equipped fighter. Before the ghost ship can have its course redirected toward the shuttle, Apollo dives our ship right at it, then pushes a multilined template in front of him. Laser fire shoots out from the front of our ship. A few tongues of flame, and the ghost ship is a real ghost now. I hope Apollo was right about which ship Boxey's in.

The last ghost ship comes back out of the clouds. It's heading directly for the highside of the shuttle. It looks like there's no chance the rescue ship can get out of the way, but at the last possible moment it surges forward with a blast of power and the ghost ship goes unsinged through its flaming wake. The ghost ship goes into a deep dive. Apollo mutters:

"No, it can't crash. It can't—"

It doesn't. The attacker is pulled out and buzzes the ground. If Boxey is really in it, he must be having one hell of a fun ride. That Cylon pilot's showing considerable skills at precision flying by remote.

Apollo turns to me, talks quickly:

"Okay, Croft, it's up to you now."

"Up to me what?"

"Listen and don't interrupt. The climbing stuff, you know how to use it. Anchor the rope here, and climb down to the ghost ship, get Boxey out with your fancy equipment. That's it. It's our only chance."

"It's not even a chance, it's—"

"Do it!"

The desperation in his voice puts an end to it. Sure, I'll do it, I say to myself even as I start gathering the equipment, what do I care? I might as well die, too, like Leda. Even as I contemplate my own death, I work out a plan. It probably won't work, it shouldn't, but I don't like to try anything this dumb without a plan. Why shouldn't it work? All I've got to do is work my way down to a ghost ship that's engaged in attacking a shuttle while the revered Captain Apollo keeps still another ship that he's never flown before steady enough for me to do my job without falling from the rope to the icy surface below. I can do that, can't I?

As I anchor the rope to an ice-ax which I've wedged between the base of the copilot seat and another jutting piece of ship whose function I can't even guess, I notice that the belay's no worse than some I've set up on mountainsides. I tell Apollo a few hand signals I'll be using that'll let him know how to fly while I'm operating below. Then I grab three molecular-binding pitons, and using my famous Scorpion slip knot on each, I connect them all with a length of rope. Attaching another piece of rope to a second ice-ax, I coil it and secure it on my shoulder. I check to verify that my laser pistol is still in my holster. Taking still more rope, and with a few more applications of my famous Scorpion knot-work, I jerry-rig several loops at the end of the climbing rope I'm going to use. Some of the loops are small enough to slip a boot into, which is exactly what I intend to slip into them. Another two loops are big enough to fit me rather snugly, albeit without much style, at chest and waist levels. I weight down the main climbing rope with a lot of junk I find around the interior of the Cylon ship. Apollo keeps looking over his shoulder, as if to say: Aren't you ever going to be ready?

"Good flying!" he shouts suddenly. Apparently the pilot of the shuttle has executed another great maneuver! Swell!

After setting the rope to its stiffer cablelike tension and kicking open the side hatch of the Cylon fighter, I throw the rope out the hatch. The weight at the rope end keeps the rope from dragging directly behind the ship, but the angle downward still looks less than favorable to me.

"Check with you later, Apollo," I scream, and don't wait for his answer. Grabbing the rope and gripping it tightly, I hurl myself backward out of the open hatch of the ship.

As I descend I try not to notice the intense cold, the fierce wind, the memories of Leda clinging to the rope in the elevator shaft. The cold and wind are easy enough to ignore—they're no worse than on some mountains—but the memories of Leda are hard to dispel.

I reach the bottom weighted area of the rope and slip my booted feet into two of the loops I'd knotted. Looking down, I can see the ghost ship below me. It's heading toward the shuttle again. Somehow Apollo's keeping pace with it. Concentrating on the ghost ship itself, I'm only half aware of the evasion maneuver of the shuttle. Waving my hand in the gesture telling Apollo to descend closer, I then watch the ghost ship come toward me. Suddenly I'm right next to it. I have to act fast, since I don't know when the Cylon guidance pilot might pull the ship away from me. Checking that the chest and waist loops are secure, I quickly slip my body into them, thus freeing my hands to work. I gesture to Apollo to edge me closer to the ghost ship. He does. I jam the three pitons, set on metal penetration, into the side hatch of the ship. Just in time. Before I can do anything about attaching the ice-ax to the rope linking the pitons, the ship seems to drift away from me, the hatch now out of reach. That's okay; I figured on that. I take out my pistol and quickly but deliberately fire toward the hatch. Although I'm not up on the technology of the superstructure of this bloody ghost ship, I-place the shots where the locking mechanism and single hinge of an ordinary Cylon spacecraft hatch should be. My shots seem to be accurate, at least the abstractly designed scorch marks at each area look right.

Well, lucky so far. The wind tearing at my clothing makes me realize just how fast we're going, and for a moment I am terrified. I'm putting my life on the line, just trusting Apollo's piloting skills. Well, he came quite well recommended, I try to tell myself.

As the ghost ship makes another run at the shuttle, it passes very close to where I'm hanging. I get a good view of the cockpit. The kid's in there, all right. He's enjoying himself! He's all wide-eyed and excited.

Apollo pulls up slightly and follows the ghost ship's run. Again the shuttle executes a smooth evasive action. Following the path of the ghost ship, I signal Apollo to lower and move to the left, which he does smoothly. This time the hatch is just out of reach. Okay. I slip the ice-ax in its coil of rope off my shoulder. Feeding out just a bit of the rope, I then fling the ice-ax toward the pitons on the hatch. First time, it just misses and I have to reel it back in like a fishing line. Taking a deep breath first, I then throw the ice-ax again. This time its point catches hold of the rope linking the pitons, its long surface hooked snugly onto two of the connecting strands. Replacing the coil of rope on my shoulder and taking a firm hold on my end of the section of the rope leading to the ice-ax, I signal to Apollo to slide rightward abruptly, away from the ghost ship. The rope jerks tight and for a moment I don't know if it's going to hold; then suddenly there is a loud cracking sound and the hatch pulls away from the ship, and begins to plunge downward. I shake the coil of rope off my shoulder before the heavy weight of the hatch can break off any piece of my anatomy, and don't even bother to watch it all hurtle to the ground.

The hole left behind in the ship is more jagged than I'd have expected. Apparently the hatch pulled away pieces surrounding it. Quickly I slip out of the chest and waist loops and grab onto the climbing rope. After signaling Apollo to head back toward the ghost ship, I grip the rope with both hands and release my boots from the footholds. As Apollo executes the sweep toward the ghost ship, I kick back with my legs as hard as I can under the circumstances, then forward. My aim has got to be just right. The side of the ghost ship comes close to me much too fast, and I don't have time to think. All I can do is swing my legs outward, aiming for the hold in the side of the ship. Apollo holds the Cylon fighter steady. I almost miss, anyway. My leg scrapes a jagged edge of the hole as both legs begin to go through. Letting the force of the swing carry me, I let go the climbing rope and plunge through the unevenly shaped but wide opening. I don't know why I don't break every bone in my body, as I hit the opposite wall and bounce back toward the other side, just missing going out again through the jagged hole which I'd so clumsily entered.

I lie on the floor of the ship, trying to catch my breath, trying to make some part of my body move. Suddenly the kid is standing over me, each of his eyes as large as the hatchway opening. Beyond him, I see Apollo's ship hovering high above the cockpit.

"Where'd you come from?" Boxey says.

I reject all the bad jokes I could make for a reply to that question and just say:

"From up there, kid."

CHAPTER TWENTY-EIGHT

It was all Athena could do to keep from watching the rescue attempt of Apollo and Croft. Instead, she kept her attention on the controls, carefully timing her evasive maneuvers each time the ghost ship approached. It seemed that each escape from it was narrower than the one before. She could hardly believe she'd heard right when an officer reported that Croft had jumped from the rope and through the open ghost-ship hatchway. She now understood completely why the computer had kicked back Croft's name during the search for personnel. She was also glad that Apollo had worked himself onto the mission roster. There were a lot of good pilots in the *Galactica* squadrons, but with the possible exceptions of Starbuck and Boomer, only Apollo could have flown a strange ship with that much accuracy and precision. Well, as far as precision flying went, she wasn't doing too bad herself, she thought, as she plunged the shuttle downward to evade another diving attack.

"What's happening out there?" she asked the crew member who was keeping track.

"Nothing. No, wait. Something. The guy just made some gesture out that hole. Apollo's bringing his ship closer, the rope's right next to the hole. The guy's coming out. He's carrying something, like a big pack. It's Boxey, I think, it looks like Boxey, and they're both on the rope now, clinging to it."

"Confirm that it is Boxey, please."

The crewman squinted at a picture on the monitor, then shouted joyously:

"Confirmed! It's Boxey, all right!"

"How far are they away from the ghost ship?"

"Not far. No, wait. Apollo's ship is slowly veering to port. He's carrying them away."

"Are they out of range of any explosion?"

"Yes, I think so."

"*Confirm* they are out of range."

The crewman paused before answering.

"Out of range. *Confirmed.*"

"Escort leader!"

The voice of the escort officer came over the commline: "Yes, Ensign Athena?"

"Destroy that ghost ship. And the guidance ship, too. Both of them. Immediately."

She watched the ghost ship explode with great pleasure. Other vipers from the escort chased after the guidance ship, which now dived toward the ground. A shot from one of the vipers crossed the Cylon ship highside, and it began to wobble. Incredibly, the Cylon pilot was able to keep it steady for a crash landing on the Cylon surface. A clear view of the Cylon ship became lost in the swirling snow created by the crash landing.

In the distance Athena could see Apollo descending his ship carefully, delicately, toward the airfield, Croft and Boxey hanging from the rope. The rope seemed to just touch the ground when Croft, holding onto Boxey, jumped off and went into a gentle roll along the ground. After a moment of lying there, both Croft and Boxey stood up and shook themselves off. Boxey leaped up at Croft's chest and hugged him. Even from this height, it looked to Athena as if Croft didn't mind.

An aide distracted Athena's attention from the events

below by telling her that Commander Adama was on the commline and wanted to talk to her.

"Yes, Commander."

"I just wanted to tell you—good work. We were . . . impressed with the flying skills of you and Captain Apollo."

"Yes, sir. I'm taking the rescue unit in now for a landing."

"You'll have to make it quick. The Cylon pursuit force is still on our tail, and we won't be able to keep them at a distance for long."

Athena resisted smiling until the image of her father had faded from the screen. The guarded praise he'd given her had been worth all the medals in the fleet.

"Prepare to land," she ordered her crew.

Beside the rescue shuttle, Ravashol gripped Apollo's shoulders and said his farewells.

"Peace be with you, Apollo. May you reach your destination."

"Peace be with you, father-creator," Apollo replied.

Apollo and Ser 5-9 embraced.

"And thank you and your people for your help," Apollo said. "If you and Tenna had not led the way up Hekla, I don't—say, where is Tenna? They were *all* here a few moments ago."

Ser 5-9 hesitated before answering:

"I believe they went into the shuttle to say good-bye to your Lieutenant Starbuck."

"I should have known. Starbuck!"

Inside the ship, Starbuck was busily bestowing kisses on three Tennas, each one in turn. They all seemed to be enjoying the ritual immensely.

"Time to go, Lieutenant," Apollo said, trying to keep from laughing.

Starbuck appeared reluctant. He sidled conspiratorially over to Apollo and whispered:

"Can't they come with us? There're only three of them, and—"

"No, Lieutenant. We can't interfere with these people any more than we already have."

"It hasn't been such a bad interference," one of the Tennas said.

Apollo's observation to Ravashol had been more correct than he'd even suspected; the clones were becoming more and more human.

"Captain," Starbuck urged, "this is a chance in a lifetime. Three versions of the same beautiful woman. Can you imagine?"

"Only too well can I imagine. Another time, Starbuck."

"But, Captain..."

"I'm sorry, Starbuck. Good-bye, each of you, and thank you. We are all in your debt."

"I just wanted to pay off some interest," Starbuck muttered; then he said in a way that took in all three women: "Good-bye, Tenna."

All three bade him farewell together, an identical sadness in their eyes.

As Starbuck watched them disembark, Boomer patted his shoulder and said:

"Win one, you lose one."

"I just lost all three," Starbuck said.

He turned and saw Athena glaring at him from the entranceway to the pilot compartment.

"I think I'm on a real losing streak," he mumbled to Boomer; then he stepped forward, saying, "Athena, we were all just friends. *Really*."

She continued to stare daggers at him.

"By the way," he said, in his best disarming fashion, "I heard you flew the pants off this rig."

Her mouth made a nervous movement at the corners, as if it very much wanted to smile.

"But I missed it. Tell me about it, huh?"

She said nothing, but nodded toward the cockpit of the shuttle. He followed her in, and took the copilot seat as she began to run an equipment check preparatory to launch.

For the first time in recent memory, Imperious Leader felt stunned. He had had to verify the report three times with his executive officers. The laser gun had been destroyed. Contact with First Centurion Vulpa and his garrison had been lost—apparently the communication systems there had been destroyed along with the cannon.

Some human ships had been detected leaving the ice planet. Then, abruptly, the human fleet itself had escaped. None of his officers knew how, although they suspected the *Galactica* had successfully created another camouflage force field. None of his officers knew where they had escaped to.

The trap should have worked. It was as if it had been sprung and had captured its quarry, and still the humans had found some way to wriggle out.

He came out of his reverie to find the Starbuck simulacrum looking at him and smiling.

"How did they escape?" Imperious Leader asked the Starbuck.

"Escape?" it answered. "That's just so much bilgewater, bug-eyes. We beat you, that's all. We beat you again. And we're going to keep on—"

Imperious Leader leaped at the Starbuck, intending to strangle it. His hands went right through the Starbuck's neck, and did not alter one degree of its smile. With one gigantic effort, Imperious Leader pushed the entire simulator off his pedestal. It crashed to the floor of the chamber. Sparks flew in all directions. For a moment, the Starbuck stood at the center of the wreckage, then suddenly flickered out.

CHAPTER TWENTY-NINE

Croft:

After what I've been through, the bridge of the *Galactica* seems incredibly claustrophobic, even though it's an immense chamber. But I can't stop my shoulders from contracting at the box that I feel enclosed in. Boxes, prisons, cells. That's my life. Maybe I should have taken the opportunity to escape with Wolfe and Leda. They might be still alive and I might not feel so trapped. Still, as I look around at the joyful crowd gathered on the bridge, I can't help but feel that their lives were traded for the lives of all around me, all personnel and passengers on the many ships of the fleet. Perhaps it was the proper trade.

Adama is in his commander mood and praising Apollo and the expedition for the successful completion of the mission. He tosses a couple of bouquets to Athena and Apollo for their flying skills. I try to feel a part of it all emotionally, but all I can feel is that it was just a job I did. I wouldn't downplay my part in it, especially the rope-swinging act I did with the kid, but I still don't feel that I belong here, drinking in the rhetoric of praise. They used me because they had to. Otherwise, they would have left me in my stinking hole. The hole they're going to send me back to.

Adama has moved to Cree and is eulogizing on how brave the young cadet was. Well, that's true enough. I'd rather have been hanging on that rope and falling in that avalanche than be subjected to Cylon torture. Good work, Cree, you deserve the praise.

Suddenly Adama is standing in front of me. I try to straighten up into some semblance of attention, a reflex from the old days, but my bones are so much in pain I can hardly move them.

"And Croft," Adama says in his resonant voice.

"I guess it's back to the old grid-barge," I say, and try to smile as if I don't mind.

Adama smiles back. The monster, *smiling* about sending me back.

"No," he says after a pause. "I think you worked out the rest of your time down on that ice planet. You're needed on the *Galactica*, Commander."

I almost don't hear him say the last word. Commander. Reinstatement in rank. If only Leda were here, she might just—I've got to stop thinking of her now. Anyway, she'd only have said that reinstatement in rank was just so much bilge.

Adama grips my shoulder for a moment, then moves on. Now he faces the kid and his daggit pet, which is doing a good mechanical version of a happy drool.

"Boxey," Adama says, "if anyone should be sent to the grid-barge for disobeying orders..."

The kid looks scared. I almost want to protect him. The daggit squeals.

Maybe a good scare'll cure the kid of sticking his nose into dangerous places.

But I doubt it.

CHAPTER THIRTY

First Centurion Vulpa pulled his heavy body up over the hanging cornice. The sound of the metal in his uniform scraping against the ice surface sent echoes rolling down the mountain. He glanced down at the uniform. Many of the black bands awarded him as decoration for valor had been scraped away by his climb. Breaks in the suit that had occurred during the crash landing of his ship had rendered it only barely functional. He had had to continue to wear it as protection against the rising cold temperature.

There was only a little farther to go. Exercising all the willpower that two brains could offer, he climbed upward. By the time he had reached the summit station, he knew he had no more powers of exertion left in his body. He lay still for a long time.

Finally he could force his body to rise. Without looking around him, he began stepping heavily across the wreckage until he reached the center where the remains of the once-powerful weapon stood. Its shell still rose mightily toward the sky, dark gray and gloomy. But it stood on a mangled foundation. The awesomely powerful energy pump was in jagged ruins. Fragments of the station, broken, split, bent, lay about the still-intact flooring. At points Vulpa could see a helmet or uniform from one of his warriors perceivable beneath some part of the ruins. A bridge of burned metal had formed across the gaping elevator shaft. Except for the shell of the gun, nothing tangible revealed what it once had been.

Leaning his heavy body against the shell of the weapon, Vulpa resolved to go into a meditative state. The ability to do that in the midst of a disaster such as this was a second-brain quality for which he was extremely grateful.

He could meditate here, oblivious of the wreckage around him and what it meant to his life, for a long time.

Perhaps for the rest of eternity.

Or until a reinforcement garrison arrived.

Or until he died.

It did not matter.